THE EMBERS
OF
TRADITION

THE EMBERS
OF
TRADITION

(ONE MAN'S MEAT...)

CHUKWUDUM OKEKE

atmosphere press

Published by Atmosphere Press

Cover design by Josep Lledó

The US Copyright Data for the book is as follows below:

Registration Number/Date: TXU002095028/2018-04-19
Previous Registration/Date: TXu002-055-358/2017-05-22

atmospherepress.com

This book is dedicated to my parents, Nathaniel Nwakaibie Okeke and Joy Nwanyankwo Okeke. I learnt humility from them and everybody was loved and welcomed to our house.

CHAPTER ONE

Nweke liked the scenario, even if it represented a mere delusion. He woke up early that morning and sluggishly climbed down from his raised mud bed. Nweke made his way to the only door that led out of his mud hut. He bent down his head low enough to pass through the low wooden door, wiping his face with the back of his right palm as though he was wiping away the early morning sun's rays hitting him in the face. He emerged from his hut into his compound, face-to-face with Ikenga, his personal god. He looked into the emotionless, yet mystical and awe-inspiring eyes of Ikenga with a feeling of satisfaction that it was watching over his compound and his barn. Then, with that happy feeling, Nweke greeted his Ikenga,

"Father, 'diije daalu.' I know that you are full of thoughts about the welfare of me and my family." Nweke addressed his Ikenga as Father.

At other times, Nweke passed by his Ikenga without a word, save for a casual glance often loaded with meanings only known to him.

Nweke was a dark-skinned man of average height and wasn't a man of many words. He compensated for his lack of words with a hot, unpredictable temper and his fists. Despite that, he worked very hard, and like every real man in Akpu, he took the welfare of his household very seriously. So it was not surprising that Nweke's barn housed one of the largest stockpiles of yam harvests in the history of Akpu Town.

Akpu Town was located in the South-Eastern part of Nigeria, a tropical rain forest region of West Africa just above the Equator. The Dry Season, hot and dry, and the Rainy Season, hot, wet and humid, were the major seasons in Akpu. But a third season called the Harmattan Season was mild, dusty and dry. It was chilly in the night and morning but the opposite, hot, in the afternoon. It was dusty due to the wind that blew the Sahara desert dust from the North down to the Atlantic coast. Akpu Town was very rural and had not been affected by the perks of Western civilization like electricity or paved roads. The highest school in Akpu was the Church Missionary Society, CMS elementary school. The people of Akpu were content with their oil palm lanterns and the village pathways of red soil. On hot days, usually every day except rainy days, school children sometimes had blisters on their bare feet from the hot soil. But it rarely spoiled their joy. The pathways, as well as the playgrounds and streams, were diligently maintained in turns by the various youth age-grade groups. Akpu was therefore a very neat and clean town guided by strict rules put in place by the council of elders with a ceremonial Paramount Chief at the head. But Akpu had a major roadway passing through it linking Akpu to Offiah in the West and Ogwu in the East.

Nweke was in his barn very early on this clear and sunny day sitting under the shade of the landmark tree ogilisi, kola nut (orji) and pear (ube) trees that surrounded his barn. These trees, planted on purpose, also provided shade for the yams so they didn't rot from the intense heat of the West African sun. The barn 'Oba Ji' was where yams 'Ji' were kept all year round. And yams were the most important farm produce. They were the evidence of economic wealth and riches in Akpu and all Igbo land. His barn was built in the open air for ventilation and stretched for about seventy yards long and fifty yards wide with dozens of rows of upright stacks of yam tubers tied to one another against the palm sticks and supported with bamboo sticks. His barn was so high that he had a bamboo ladder on which he stood while tying yam tubers on the upper part of the stakes. Members of Nweke's household had no business in the barn, except Nweke sent them to bring the yams meant for consumption. Some yams were exclusively seedlings for planting and not to be eaten. Nweke had just received from his extensive farms heaps of freshly harvested yams to be tied to the upright stakes. His happiest moods seemed to always coincide with a fresh arrival of a bountiful harvest of new yams.

Nweke's compound was quite large commensurate with his stature as an Ichie in Akpu. A carved wooden gate led into his compound. There were many economic trees in his compound like the kola nut, ube, oloma, udala and mango trees. As you entered Nweke's compound, his hut was on the right side. His Ikenga was on the left side, whereas the barn was straight ahead. The barn was a few yards away from Nweke's hut and was the most important economic part of the Obi, the man's compound. Next to Nweke's hut on the right was the wooden door leading into his wives' compound. The door was on a lower mud fence separating the wives' compound from Nweke's compound. Besides the door, the only other connection between both compounds was a couple of cylindrical holes in the wall which served as look-outs, equivalent to pinholes on modern doors. Nweke's hut had some esoteric uli drawings on it. Some of the drawings were replicas of famous ancestral spirits of the village like the Otaka. The wives' huts were also decorated with artistic uli designs but not ancestral spirits.

A higher mud fence went around the entire compound of Nweke, enclosing both Nweke's compound and the wives' compound, protecting them from human, animal and spiritual intruders. This higher mud fence formed part of the length of the barn. Any spiritual invaders who dared to cross over the mud fence into Nweke's compound were trapped on the fence until exposed by the morning light. Some witch doctor concoctions embedded in the fence at the request of Nweke were responsible for that. The mud fence was also home to many spiders and reptiles. On various cracks on the fence and other hidden parts of the fence, the spiders wove the white silky covering for their eggs. The spider's web also served as the voice of the Ancestral Spirits, and only Nweke had this knowledge in his compound. Only the initiated into the masquerade cult had this privileged knowledge. It was amazing that for the centuries of Akpu's existence, the womenfolk and uninitiated men did not have the faintest idea that a spider's web, though hard to find, had any other kind of use to anybody except to spiders for the protection of their eggs.

An udara (African cherry) tree, standing on an empty plot of land on the other side of the fence, had some of its branches drooping over the wall fence into Nweke's compound next to the barn. Nobody complained about this intruder. The udara tree branches were welcome intruders because they had obvious sweet intentions.

The most important spiritual part of Nweke's compound was the Ikenga or Chi, the man's personal god. Nweke's Chi, partially facing the left side of his hut and the barn, was like a carved midget seated on a chair made from the wood of a mahogany tree. The god itself was probably related by blood to its stool, as both of them were products of the same parent, the mahogany tree. The gods were made by a select club of gifted carvers, or god designers. It was a secretive and exclusive profession known only to initiates of the masquerade cult. Although these carvers could render their carving services to the public at large, only a privileged few initiates knew that they designed masquerade heads. In Akpu, there were not more than half a dozen god designers. The village gods were designed according to their characteristics and according to the expectations of their adherents. Nweke's eldest son, Ekigwe, had noticed the differences between his father's Chi and Akilika's Chi. Akilika was Nweke's best friend and lived in Nweke's neighborhood. Akilika's Chi had a pointed nose and looked good. On the contrary, Nweke's Chi had a flat nose and looked unkempt. Ekigwe had been pondering over this discrepancy. So one day as Ekigwe strayed into his father's compound, as was his habit, he addressed his father, "Nnam."

"My son," answered Nweke.

"Why is your Chi always looking so ugly compared to Opulozo's Chi?" Opulozor was Akilika's Ozo title name.

"Even your Chi's nose is looking like somebody hit a

pestle on its face. Opulozo's Chi has a straight and pointed nose."

"Let a tiger tear off your jaws," barked a shocked and enraged Nweke who immediately went after Ekigwe. Ekigwe had already dashed off in anticipation of his father's reaction. But Nweke continued in his rage, as if Ekigwe was still there hearing him, "Anu Offia (wild beast). You'll easily notice the difference between Opulozo's personal god and my personal god. But you will not be quick to notice the difference between your idleness and the productiveness of your father. It is always things that do not concern you that you focus on. If you were not so foolish, you would have asked me why my Ikenga is more powerful than Akilika's god. Akilika's Ikenga is not a man. It is a lady and that is why it is looking pretty. Men are not judged by their looks but by their power and their pockets. But only wise men realize this, foolish boy. You did not look at Akilika's barn? Can you compare his meager harvest with mine? If Akilika had enough cowries for a dowry, wouldn't he have happily married a second wife to help him with his farm work? Efulefu! Just don't let me lay my hands on you."

Nweke then turned to address Ikenga, his personal god, "You are just sitting there quiet as if you are not hearing my son. Is it not to you that he is pouring out all his insult? If you gave me a good son, will he be insulting you like that?

"The challenge is yours, not mine. I meet my obligations to you, don't I?" continued Nweke in his frustrated monologue. Ikenga kept moping away unperturbed. In spite of Nweke's rage, it still crossed his mind that he could redesign his god. But he brushed the thought aside with "Odonigwugwu" meaning, "I'm done with it. It's their business, not mine!"

Ekigwe had never been an apostle of his father's Chi, but he had always been very curious and studious about it. Ekigwe could never come to terms with why his father chose to address a piece of wood carving as his father, and by extension, Ekigwe's grandfather.

Meanwhile, chickens roamed about in both compounds, ceaselessly looking for something to eat that one was tempted to wonder if they ever got full. As the chickens 'tuck-tuck-tucked' in the women's compound towards the maize spread on a mat to dry for preservation toward the dry season and associated famine, Mgbogafor could be heard shouting at one of the children to go and drive away the chickens.

"Oliaku," screamed Mgbogo as Mgbogafor was fondly called.

"Yes, Mother."

"Okuko! Okuko!!" Mgbogafor shouted at Oliaku.

"On my way, Mama," responded Oliaku who already knew what Mgbogafor wanted her to do. Next, you could hear the chickens 'kack-kack-cackle' as they ran in all directions for safety. But while the chickens were free to roam about, the goats and sheep were usually kept in their sheds fenced in with palm and bamboo sticks.

As far as Nweke was concerned, the only useful service rendered by Ekigwe was taking out the goats and sheep for grazing. Ekigwe seemed to enjoy it because it offered him the chance to leave the compound with his catapult. Often one of the python snakes of the village god relaxed on top of the mud fence, seemingly enjoying the morning sun. But sometimes, it was a sort of an uninvited company to Nweke in his work at the barn. Sometimes Nweke talked to it, usually a greeting, "Nnayi, have you come to know how your children are doing?" Nweke would address the python snake. But sometimes Nweke simply ignored the python snake.

As Nweke tied the yam tubers, he heard a plop. A ripe udara fruit had fallen into the barn, offering Nweke an opportunity to keep a precious something for his favorite daughter, Adaobi. Adaobi loved udara fruit and was always expecting her father to give her some udara. In spite of the heaps of yam tubers waiting for Nweke's attention, he was in his best elements proudly tending them.

"After all, is it not the prayer of every farmer to have a bumper harvest?" muttered Nweke as if to encourage himself concerning the enormous task he took upon himself without any helping hand.

Nweke was always in his best element whenever he was alone in his barn tying his yams to the stakes. He did not trust anyone with his precious yams, or with anything else for that matter. "Why should I trust anyone when even the gods are not to be trusted?" thought Nweke to himself. His relationship with the gods could be described at best as a quid pro quo. You 'rub my back' and I 'rub your back.' So far they seemed to have been rubbing his back. Nweke and his gods were like monkeys who say, "If I fall for you and you fall for me, it is play."

As long as the gods met their obligations toward Nweke, he could be relied upon to meet his obligations toward the gods and even fervently defend them. The number one obligation the gods owed the people was a bumper harvest, and Nweke was unquestionably one of the greatest farmers in Akpu.

Nweke had great expectations from the village gods but also he had a private skepticism regarding their integrity. He could be described as a follower and a team player, but not a believer. In this, he didn't seem to have a choice. If he did, he probably would not follow the gods. But then he would certainly be the only noble man in Akpu who didn't follow the village gods, and that was as good as being a mad man and an outcast.

The only person Nweke could be said to trust was his friend Akilika. And that was even because Nweke and Akilika had entered into a blood covenant called 'Igbandu,' a tradition of the Igbo. The blood covenant between Nweke and Akilika was particularly necessary because gossips about their past would have made their friendship very uneasy for both men. It was better to be at ease while exchanging kola nuts and snuff-boxes without the fear of poison. Trust was expensive and fraught with risks.

Nweke once told Akilika, "I am often tempted to regard our gods like the kotma. The Oyinbo DC (District Commissioner) will tell kotma what he should say to the people." Because the people didn't understand English, the kotma would translate the message to them adding 'a live chicken each' to the Oyibo DC message. Of course, he kept the live chickens. "Chukwu Okike tells the village gods, his messengers, what to do, but they add their burden of chickens and goats and still won't do what Chukwu Okike instructed them to do."

"Ogbuefi," Akilika called Nweke by his title name.

"Opulozo," answered Nweke, calling him by his own title name.

"Chukwu Okike should have made you his chief messenger instead of the gods," responded Akilika, laughing aloud.

"It's not too late," replied Nweke.

"When I join my ancestors, if you're still here, I'll reward you better than your Ikenga," continued Nweke with a countenance that suggested he indeed believed in what he was saying, and both of them erupted in more laughter.

But trust was probably Nweke's albatross. He had to probably learn to trust himself first before he could trust his gods or even his tradition. Nweke was a far cry from the Nweke of years ago. In his younger years, Nweke's zealousness, or often overzealousness, was a recurring subject of discussion, a proverb in Akpu town till today. Nweke was a prosperous young man in Akpu. So when the going was good, he was so zealous about the gods that he soiled his hands with blood. Nweke's action caused a subtle enmity and mutual suspicion between the two towns till today. Okwe shared a boundary with Akpu, but there the relationship ended.

The symbol of the Akpu gods was the python. Okwe town worshipped the tortoise as the presence of their god. Suffice it to say that in Akpu nobody touched the python, let alone kill it. In Akpu, although the tortoise was also a god, albeit a lesser god, it was also forbidden to kill it. However, in Okwe the python was not a god, but a mere dangerous snake. Its meat was also considered very sweet, a delicacy of the highest order. Only a person who greatly honored or loved you would serve python meat, or any other snake for that matter, to you. But the python was considered the sweetest of snakes, so it was the sweetest of the sweetest.

There was a teacher at Akpu CMS Church Elementary School. His name was Mr. Osondu. Mr. Osondu was transferred from Okwe Misson School to Akpu. As he came to Akpu, he brought an Okwe boy, Ebuka, as his houseboy. Ebuka helped Mr. Osondu do simple house chores like sweeping, dressing the bed, fetching firewood and going to the stream to fetch water for cooking, washing and for the teacher's bath. Ebuka usually bathed in the stream. Ebuka's parents did not give Mr. Osondu their son as a servant because they could not take care of him but as a way of training him to be responsible and well-behaved. Teachers were known to be great disciplinarians.

One day, Ebuka saw a python in his master's compound and was very scared. Ebuka did not realize that pythons in Akpu town were harmless because they represented the gods. The pythons had an unwritten agreement with the people of Akpu. The pythons harmed nobody. And tradition forbade Akpu people from killing a python. In school the next day Ebuka told his friends about this monstrous python that he saw in his compound. One of the boys noticed the fear in Ebuka as he reported about the python.

"Ebuka, why are you so scared about this python?" the boy queried Ebuka.

"Don't you know that the pythons are harmless?" continued the boy.

"They are not harmless. There was a man killed by a python in my town last year. Is that harmless?" retorted Ebuka.

"Well, that's in your town. Here the python does not harm anyone, and no one harms the python. It represents the spirit of our ancestors. So, how will our ancestors harm us?" replied the boy to Ebuka. Ebuka was dumbfounded and talked no more.

Soon Ebuka got used to seeing pythons, especially when they were sluggishly slithering across the village pathway. They didn't cross in haste because they knew that nobody was after them. Ebuka didn't fear much any longer but always kept a safe distance. Ebuka took extra care in making sure he closed the doors of his house firmly. He imagined waking up one morning and seeing a python relaxing in a corner of his room. That thought sent shivers through him every time.

Besides the python enigma, the Akpu environment did not present any problems to Ebuka. He got along well with other kids in his school and was well-liked. After all, Ebuka was very benevolent toward other kids in school. He always came to school with a bag full of ripe mangoes. There was a big mango tree at the teachers' quarter where Ebuka's master lived with him. Ebuka would pluck ripe mangoes every evening in readiness for school the next morning.

He made many friends because of his mangoes.

Ebuka's friends in school also got a chance to pay back his kindness sometimes. Often a student accompanied Ebuka to the village stream. This was because Ebuka detested the crab found in great numbers at the stream. The funny sideways movement of the crab disgusted Ebuka. He always imagined a crab grabbing his toes once he stepped inside the stream. That thought always brought up goose pimples on Ebuka, who often made a shrill sound. Ugo was the most trusted friend that always followed Ebuka to the village stream. Ebuka would stand some yards from the stream while Ugo filled his clay pot with much-needed water from a special part of the stream where the water was cleanest. Ugo will then help Ebuka lift the pot of water atop Ebuka's head for the trip home. Of course, back in school, Ugo always selected the choicest mango or two before the other kids.

In spite of all this, Ebuka was occasionally homesick and longed to be back with his parents in Okwe. Therefore Ebuka's joy knew no bounds when his first holiday break in Akpu was around the corner. It was vacation time for the Akpu Mission School and Ebuka's teacher planned to take him back to his parents for the holidays.

Ebuka started to prepare to go home for the holidays. First, he went to the stream, and with the ever-ready help of Ugo, washed his few articles of clothing: 2 pairs of khaki shorts and shirts and two singlets, as well as a cotton wrapper which he neatly folded into his small multi-colored aluminum box. Ebuka made sure that he collected his report card detailing his excellent examination results and put it in his box, anxiously waiting to show his parents. His school vacated on a Friday, and early Saturday morning, Ebuka's teacher took him to his town. It was a long walk through a narrow dirt road. Occasionally, leaves from the brush on both sides of the road gave them an uncomfortable rubbing. Ebuka carried his box on his head with a soft pad made out of banana leaves. They arrived in Okwe town a bit sweaty and dusty, but Ebuka was very happy regardless. Expectedly, Ebuka was received happily. His first action was to eat his mother's food which he had been yearning for all these months.

Now back in Okwe, Ebuka couldn't wait to tell his family how the dangerous python moved about freely among the people as if it was part of the citizenry, and a royal one for that matter. "Mother, I have a very interesting story to tell you," requested Ebuka very excitedly. He was so excited that the rest of the family gathered to hear Ebuka's story from his new town. It was like a gathering for a moonlight night's fairytale.

"My son, I hope it is a good story?" asked Ebuka's mother.

"It is a good story, Mama. But I already told you that I have an interesting story to tell you," replied Ebuka.

"That's true my son. Please forgive my forgetfulness. Your mother is getting old," apologized Ebuka's mother.

"Hahahaha," Ebuka laughed. "Are you as old as Nnebue?" Nnebue was considered the oldest man alive in Akpu. All his age-grade men had passed away, with only him remaining. Even his first son died at an old age. But that was a bitter pill to swallow for Nnebue because fathers were not supposed to bury their sons, but the sons were to bury their fathers.

"My son, you don't have to be as old as Nnebue to be considered old," she answered her son with everybody laughing.

Ebuka's family, eager to hear what happened with him and the teacher gathered around him and listened attentively. Ebuka was so excited that he could attract the attention of the entire family. He then proceeded with his story, "Do you know that in Akpu Town, the people don't kill the python, and the python doesn't kill the people?" Ebuka started.

"What?" was Ebuka's mother's impromptu reaction. She was completely alarmed. "My son, that cannot be true," charged his mother with trepidation.

"My son, don't go and give yourself as food to a hungry python thinking that the python has become your friend, please please please," warned Ebuka's mother. "Let everybody help me warn Ebuka, please," continued Ebuka's worried mother.

"Mother, I don't go near the python regardless," Ebuka was laughing as he assured his mother.

"You better not," commanded the mother, obviously relieved.

"Do you really mean it, Ebuka?" quipped Anayo, who had been pensively quiet.

"Yes, brother. Come and see for yourself."

"Are there many pythons in Akpu then?" continued Anayo. Everybody laughed, oblivious of the clandestine plan that Anayo had instantly developed for the Akpu pythons. But the rest of the family seemed to be listening with nonchalant amusement and considered Ebuka's tale as a child's enchantment.

"Anayo, will you please allow Ebuka to tell us his story? When he is through, you can ask him your many questions, please," their mother appealed.

Ebuka's parents understood that the python was a god in Akpu Town, but Anayo, who had been quietly listening, was thinking about the sweetness of the python, especially in a hot peppered soup. From that time, Anayo started to plot and calculate how he could go to Akpu Town to kill and smuggle pythons to Okwe Town. His plan was not only for his eating, but also to make money. He planned to sell the python meat as a great hunter of python without revealing that he was poaching some people's god.

Anayo kept his plan close to his chest. But he planned

that when it was time for Ebuka to travel back to his master, the teacher, he would take Ebuka back to Akpu Town. While his vacation lasted, Ebuka had turned into a moonlight night storyteller, as he would compel his mother to listen to another story out of Akpu. One such story was the story of the stream and the crab.

Time went fast, and the holiday season was coming to an end. At least so it seemed to Ebuka, who was having a lot of fun playing with his many neighborhood friends.

Soon it was time for Ebuka to return to school. Ebuka dusted his box and washed his clothes in readiness to return to school. His mother bought him new exercise books, which Ebuka brought close to his nose to smell the new aroma.

The holiday was over, and Ebuka was set to return to Akpu town. Anayo volunteered to accompany him to Akpu Town's school. Ebuka was excited that his big brother would accompany him back to his Master in Akpu, but Ebuka was not aware of his brother's clandestine plan which was the real reason for his nice gesture. Usually, Ebuka's father, who was pleasantly surprised at Anayo's unexpected largesse, would have played that role. So Anayo accompanied Ebuka to his Master and intentionally spent a long time with Ebuka, planning to leave quite late because he wanted to look for and kill a python under the cover of darkness. It was a great price to return home with.

The same evening, Nweke was getting ready to go out.

"Nnayi, I am about to serve you dinner. I see that you are on your way out. Please wait and eat before you leave. Is it Ezulu's condolence visit?"

"Woman, when did they make you an Ichie?" responded an angry Nweke. "And what concerns you with the funeral of an Ozo titled man?"

"I am sorry Nnayi for asking," pleaded Mgbogafor. "I just wanted to tell you that I will be leaving early tomorrow morning by first cock's crow to go to Nkwo Agu market," continued Mgbogafor.

"It's like you have become so deaf that you are the only person in Akpu that did not hear the Town Crier?" queried Nweke angrily.

Mgbogafor heard the Town Crier but had forgotten. Her mind was focused on why Nweke was refusing her dinner. "Has the second wife served him dinner?" wondered Mgbogafor.

The second wife Obuteaku, fondly called Obute, was younger and was noticeably Nweke's point of weakness. "But it's my turn to serve him dinner today," continued Mgbogafor, thinking aloud.

Nweke often did not eat when they had their traditional meetings.

Meanwhile, Ebuka's master was concerned that Anayo was staying around too late.

"Anayo, I am not driving you away, but I don't think it is wise for you to travel back to Okwe late for obvious reasons," advised Ebuka's master.

So Anayo left Ebuka at his master's house and went away. Anayo kept perambulating circumspectly in Akpu village with his eyes on the lookout for his prize, the python. At almost nightfall, he finally found one and carefully followed it. At a safe spot, Anayo scouted the surroundings to make sure nobody saw him. He immediately put his right foot very hard on the snake toward its tail section. As soon as the python snake raised its head in reaction, Anayo hit a brutal blow on its head with a heavy stick. Then while the snake was tumbling in pain, Anayo finished it off by cutting off its head with a machete he prepared for this job. He thus killed the harmless and unsuspecting python and loaded it in a sack he brought along. Anayo heaved a sigh of relief that his mission was accomplished. But he didn't know that his accomplishment was nothing but the beginning of a personal tragedy.

Unknown to Anayo, there was an announcement the previous night by the Akpu Town Crier that the night masquerades were to be out that night. A great Ozo titled man, and also a very old man, Ezulu, had died in Akpu. As was the tradition, the burial of such men attracted the appearance of the highest ancestral spirits, called Ayaka. The Ayaka appeared only at night. The Ayaka, unlike the day ancestral spirits, the masquerades, came out without masks. The Ayaka were initiated men in their normal human form. Some even sang and spoke with their regular voices, although most spoke with the guttural voice device. Usually, another night masquerade, Ogbadu, preceded the Ayaka. The Ogbadu was like the forerunner of the Ayaka. Once you hear the Ogbadu, prepare to expect the Ayaka. It was as though the ancestral spirits came out in numbers to welcome the latest arriving fellow ancestral spirit, Ezulu, during his burial. People were warned to stay in their homes because any night the Ayaka, the most sacred of ancestral spirits came out, no human was supposed to be out.

Anyway, Anayo was happy and felt accomplished as he cheerfully traced his way in the dark along the narrow dirt road out of Akpu town. He hung the heavy bag on his left shoulder. Happy thoughts of what he would do with the huge python meat and the accompanying respect filled Anayo as he jollied along in the quietness of the night.

Anayo was close to the border between Akpu and his own town of Okwe when he heard in a distance a certain guttural voice commanding him to stop. Surprised, Anayo halted momentarily. Then he continued his walk home. Then in a matter of seconds came another voice, "What is this daring but foolhardy foul odor I perceive?" came the angry query. Anyone uninitiated to the masquerade cult, or a stranger, was usually referred to as a 'foul odor' by the ancestral spirits who came back to the community as masquerades. Anayo smelt danger and stood still and silent. His heart beat very fast and he was sick in his stomach. He understood that he had run into Akpu Town's night masquerades, certainly a delicate and a dangerous situation. It was indeed unfortunate.

"To worsen matters, I have their god inside my sack, stone dead," lamented terrified Anayo. "No wonder their god has trapped me," he hopelessly concluded. As the sound drew closer and louder, Anayo took a futile detour but was greeted with a louder and closer challenge.

"O bu onyeeeeee?" queried a night masquerade, meaning "Who is that?" stressing the 'who.' Then the masquerades, noticing something unusual, changed their chant to a war song, "Eme n'enu n'obu agha. Eme n'ana n'obu agha. Ka......" It was very unusual for an initiated Akpu man to say nothing to identify himself in the circumstances. Therefore, the ancestral spirits smelled a rat.

Seeing he was surrounded, Anayo dropped the sack containing the python and tried to run, but ran into the waiting and chilling hands of the ancestral beings.

Concerning Anayo, a night masquerade commented, "A frog does not run during the daytime in vain." Apparently, night was the daytime of the ancestral spirits. The masquerades were asking Anayo who he was and his mission on the night of the spirits. They had not yet seen the sack containing the python, their god. Anayo, considering himself already dead, was limp with fear.

Then came the alarm.

"Abomination! Abomination!" came the desperate and piercing cry disrupting the still of the night. A masquerade had seen the slain god of Akpu. The peace of Akpu had been irretrievably jolted. Anayo's spirit sagged, and he was paralyzed with fear. That was the moment Anayo died. The masquerades then cried and lamented the death of one of their own gods and chanted more war songs.

Nweke was one of the night masquerades that held Anayo that night. At that time, in his younger days, Nweke was a fanatic of the Akpu tradition and the gods. But Nweke's fervent disposition towards the gods was probably not due to his trust in the gods but more due to his eagerness to belong and show manliness. It was manly to be traditional.

"This man's head cannot atone for the murder of the royal python, let alone save Akpu from the coming consequential calamities. And all we are here doing is lamentation," screamed Nweke about Anayo. As the words left Nweke's mouth, he drew his shining machete, and in an instance, Anayo's severed head was on the sand and his lifeless body twitching. The masquerades had the dead python and the dead stranger in their hands. For a moment, everything was quiet. Nweke wiped the blood off his machete on the earth and walked away in a rage straight to his house, leaving the other night masquerades behind. Although Nweke killed the stranger in vengeance, he was privately deeply depressed that his god could so easily succumb to becoming the prey of an ordinary stranger. Many thoughts ran riot in Nweke's mind. Even though he would not openly acknowledge it, Nweke knew and felt sad that he could not trust himself to tame his temper and his overzealousness for the gods.

"Should I have controlled my anger and let the gods do the vengeance?"

"But the gods have already shown that they are incapable of vengeance by falling victim to a miserable stranger in the first place," declared Nweke to himself, trying to justify his actions. "If our god can't even defend itself, how can he defend me, let alone the entire Akpu Town?" thought a worried and frustrated Nweke.

"Do the gods really deserve my commitment?" asked Nweke rhetorically.

"Somebody has to give an explanation to this," he mournfully concluded. But deep in his heart, Nweke knew that he needed nobody's explanation. The explanation was simply his own posturing and show of manliness. Nweke had simply fed his ego with a very expensive diet. He had to live up to the people's expectations and earn his high placement in the community. He was an Ichie, a chieftaincy title in Akpu, as well as a rich and respected Ozo titled man. Before noon, news had spread in Akpu Town that a royal python was murdered by a stranger from Okwe. Nobody did mention that the stranger was also brutally murdered. The elders of Akpu had an emergency meeting that evening to deliberate on the

23

sudden and troubling catalog of developments in Akpu. Meanwhile, the family of Anayo in Okwe was looking for him and worried about his disappearance.

The meeting of the elders of Akpu was very tense and divided on how to respond to the sudden and unexpected emergencies. All the elders agreed that the gods gave an instant response to the strange interloper by killing him. But they disagreed on the method by which Nweke killed the stranger. One group said that Nweke characteristically was overzealous and shouldn't have taken the place of the gods.

"We have lived in peace with our neighbors in Okwe for centuries, but now nobody knows what Nweke's overzealousness will result in. If Nweke didn't cut off the man's head, we could have told Okwe that the royal python strangled their son while he tried to kill it. Then we would have been free from blame," remarked Odu.

"Taa kpuchie onu," a hardliner, Ekeocha yelled at Odu, meaning 'Keep your mouth shut.'

"Are we afraid of the hungry Okwe people? Are they not gluttons who are known to have lost control of their throats due to poverty? I heard that if a rabbit runs out from their burning house, they'll abandon the house and first chase after the rabbit," blurted an incensed Ekeocha.

"You should be thanking the gods that Nweke instantly acted like a man and prevented the anger of the gods that a royal python was killed in the full glare of the ancestral spirits while everyone else was paralyzed into a stupor."

"We still have men with balls in Akpu," continued Ekeocha.

"Yes, we welcome peace, but we are not afraid of war. They are taking the peace for granted. That is why an

Okwe man had the effrontery to think that he could eradicate his miserable poverty by converting our royal python into a delicious meat," continued Ekeocha, concluding angrily with this proverb, "Dibia n'agwo otolo, o tiili iki e na mpio?" meaning, "A doctor that treats an infectious disease is not exempt from infection."

"Nobody has the exclusive right to violence," was the only reply from Odu, a usually calm elder and wine tapper. He was essentially saying that nobody should underrate the strength of the peace-loving Okwe people.

Not done, Ekeocha, overtaken with emotion, angrily shouted, "Be careful what you say, Odu, for I can see that your ineptitude is leading you along a dangerous path. Let your utterance not be heard outside this meeting because it will be tantamount to killing an ancestral spirit, which you all know very well the consequence. Nweke was an ancestral spirit that night that he killed the stranger. So an ancestral spirit and not Nweke killed the killer of the royal python."

Odu did not reply to Ekeocha, but he muttered to himself, "Just imagine this. The buttocks farted, but it was the head that received the hard knock!" Odu felt that Ekeocha unfairly rebuked him for a crime committed by Nweke but he dared not say it aloud for obvious reasons.

Then, as the import of Ekeocha's outburst and revelation hit home, a great hush fell over the room. There arose murmurs among the elders as they realized that they had overlooked a dangerous and important aspect of the evolving episode. The Odu faction piped down on the critique of Nweke as this revelation unfolded. The meeting of the elders also disagreed on how to handle Okwe for the abomination of murdering the royal python. The hardline group ignored the murder of the Okwe man, Anayo, but insisted that Okwe should be given an ultimatum concerning the murdered royal python.

"Okwe should be given one market week to tell us why their son sneaked into Akpu on a solemn night to commit an abomination against Akpu," charged a hardline elder. "If they give us an acceptable explanation, we then tell them what to do to atone for their sin. Otherwise, they should prepare for war," concluded the elder.

"Akpu Kwenu!"

"Yaa!"

"Kwe nu!"

"Yaa!"

"Muanu!"

"Yaa!"

"Zuanu!"

"Yaa!"

Akunne, though a moderate, was well respected by both sides of Akpu elders. He stepped in to defuse the rising temper. After he saluted the elders the proper way according to the Igbo tradition, which the earlier speakers failed to do, he rightfully gained the attention of the meeting. But he kept silent for a while, letting the tempers calm down and the expectation mount. Then Akunne put a thumb-full of snuff in his nostrils and sneezed twice. He cleared his throat and cast a deliberate glance around at the elders gathering.

"Mbelede ka eji ama dike," Akunne finally spoke.

He essentially said that brave men are known during an emergency.

"This is an emergency and Akpu is a town of brave men," he continued to the agreement of all. "Both Ekeocha and Odu spoke well, but the connecting link was lost in the understandable emotion of the moment."

Akunne kept quiet again raising, the expectation of the elders.

"If we could travel to yesterday, we would have told Nweke, though an ancestral spirit, to wait for our deliberation and instruction. Yet, this is an opportunity for the elders to show the wisdom for which Akpu is famous. Yes, Okwe will say that we killed their son, but their son sneaked into Akpu uninvited and killed something bigger than their son."

There were whisperings of unanimous agreement with Akunne among the elders.

"As atonement for killing the royal python, we would among other things require that they give Akpu a man. Is it not true?"

There was a thundering unanimous agreement, "It is true, Akunne. You spoke our tradition."

"Then, have they not inadvertently given us a man?" continued Akunne.

Another unanimous agreement followed.

"All our neighboring towns know how strong we are and how foolhardy it is for any town to incur the wrath of Akpu, but we are not warmongers. We don't fight a fight of blame."

"It is now up to us to send an emissary to Okwe and ask them to come to Akpu in peace so that we resolve these issues amicably," concluded Akunne.

Akunne greeted the elders and sat down. There were expressions of satisfaction among the elders and praise for Akunne.

"A man is not just a person who has something

27

dangling between his thighs. Akunne has shown us what a real man is," commented an elder.

The elders thanked Akunne and proceeded to select the emissary to Okwe.

Three elders were selected to go to Okwe in two days' time to invite them for a meeting and settlement. Before the emissary proceeded to Okwe, rumors were already circulating in Okwe that their son was brutally murdered in Akpu without provocation when he went to visit his brother. So Okwe elders had an emergency meeting of their own to deliberate on the murder of their son.

The elders invited Anayo's father to tell them about Anayo's mission to Akpu and what happened to him.

He was looking bewildered and obviously fighting tears. It was not manly for men to cry in Igboland.

"I greet you, my elders," greeted Anayo's father with a bow.

"Your son has gone to join our ancestors, and our ancestors will take vengeance on Anayo's killers. So take heart," spoke an elder, commiserating with him.

"You may now go on, our son," requested the elders.

"On the last Nkwo market day, which was last Sunday, my youngest son, Ebuka, was to go back to his master, a teacher in Akpu because the school break was over. Anayo escorted Ebuka to Akpu because Ebuka is too young to travel alone. We expected Anayo to return home in the afternoon, but till now, we have neither seen Anayo nor heard anything about Ebuka. If not that you invited me, I would have been on my way to Akpu to ask Ebuka's master about Anayo's whereabouts. And now you are here telling me that my son is dead?

"Toaaaaa," he screamed, tears welling in his eyes.

"Anayo, so that's how you went to escort your brother back to his station. And your mother does not even know that you are never coming back?"

"Toaaaa, is it true, Anayo, that you have gone to the land of no return?"

Then some elders helped him to sit down and tried to console him.

Okwe elders were still in that meeting when they got the news that the Akpu emissary was in town. The Akpu emissary was directed to the elder's meeting. The atmosphere was so charged that it felt as if one could touch it. Nevertheless, as Igbo elders, they had to differentiate themselves from young men. In Igbo culture, young men could be excused for irrational and emotional behavior, but not elders. So Okwe elders had to observe proper Igbo protocol in welcoming their visitors. The Igbo say that what a man would do is lodged inside his chest. Besides, Okwe elders understood that these men from Akpu were just emissaries, even though they were elderly. An Igbo proverb says, "If you send me a message to the king, I will deliver. But if you send me to go and carry him, I will retreat."

So Akpu elders entered the venue of the Okwe elders meeting, which was at a mud house Town Hall at the village square. They were offered seats facing their hosts, the Okwe elders.

"Welcome to Okwe," declared the chief spokesman of Okwe elders. Without the usual prayers that go with the presentation of kola nut in Igboland, the spokesman presented kola nut on a carved wooden tray. "We have kola nuts," he declared in an unmasked bitter tone.

"Thank you for the kola nuts, but we're not here to eat kola nut," responded the leader of Akpu somewhat rudely.

"The kola nut could wait until after the urgent business of the day," concluded the Akpu delegation spokesman with a firm and serious emphasis.

The spokesman of Okwe then spoke, "Since our guests have refused our kola nuts, our ears are open to hearing your urgent message."

"Our message is very straight forward. A son of Okwe sneaked into Akpu under the cover of darkness, even on a solemn night, and committed an abomination against the gods of our land," started an Akpu elder.

"Don't speak in proverbs. What did he do?" charged an Okwe elder.

"Yes tell us what he did," added another Okwe elder, the tension mounting.

"He murdered a royal python in the full glare of the ancestral spirits. In the process he lost his own life," continued the Akpu elder.

"So you murdered him?" interrupted an Okwe elder.

"That is why we came here to invite you for a meeting in Akpu, so that we tell you what you need to do for the cleansing to avoid trouble between our two communities, and also to claim the corpse of your son," concluded the Akpu elder. At this point, tempers had risen to a dangerous level.

"So your dead royal python retaliated and killed our son? And you have staggered into this place like drunken men to tell us that you murdered our son because he killed a snake?"

"Toaaaaa!"

"Okwe elie nsi," screamed an Okwe elder, meaning,

"Okwe has eaten excrement! — grossly insulted."

"Tuffiakwa!" shouted another.

"Simple common sense should tell you Akpu men that if you have to fight for your god, it's a weak and powerless god, and it's time to dump him. Your god ought to fight for you, instead of you fighting for your god. Our tortoise may be small in size but it's very powerful. It's the tiny dry meat that swells and fills the mouth!" concluded the elder.

"Besides, it is an abomination in Igboland to kill a stranger except in war," contributed another Okwe elder.

"Not when the stranger declared war on Akpu," countered an Akpu elder.

"Can you tell us how an innocent Okwe man declared war on Akpu?" queried an Okwe elder.

"He was so innocent that he sneaked into Akpu under the cover of darkness and killed a royal python. That was equivalent to a declaration of war," answered the Akpu elder. "Even the ancestral spirits were chanting war songs after he killed the royal python. That was when an ancestral spirit killed him," continued the Akpu elder.

"Oh, your weakling ancestral spirits were sleeping when he killed your royal python and woke up immediately after," mocked the Okwe elder.

"You and your ancestral spirits must be mad," concluded the Okwe elder.

"Enough of this evil vituperation," thundered the leader of the Akpu elders. "We came here for peace, but it is obvious that you have chosen the dance of the madman at the market square."

"It is obvious that Okwe people have never heard this

Igbo proverb, 'If a young boy is not strong enough and goes to investigate what killed his father, what killed his father will also kill him.' There is no doubt that you are as small and as slow as your tortoise god. We'll meet at the battlefield," concluded the enraged Akpu leader.

And at this point, Akpu men stormed out of the meeting because the Okwe elder referred to their royal python as a weak and powerless god and a mere snake.

"If not that they were guests, they would not have left here alive. But the lion does not eat dead meat," continued the Okwe elder. The battle line had thus been drawn.

Meanwhile, Anayo's father, grief-stricken, walked home to his family whose ears were on the road itching for the news about Anayo and obviously expecting the worst. The man's countenance said it all. As soon as they sighted the man and observed his hopeless mood Anayo's mother gave out a spontaneous outcry of grief, "Alu emee muooooh."

The rest of the family joined her in the mournful chorus.

"I knew that a terrible thing had befallen my son because Anayo had never spent a night away without notice."

"But whoever is responsible for the death of my son will never know peace. The gods will pursue him till he curses the day he was born," the women who had gathered on hearing Anayo's mother's outcry agreed to the curses. Anayo's father walked into his house quietly, saying nothing to anybody. Nobody had the courage to say anything to him.

Later, when the Akpu men got home, a meeting of the elders was sitting. So they returned right into the midst of elders, anxious for an answer. By the time the emissaries narrated the insult given to the royal python, the drums of war started beating.

"If Nweke didn't act like our brave forefathers, this is the kind of shame we would have had to live with. The cowards of Okwe calling our royal python a mere snake. Ten heads from Okwe are not enough to atone for the abomination Okwe has committed. They have spat into our very eyes, but they will hear from Akpu," boasted Ekeocha.

Within days, the news spread that an Akpu woman was missing. Her family reported that she went to a distant market overpassing Okwe, but for three days she hadn't returned. The evening of the third day of the woman's disappearance, the drums that signaled trouble or war started to beat, and people were troubled. The drums were beating all day:

"Obodo Dike."

"Town of the brave."

That same night, the Town Crier beat his own ogene, Gom, gom, gom.

"People of Akpu, men and women, hear the message from the elders. Nobody should go to Okwe town or pass through it from henceforth. I have delivered the message as I was instructed."

Gom, gom, gom.

After some minutes, you would hear his message again, and it faded steadily until it was so faint that you won't understand what he was saying. Everyone in Akpu knew that there was trouble. Certain young men's age-grade societies were having regular meetings bordering on the eventuality of war. But spiritual war was more real than the war of machetes and Dane guns because the Colonial Government would send troops. There would be no victors or vanquished, only a number of heads brought home. Nweke was bound to bring heads home if war broke out.

The first test of strength between Akpu and Okwe presented itself. In two market weeks, a neighboring town Abam would hold their feast, which was famous for its masquerade festival. The last day of this feast was the largest gathering of masquerades in that province. All the surrounding towns sent their best masquerades to this 'mmanwu festival.'

There were two classes of competition here. The first was the Flogging masquerade competition. This competition was to determine who could most withstand the pain of the whip. It was a display of youthful strength and manliness. It was so rated that 'echi ka mmuo gi g'eje Eke' became a popular cliche in Okwe. Literally speaking, it said mockingly, 'tomorrow your masquerade will go to Eke.' Someone telling you that what you just boasted you'd do was not within your reach to achieve.

The second was the fetish and magical masquerade competition. During this competition, the dangerous masquerades cast bewitching spells and enchantments on themselves. The weaker masquerades fell under the weight of the spell. It was akin to the battle of the gods. D-day had come and all the flogging masquerades, their hands filled with long flexible whips, were assembled at the Eke market square. Masquerades outnumbered human beings so much that it was hard to see a human being in the market square. It was usually a fun display where the stronger masquerade drove its opponent out of the square with a stronger whipping power. But this day's contest would prove an unfriendly and a fatal event for two towns. Akpu masquerades entered the arena chanting their signature tunes.

"Onye akponiganiga n'ezi oyibo. Odi Igbo na nso anya."

"Onye akponiganiga."

"Onye akponiganiga n'ezi oyibo. Mmanwu anyi no nuzo."

"Onye akponiganiga."

The import of the song is:

"Let nobody put up a show of reckless impunity on a major road because the Igbo don't approve of it."

Refrain

"Let nobody put up a show of reckless impunity on the major road because our masquerade is out on the road."

Refrain

Actually, they were the ones putting up the impunity show because they insinuated that while they were on the road, every other user should give way. They were the kings of the road! The masquerades were all charged up and itching for action. Some of them moved back and forth, leaping up and shaking their bodies, the tiny bells attached on some of them ringing ceaselessly. They moved back and forth, partly as a frenzy for the severity of the situation, and partly as a required spiritual movement in the spiritual warfare.

The whipping event of the festival started. People usually gathered from a distance to watch the masquerades display their strength and tenacity. But soon all eyes were focused on the Akpu versus Okwe masquerades. People outside these two towns thought that the masquerades from Akpu and Okwe towns were exceptional that year. Little did they know that the display of unusual tenacity was premeditated until a fight broke out among the two towns' masquerades.

The masquerades defied the rules of the whipping competition and flogged each other indiscriminately, inflicting serious injuries until it degenerated to physical bodily fights. Then they tore the masks of opposing masquerades open and some masquerades were stabbed. It was not only a bloody contest but also an abomination. It was an abomination in all of Igboland to expose a masquerade to the public. As soon as the people of Abam discovered the abomination about to take place, they sent both men and masquerades of Abam to surround them and shield them from public view. The men and masquerades of Abam town separated the warring masquerades, but it was too late, as many casualties had been recorded. People ran helter-skelter for safety, unable to understand what went wrong. After the dust settled, there were a few deaths, especially deaths of Okwe masquerades, and some were still in a clinic receiving treatment. At the venue of the fetish masquerades, no less vicious spiritual war was going on, albeit an invisible war. But the manifestations of the invisible war were visible for the trained and discerning eyes. These masquerades cast evil spells on each other, sometimes stretching their hands as if they were indeed shooting visible arrows. The receiving masquerades would often sway and stagger, then steadying their gait, would retaliate with their own darts to the enemy masquerades.

Two masquerades stood out like David and Goliath.

Okwe brought an Ijele masquerade in its squad. The Ijele masquerade was the biggest masquerade in terms of size. But it was also normally very strong magically because the followers of the Ijele didn't want it to fall while displaying its moves because of its excessive size.

Akpu's magically strongest masquerade was comparatively small-sized but mysterious and ugly looking. It had smoke emanating from the top of its head and a live bird hanging precariously from its head looking tortured. The masquerade, seemingly unperturbed about the condition of the bird it had in tow, marched briskly forward, then took a few steps backward. Men beat heavy banana stems and palm fronds before the masquerade, and a flute man blew his flute with a sense of urgency which made the masquerade charge forward again like one drunk or possessed. The flute was akin to a strong alcoholic drink to the small masquerade. This masquerade had bells attached to its mask all over, making jingle sounds as the masquerade moved backwards and forwards.

The Akpu's number one fetish masquerade was now face-to-face with the Okwe's leading fetish Ijele masquerade. The smaller Akpu masquerade moved forward, then stopped abruptly as if blocked by a wedge that only he could see. The Ijele stood still and wasn't taking its rhythmic dance steps. It was surrounded as usual by a lot of men, but this time it was obvious that all was not well with the Ijele. The smaller masquerade seemed to have regained its balance and initiative, and so charged forward again, right hand stretched forward toward the Ijele. The Ijele swayed briefly, moved forward and fell, causing a lot of brown dust to rise toward the sky. It was a very rare occurrence and signaled the end of the spiritual warfare between Akpu and Okwe. Akpu was victorious in both spiritual and physical battles. Akpu men started to head home, jubilating on their victory of the phase one battle, whereas Okwe men and masquerades started trooping home dejected.

But some Akpu men and masquerades, not done, did more havoc. A masquerade from Akpu suddenly took off and raced to a masquerade he thought was an Okwe masquerade. The Akpu masquerade was apparently intoxicated with his own witchcraft, and so rushed and tackled an Abam Town masquerade. He stabbed the Abam Town masquerade, and he was bleeding. He held him down and mocked, "Cowardly ancestral spirit. Today you will die the second time because I will kill you and send you to your ancestors again. See how you're bleeding like a chicken because I have sacrificed you to my Ikenga."

Unsure of what was happening, the men and masquerades of Akpu and Okwe turned back and raced to the arena. Abam Town masquerades rushed as well to the arena to rescue their masquerade. In the ensuing confusion, there was a free-for-all fight. No one talked about abomination again because things had gone out of control such that the wounded Abam Town masquerade was lying motionless and apparently dead. Several other men and masquerades were littered all over the arena and the adjoining roads. Some of the dying men and masquerades were twitching as they gave the last struggles of life. Women and the uninitiated had completely disappeared from the entire arena and its vicinity because the things happening were not safe for them to witness. It was an abomination for any woman to witness what was going on.

"We have never witnessed a situation close to this in the history of Abam Town," declared an elder from Abam.

"Akpu town has an explanation to make concerning the calamity that happened today. They undoubtedly have huge reparations to pay."

"And cleansing for the abominations that occurred today," added another.

Suddenly, a huge troop of men with some masquerades from Abam Town had amassed and were approaching from the eastern end of town chanting war songs. They were armed with machetes and Dane guns, and it was obvious that Abam Town had prepared for war and the men appeared very thirsty for blood. The assembled troops from Abam far outnumbered the members of both Akpu and Okwe towns. Nobody knew exactly what the mission of the amassed Abam troops was except maybe to avenge the deaths of their kindred human or ancestral. As the men and masquerades of Akpu and Okwe heard the noise of the approaching Abam troops, they scurried in retreat for safety. The advancing Abam troops soon reached the arena and paused their advance as if to reorganize before continuing their movement to a place no one was exactly sure about. The arena is now filled with only the men and masquerades of Abam town. The men and masquerades of Akpu and Okwe had all gone back to their towns.

Back in Akpu Town, rumor had it that the men of

Abam were on the verge of attacking Akpu. Akpu Town, therefore, prepared their own men for war. The atmosphere was tense and pregnant because nobody knew when Abam men would attack Akpu Town. Meanwhile, Okwe Town equally prepared for war, not knowing the intentions of Abam. Akpu Town was now in enmity with both Okwe Town and Abam. Men and women of Akpu started to go missing from time to time. They would go to the market and never return. To worsen matters, there was an outbreak of leprosy among an unusual number of Akpu men. Akpu people were in a panic and sensed that all was not well with the town. The elders of Akpu, therefore, went to the oracle and the answer was predictable.

"You have committed untold abominations against Abam town. Go to Abam and find out what you should do," declared the Chief Priest of Akpu town.

"Next, you should go to Okwe and also find out what you should do to avoid the looming calamity. The gods are angry with you for your recklessness and impunity toward Okwe and Abam. You should look for the black sheep while it is still daylight. I have delivered the message as instructed," concluded the Chief Priest.

Meanwhile, Abam town had banned both Akpu and Okwe towns from participating in future Abam festivities till further notice.

CHAPTER TWO

Ekigwe's heart was no longer with Akpu tradition but with the Christians. Ekigwe was simply playing it safe because of his father whose rage was worth fearing. So Ekigwe looked for other distractions, like hunting with his catapult. Nweke especially looked forward to the coming Opoto feast. He hoped that this Opoto would herald the return of his "lost" son. Ekigwe was ripe to be initiated into the masquerade cult (Ima Nmuo). Ekigwe was also of age to be initiated into the Amanwulu and age-grade societies. Nweke hoped that after these initiations, his son would grow up into a responsible man interested in his people's tradition and in his father's farm work. Ekigwe was indeed of age the previous year for the masquerade cult initiation but he ran away into hiding on the night of initiation. Ekigwe had heard gory tales of the initiation process. His schoolmates who were already initiated had, sometimes deliberately, exaggerated their account of how Ekigwe would be introduced to the spirits of the dead regardless of whether they were his ancestors.

"They are dead," Ekigwe would grumble to himself.

"Why won't they just stay in their domain and leave us

living people alone?" Besides, the thought of confronting the terrible howling spirit tigers (Agu Nmuo) sent shivers down his spine.

The sound of bells from Nweke's wooden gate attracted Nweke's attention. He turned his eyes away from the heap of yams he was sorting to look for who was at the gate. It was no other than the most frequent visitor, Akilika.

"Opulozor!" Nweke called his friend.

"Ogbuefi!" Akilika called Nweke back by his own titled name.

"Here is a chair," Nweke pulled a carved wooden stool for Akilika. Akilika sat down to their usual banter.

"I wonder what can ever take the place of yams in your life," Akilika remarked jokingly to Nweke.

"Maybe you want me to farm cocoyam. I leave cocoyams for you but please leave yams for me," joked back Nweke to Akilika. Both men burst out laughing. Cocoyams are the exclusive preserve of women just as real men are known for yams.

"I am trying my best to stack these yams before Opoto so that I can celebrate Opoto with peace of mind. I also want to focus on Ekigwe to make sure he does not dodge the Maturity ceremony, Ima Nmuo, like he did last year."

Ekigwe's fear troubled Nweke so much that he told his friend Akilika that he wondered whether his son was a woman that mistakenly came out in a man's form. Akilika counseled Nweke about his fears for Ekigwe, "Ogbuefi, you asked the gods for a son and they gave you a son. Therefore, whether it was a woman that came out with a man's penis, we don't know. What we don't know won't know us. Be patient with Ekigwe."

"Opulozo, you've spoken well. But you know, women often know more than we are ready to give them the credit for."

"Ogbuefi, which women?" asked Opulozo.

"You remember that my mother questioned my marriage of Ekigwe's mother?"

"No, I don't remember. But so what?" asked Opulozo, wondering how this came into the discussion.

"Well, Ekigwe's behavior often leaves me wondering if my mother knew something that I didn't know," continued Ogbuefi, sounding sneaky.

"Come out plain and stop talking in parables!" charged Opulozo.

"I am not sure where that pregnancy came from because a tiger cannot give birth to a chicken," Nweke finally landed.

"It is time for me to go home," declared Akilika insinuating that Nweke had nothing else important to say. Akilika excused himself from his friend and departed for his house before Nweke accused him of being responsible for the pregnancy that produced Ekigwe.

Nweke hoped to finish his lonely work of tying the yams to the stakes in the barn in time to free himself to fully celebrate the upcoming feast. The air in Akpu village was filled with the aroma of the great feast called Opoto only a few market weeks away.

Opoto was celebrated not long after the Awanji (Alonmo) feast. Awanji was a spiritual celebration performed before anyone ate the new yam. It was celebrated throughout Igboland to thank the gods for a good harvest and also to allow the ancestors to eat first before humans ate. Although spiritually, Awanji was

43

superior to all feasts, Opoto was practically the king of all feasts in Akpu Town. It was celebrated to thank the gods of all the surrounding villages for ushering them into the new year. Opoto was the reward of a year of hard work. The harvest time was over and Opoto was a celebration of the end of the harvest, and especially a celebration of rest and relaxation after a season of hard work, planting and weeding before another season began. It was a season for real men, successful farmers, to show off their prowess as great farmers through their extensive barns of yams. Great farmers were known by their massive barns of yams (oba ji), which sometimes stretched over a hundred yards of endless rows of yams craftily tied to each other on erect palm stems.

Akilika just walked into Nweke's compound. As Nweke once told Akilika, "You know that you are no longer a visitor in this house." So Nweke told Akilika to pull a stool and sit down. What was always their key subject if not yams?

"This year's harvest has become one of the greatest in memory," Nweke told his only close and trusted friend, Akilika, with an air of pride and professionalism. Akilika put a thumb-full of snuff in his nostril as if in acknowledgment of Nweke's comment.

"It's ample evidence that the gods of Akpu are happy with us," added Akilika to Nweke's obvious delight.

"Well, the great sacrifices of goats and rams you made this year are also the greatest in memory," Akilika continued to Nweke's further delight.

One of Nweke's wives once said that if Nweke gave his family half the attention reserved for his yams, that his family, rather than his yams, would be the envy of Akpu village. By all standards, Nweke was undisputedly one of the most successful and wealthy farmers in Akpu. He married seven wives to help him in the farm business.

Akilika was also a successful farmer, although not in the league of Nweke. But he was successful enough to take on the Ozo title.

In the weeks leading to Opoto, it was Nweke's routine to be in his barn early in the morning, tying his yams to stakes in preparation for the great feast of Opoto. Nweke could not afford to employ many hands in the barn because, unlike the planting and harvesting of yams, work in the barn was very delicate and intricate. Careless hands would break most of the yam seedlings. Nweke had a distrust of the youth.

"The youth of today have become softened and distracted from our forefathers' traditions because of white man's new religion and culture," he lamented in veiled reference to his son Ekigwe.

"As long as they bring the spoils of the white man like the bee which brings pain and pleasure, we can stomach them. That was what Aforcha did and was at last celebrated by the people of Akpu," responded Akilika almost weary of Nweke's complaints.

"Aforcha is a different breed, Opulozo," responded Nweke. Aforcha was one man that Nweke esteemed a lot in Akpu.

"Yes, Aforcha was very smart with the white man. He took the good things about them but he did not surrender himself to them," emphasized Nweke.

"How could Aforcha have taken any good tradition from them if he did not go near them? He incurred the fury of his father and was driven out of the family. Today he is bigger than the king," emphasized Akilika.

"So Opulozo, what are you saying? Which side are you on?" queried Nweke.

"Ogbuefi, you should not ask me such a question. You know I am a Chief and I know Akpu tradition. But it is common knowledge among Akpu elders that you keep your good sons close to our tradition. But if you have a weak or a rebellious son, he can jolly well join the Efulefu. If he perishes, so be it. But if perchance anything good comes out of him, he is still your son. When Aforcha came back from the dead, so to say, did his family and indeed did all Akpu not celebrate him like a king?"

"Opulozo!"

"Ogbuefi!"

"You have spoken like a man," acknowledged Nweke of his friend.

"Thank you, Ogbuefi, but I must add that what we are missing is pragmatism. I have been observing this trend about people who leave our tradition to follow the white man and his god.

All of them end up controlling everybody with their money and influence. Just think about Aforcha's bicycle, his powerful light never before seen in these towns. I think he called it 'Ntili.'

Who does not like something good? Remember how the whole village gathered around his house daily. Our problem is that we follow our gods with both eyes closed. But the white man does what works for him, a bit of his god and a bit of common sense. We fantasize too much, Ogbuefi.

Life is not fairy tales. It's time we stop fantasizing, start thinking and start taking action."

Nweke uncharacteristically sat through Akilika's sermon without a word, but one could see he was thinking, especially of Aforcha's success. Nweke escorted Akilika to the gate and both men retired for the night in their huts.

Because the tradition dictates that after the feast, it became forbidden by the gods for anyone to harvest any yams, Nweke and all Akpu persevered to finish their harvest before the feast of Opoto. Any yams not harvested by this time were left for the poor and wretched of the village to help themselves.

Anyone who violated this rule was visited with the plague, understood by all to be leprosy. But nobody called it by name because leprosy would hear and pay an unpleasant visit to the caller. It was instead called Mkpobuna, which could be vaguely translated as stubbing your toes. Tending yams in the barn was a lonely routine for Nweke. Lately, his first son Ekigwe, a teenager, was no longer showing interest in his father's farm work. Nweke had been pondering over what might have been diverting his son's attention.

"Is it Ekigwe's habit of going out daily with his catapult to target some game-squirrels and birds, or is it something else that I don't know?" Nweke continued to wonder aloud.

"Times have indeed changed," commented Nweke, shaking his head in disbelief. Nweke especially looked forward to the coming Opoto feast. He hoped that this Opoto would herald the return of his "lost" son. Ekigwe was ripe to be initiated into the masquerade cult (Ima Nmuo). The uninitiated (Ogbodu) could not stand before a masquerade. The masquerade would even cry out that he smelt the foul smell of the uninitiated.

"Ogbodu n'esi," the masquerade would cry out anytime the uninitiated was nearby.

Ekigwe would remember one Opoto feast when he was younger. He was standing outside their compound holding on to his father and scared stiff when suddenly an Ekwulo masquerade carrying several whips approached. The masquerade sprang briskly towards his father and in his guttural voice greeted Nweke.

"Nweke de."

Leaping up and shifting backwards, "Nweke denme denme," the masquerade repeated the greeting with emphasis.

"Mmuo na nma (beautiful spirit)," Nweke answered.

Next, to Ekigwe's shock, the masquerade greeted him, "Ekigwe de."

Ekigwe moved further behind his father, trembling with fear. While Ekigwe was still grappling in wonder about how an ancestral spirit knew his name, the masquerade told Nweke that Ekigwe's great grandfather sent his greetings from the great beyond. Ekigwe's fears about masquerade initiation were now confirmed and compounded. Ekigwe marveled greatly and wondered why his great grandfather would not come in person so he would know him. When the masquerade left, Ekigwe asked his father, "Father, how did the masquerade know my name?"

"Your great grandfather of course told him your name and also sent greetings to you through the masquerade," answered Ekigwe's father. Ekigwe was speechless.

In the period before this Opoto, Nweke had told the young men of his clan to keep watch over Ekigwe and make sure he was initiated. And as part of Nweke's preparation for this Opoto, he rose early one morning and went straight to the chickens' pen. He disturbed the sleep of the chickens and came out with a very big white hen, took it away muttering some incantations and then tied one of its legs against a bitterleaf stem. Later that morning Nweke cut the chicken's neck before his Chi (personal god). He held the neck of the chicken to direct the gushing blood on the helpless idol. Nweke then appealed to the idol to visit his son this Opoto and make him behave like a man, like his forefathers. Nweke's Chi simply starred emotionlessly into the brightening morning serenity.

The idol seemed to be saying, "Let this man continue to waste his time and blow hot air." Even Nweke, momentarily, wondered what was going on in his Ikenga's wooden mind.

"Odonigwugwu!" exclaimed Nweke exonerating himself in clear conscience.

"Nevertheless, I have done my duty. It is now up to you to do your part," Nweke reasoned aloud as if his Ikenga's wooden ears were indeed hearing him. The idol continued to stare into the morning, seemingly unperturbed by Nweke's comments.

Ekigwe, who had been sitting quietly under the kola nut tree and watching his father from a distance, broke his silence.

"Father, why is your god always asking you for a white chicken or a white ram? Is a white chicken sweeter than a red or multicolor chicken?" Immediately Nweke exploded: "Taa kpuchie onu, agu tawagi agba. Anu offia."

"Will you shut your mouth up? Let the tiger tear your jaws up you wild beast." Nweke was trembling with rage and Ekigwe was poised for a run if need be. Ekigwe could never understand why a simple question would generate such fury. Ekigwe stayed away from his father's compound till his father's rage subsided.

Ekigwe often pitied his father's personal god, who by Ekigwe's judgment moped through its hollow eyes like someone who had lost every clue, that is if it ever had any. He specifically pitied its untidiness from the many chickens' blood it had been bathed with. Ekigwe once thought that somebody should give that idol a bath. But he reasoned, "Whoever tried that, my father would skin him alive."

"But why does my father pour the blood on his idol's body instead of pouring it into its mouth? Can't he just see that it is very untidy?" Ekigwe continued to wonder.

Nweke felt he was rightfully worried about Ekigwe because apart from using his catapult to target squirrels and birds, Ekigwe's other favorite pastime was to climb fruit trees. His favorite relaxation was often to climb the orange tree by the mud fence of his compound overlooking the village pathway. Rather than use the palm tree branch stick with a hook at its tip to pluck the orange, Ekigwe would climb the tree armed with a penknife. He would relax on a v-branch completely surrounded by ripe oranges. He would then pluck oranges, peel and lick them. It was more appealing to Ekigwe because some of the oranges he plucked with the hook usually fell on a hard surface and burst open. Sand often entered such oranges. Besides, Ekigwe sometimes played pranks on passers-by. He would throw the licked orange peel across the fence on a passerby, leaving him muttering to himself and wondering where a leaked orange and peel fell from. Ekigwe would be greatly amused and would chuckle softly so the victim wouldn't hear and discover him. As far as Ekigwe was concerned, he was only having fun, albeit at other people's expense. Ekigwe and his father saw life from two different contradictory perspectives, old culture and the emerging culture.

Once, Ekigwe's hobby almost put him in deadly trouble. Bush rabbits were a delicacy in Akpu, and Ekigwe was in the habit of going after them with his catapult. Ekigwe was an amateur hunter of rabbits because it was difficult to kill a rabbit with the catapult. The rabbits would take shelter in the rabbit holes in the earth. Serious rabbit hunters usually put fire around the hole to smoke them out of their underground havens. They would then wait, machete ready, to kill the rabbits as they ran out of the hole. One day Ekigwe went rabbit hunting and met other more serious hunters in the woods. These boys put fire around the rabbit hole to make the heat and smoke force them out of the hole. Their machetes, shining and razor-sharp held up for a lucky strike, Ekigwe was hanging around them and watching to see a rabbit dash out of its hole for a daring escape.

"Get out of the way boy," came the angry warning from one of the boys to Ekigwe. "I'll rather have your head on the ground than miss this rabbit." As soon as he finished his warning, his machete ferociously sliced through the air downwards, missing Ekigwe's head by an inch. He hit the rabbit at the tail slicing it away from the rabbit which was desperate to escape alive. The rabbit left part of its tail with the hunter and escaped. The hunter blamed Ekigwe for his miss but warned him that next time he won't be this lucky. Ekigwe was badly shaken and went home but didn't say a word to his parents.

As Opoto approached, the night air in Akpu was always filled with the sound of various types of music filtering in from masquerade and ordinary dances, practicing or learning from established dance groups or from sometimes, distant villages. Every feast of Opoto promised to showcase new dances often copied from other villages and towns. These dance groups were hosted for some weeks by the groups in Akpu village who were learning the music and dance.

The howl of the spirit tigers (Agu mmuo) often broke the serenity of the night – an indication that the spirits of the ancestors were also preparing for Opoto and the appearance of the masquerades (the physical spirit of the ancestors). These spirit tigers were the nightmare of young ladies who had to go to the village stream far away at the outskirts of the village to fetch badly-needed water for cooking. These ladies could not go to the stream in daytime again because of the flogging masquerades who were considered far worse than the spirit tigers and were fond of laying in ambush for daring young ladies.

Akpu village could boast of such great masquerades from the smallest Ada masquerade to the king of masquerades, Ijele. Just as you have in humans the youth and the elders, so you also have in masquerades. When the big masquerades (Nnukwu Mmanwu) appeared in an arena, the small masquerades gave way. Akpu village had Nwadibia, the small dancing masquerade and singing masquerades like Ulaga and Ndudu as well as Atunma, the teasing masquerade. Girls liked to watch and hear Atunma, but they were always hoping that they wouldn't end up the subject of its jokes. Once, Atunma was performing at the neighborhood playground (Ogwe Nso).

One of Akilika's daughters, Oliaku, was in the crowd. Atunma started a song that was a song popular with girls for their stomping and clapping game. Atunma then started to dance toward Oliaku as he sang.

"Oliaku bia gbu m uga eh, Oliaku g'aegbulili uga eh".

Immediately Oliaku shyly dodged to the outer edge of the crowd covering her face. The crowd erupted in laughter. Atunma danced in a loop back to the center of the arena plotting another target.

"Mgbe m n'esili gi osipaka, I gwago nne gi," he continued with another girl. He was telling the girl she couldn't refuse his friendship request claiming, "When I was cooking rice for you, did you tell your mother?" That was even more embarrassing to the girl, causing a lot of laughs.

There was also Mmuo Akuko, the storyteller. Awuka was the family masquerade complete with father, mother, daughter and a foolish, irresponsible son. Maybe that's why Awuka also had a police masquerade. There was also the Ogba Mgbada (Ojionu), which was a great dancer. Some clowns in Akpu translated the rhythm of his music thus: "Would you go back to Ukwulu village again?"

And his reply was: "Let me safely return from my current trip first."

There were also the flogging masquerades called Akataka, Ekwulo and Ogolo. Although the flogging masquerade often inflicted injury to people on its way, it was still by far the most exciting of all masquerades. This was probably because it brought fear, suspense and excitement to the atmosphere, and people, especially ladies, were ever-ready to flee from the masquerade's whips. However, the flogging masquerades usually gave a difference to adult men who were initiated into the masquerade cult. It was a playful atmosphere during feasts in Akpu village. The flogging masquerade would ask a man, "Do you know me?"

And the man would playfully reply, "Who can know you?"

But of course, even if you knew the man behind the mask, it would be foolhardy and disastrous for you to utter it. How could you know an ancestor long dead before you were even born?

Izaga was the tallest of all masquerades because it walked on stilts. Okwonma was a dangerous and feared machete-wielding masquerade, but Ijele was the biggest and most celebrated masquerade in Akpu. It was like a moving town complete with all the replica and features of a town on it including trees, houses, rivers, precious stones, dancers, even masquerades meticulously crafted into its massive structure. The Ijele was full of glitter and color. Whenever the Ijele appeared, men surrounded it as it moved in case it tried to fall, which was quite rare. Only a physically and magically strong man could carry an Ijele mask.

There were masquerades that appeared only at night. Only initiated men could come out on the nights they appeared. No women stepped out on the nights that these masquerades came out. Agummuo (Spirit Tiger) was not exactly a night masquerade but a masquerade spirit. When a feast approached, the howl of Agunmuo at night was an indication that the feast was a masquerade grade feast. That meant you should expect masquerades during that feast. The Ogbadu was the masquerade that first went round the town before the Ayaka, the highest and only-at-night masquerade appeared. So Ogbadu was like the forerunner or announcer of the ubiquitous Ayaka. Ayaka was actually a hundred voices singing a frightening kind of song. The sound of Ayaka sent chills down the spine of every villager of Akpu. Everybody sort of hid in his house throughout the night that Ayaka appeared. Ayaka was actually masquerading without masks. The bearers of the masquerades came out as real humans in a large group, and that's why the rest of the population was forbidden to come out, lest they saw that it was humans that they probably knew that were involved. That in itself was a dangerous and life-threatening abomination. Wives and mothers mostly didn't know that their husbands and sons were the Ayaka. But even those who had any idea wouldn't dare to utter it, even to their husbands.

Both the day and night masquerades sang or spoke in guttural voices, which made them appear as extra-terrestrial beings indeed. Actually, they spoke and sang through a cylindrical pipe which was open on one end and covered at the other end with a white cobweb taken from the covering of the spider eggs. This was why the masquerades in their speech or song often declared that it was the spider crying. The uninitiated would not understand the meaning of "the spider was crying or speaking." And indeed, the spider could as well have some mystical symbolism that only the spirit beings understood. Ordinary beings and many uninitiated kept wondering what the spider had in common with the ancestral spirits that they kept referring to themselves as spiders.

CHAPTER THREE

On this particular night, it was a full moon and the moon shined so bright that it was almost like daylight. The happy sound of Nweke's children from many wives dominated the night air around Nweke's compound as they engaged in "Egwu Onwa (Moonlight Night Play)." The children played the popular children's play, which they sang and danced in circles, holding hands.

Akpa kolo, kpan kolo
Akpa kolo, kpan kolo
Udu moo, ogene
Udu moo, ogene
Onye Omalu,
Iya...ya...ya...ya. I yaa.
Si n'a oganaga, si n'a oganaga ngwo
Oga n'aga, si n'a oganaga ngwo

At the end of the song, whoever was the last to squat got eliminated. Other children were dancing "Igbu Uga." A more vigorous song and dance, involving clapping of hands and stamping of the feet in a peculiar fashion. The girls sang and called on their friends and sisters to come and "gbue uga" with them. The air in Nweke's compound that night was electric.

At the obi (the man's compound), Nweke was relaxing over roasted yam and ukpaka (oil bean seed) mixed with pepper in red palm oil when his friend Akilika walked into the Obi for the usual evening banter.

"Ogbuefi," Akilika saluted Nweke with Nweke's title name.

"Opulozo," Nweke acknowledged, calling him with his own title name.

"Welcome," greeted Nweke receiving him. "You are no longer a stranger in this house. I believe you have developed a talisman that tells you when your favorite food is ready in my house," joked Nweke.

"You cannot be further from the truth, except that it's designed especially for your palm wine," Akilika joked back, and they both burst out into laughter.

"There's a chair," continued Nweke drawing near a round carved wooden stool for Akilika. Nweke went to the side of the hut and brought a keg of foaming palm wine with dead bees in the foam. That was the evening flow from the raffia palm tapping, and sometimes it was sweeter than the morning flow. Nweke sat down and used the back of his palm to remove both the foam and the dead bees.

"We use the eyes to know a ripe corn. Mgbechi has no rival in Akpu as far as wine tapping is concerned," acknowledged Akilika about the wine Nweke just brought in.

"Even the bees and the flies recognize this and so have decided to die inside the palm wine so as to drink Mgbechi's wine forever," added Nweke, both busting into laughter.

Of course, the snuff boxes were ever-present in the bags of Nweke and Akilika. After eating kola nuts, Nweke and Akilika settled down to sniff snuff and to enjoy the palm wine.

A very big goat was tied to the kola nut tree inside Nweke's Obi. The goat was like a condemned man waiting for the guillotine. If the goat was troubled about its impending fate, you wouldn't know cause it seemed to always await its food eagerly. But the goat had a sympathizer, or so it seemed. Ekigwe paid a frequent visit to the goat. He would come, sad-faced, and cast a sympathetic gaze at the goat. Other kids also hovered around the goat. They were very generous to the goat. Each kid occasionally brought the goat some favorite food, especially palm fronds which the goat readily consumed. It was also not impossible that Ekigwe and the kids were counting the days left before the goat would be meat on their plates. A mixture of sympathy and a knowing of an inevitable end that favored their appetite for good meat. The goat bleated and attracted the attention of Nweke and Akilika.

"That goat is big enough to supply all the meat you need to celebrate Opoto," remarked Akilika.

"Wait till all my wives take their portions," corrected Nweke.

They sighted Ekigwe coming to drop some palm leaves for the goat.

Immediately, Nweke started to gossip about Ekigwe which prompted Akilika to comment jokingly, "Ogbuefi, our people say that when you tell a story without a mention of the tortoise, that story would not be complete or even interesting."

"I don't mind if Ekigwe is the tortoise so long as he is wise like the tortoise," countered Nweke, both laughing.

"But that's quite responsible of Ekigwe," commented Akilika.

"Hahahahahah," laughed Nweke. "Do you know that every morning, unsolicited, Ekigwe will go and cut palm leaves for the goat? He will then drop the leaves with a pitiable countenance. It always leaves me wondering whether this new commitment to feeding the goat by a boy who avoids following me to the farm is a change of heart. Is it compassion for the goat's fate or is it just to fatten the goat so that it brings more meat to his plate?" continued Nweke.

"Ogbuefi, won't you leave Ekigwe alone," replied Akilika laughing.

"Well, I will leave Ekigwe alone if he will bring this new commitment to our farm work," replied Nweke, both laughing.

One day, Nweke sent his son Ekigwe to the village market, Oye, with some yams to sell. Ekigwe sold his yams speedily because Nweke was known for his sweet yams. But instead of going home, Ekigwe lingered in the market. From Oye market, Ekigwe could see the Christian boys playing football on the Church field. He was very fascinated by the strange round object and the skill with which the boys kicked it. Ekigwe dreamt of one day becoming a Christian. He had finished selling the yams but tarried a while to watch the Christian boys play football, unaware that his father's best friend Akilika, was watching him. Akilika was in Oye market also selling his yam tubers. Ekigwe longed to join the Christian boys to play football.

He liked their excitement as they kicked the ball and the skills they exhibited. But Ekigwe wouldn't dare go near the Efulefu ballplayers. He knew that his father would not tolerate that. Nweke didn't trust his own gods. Is it the white man and his God that he will trust?

Later that evening, Nweke and Akilika were relaxing in Nweke's obi (the man's compound) as usual, chatting in between the inhalation of snuff. Suddenly, Akilika cleared his throat and called his friend Nweke by his Ozo title nickname.

"Ogbuefi," Akilika called Nweke with a deliberate and calculated cadence.

"Opulozo," Nweke answered him by calling him by his own Ozo title nickname. But Nweke's countenance immediately changed. Whenever Akilika cleared his throat in that manner, Nweke knew that something unpleasant was bound to crawl out of it. Nevertheless, Nweke held his peace and listened intently for what would follow.

Akilika cleared his throat again and told Nweke that there was fire on the mountain.

"Akwu chalu n'odu igu!" Akilika exclaimed.

The abnormal and unnatural event had occurred.

Nweke remained calm but called for his snuff-box, the burden-bearer-in-chief. Part of their ritual was sharing snuff each time they met in either's house.

Akilika told Nweke, "Ogbuefi, you did well to call for your snuff-box because you will surely need more than the snuff-box." Ekigwe brought the snuff-box to his father and left. Nweke put a portion in his left palm and passed the snuff-box to Akilika. Akilika took the snuff and placed a portion on his own left palm. They both used their right forefingers to take the snuff and place it in their nostrils, sniffed and sneezed.

Then Nweke told Akilika, "Since the Christians and the white man came to our shores, there has not been a shortage of evil news. I'm all ears Opulozo."

What followed confirmed Nweke's fears. Akilika told his friend in a very somber tone, "My good neighbor, you have to keep watch over Ekigwe carefully, because today at Oye market as I sold my yam, I could not believe my eyes when I saw Ekigwe stretching his neck and glancing admiringly towards the Evil Forest at those mad Efulefu boys kicking away their lives at some strange round object."

Akilika continued, "If I had customers buying my yam, I would not have noticed Ekigwe. But you know your yam is the best in the market, so Ekigwe sold it all in a record time. That was why he had the time to watch the Efulefus. I wish I was busy selling my yam rather than busy watching Ekigwe's folly," concluded Akilika, guilty conscience obviously setting in as he watched Nweke's countenance turn ugly.

"Of course you know the implication," Akilika continued to an unresponsive Nweke with an air of cultural patriotism. Of course, Nweke knew that the implication was nothing other than that Ekigwe was derailing from the tradition of his forefathers and following a strange religion and culture.

Nweke said nothing but immediately bent his head, as if in deep thought. His worst fears and nightmare had been confirmed. Night had fallen in broad daylight. A cold sweat enveloped Nweke instantly. And a barrage of questions begging for answers raced through his mind. The first of these questions centered on Nweke's personal god.

"Where was Okochi, my personal god, in all this?" wondered a devastated Nweke.

"Will an elder sit and watch a she-goat have a miscarriage?" continued Nweke with his musings. He gave this proverb in reference to his Ikenga, Okochi who was sitting on its majestic stool looking unconcerned.

"Where was Okochi when Ekigwe started flirting with fire – the efulefus," Nweke continued with his endless questions.

"It was either Okochi had started to doze or he is irresponsible," Nweke finally reasoned aloud.

"Hush," Akilika interrupted him.

"Don't utter such blasphemy. The gods forbid. Don't add kerosene to fire."

"The fire might as well begin to burn," said Nweke with a defiant undertone. "Could it be any worse when I don't have a son?" he continued in a feeling of melancholy.

"I can see that the fear of white man's God has consumed you," remarked Akilika. "Why don't you step aside and let the gods fight their battles?"

"Are you now stronger than the gods?" continued Akilika.

"Your son is at the middle of a tug of war between the white man's God and our gods. They are fighting for his soul but he will follow the stronger god no matter what you say or do," concluded Akilika, but inwardly he was sorry for the conflagration that he ignited.

Nweke was too incensed to talk. He replied to his friend with a thumb full of snuff he pushed into his left nostril. Akilika later took his leave but his conscience worried him that the subject he brought up had left Nweke in a state of a dangerous depression.

While Akpu village was in a merry atmosphere of expectation, Nweke was in agony and pain of spirit throughout the days preceding the Opoto feast. The joy of Opoto had evaporated from Nweke's spirit like a hawk that vanished with the chick into the vast sky. The aroma of merriment that filled the Akpu atmosphere turned into a somber air of mourning for Nweke just days before Opoto.

Nevertheless, Nweke's compound was bustling and as busy with activities as a beehive. Men were polishing the mud walls of Nweke's wives' huts and drawing esoteric designs on the walls. The women and young ladies were putting the uli art skillfully on their bodies decoratively. Others were preparing the ingredients for the major delicacy of the feast Akpu Ngu (sliced cassava mixed with crayfish in a yellow paste made from palm oil and palm fruit ash). It was eaten with smoked fish. Young men were also splitting heaps of firewood with the axe for the cooking that would be done for days. A lot of cooking was done because guests came over from relatives and friends from other villages which had no feast at that time. Most guests stayed for the whole days of the feast.

While all this was going on, Nweke's compound had an august visitor! Suddenly, one of the kids who was playing by the fence wall around the wives' huts screamed, "Eke," and the kids ran towards their mothers' huts. All eyes turned toward the kids and the wall. Behold, a huge python belonging to a nearby shrine was resting on top of the wall fence and enjoying the morning sun, and apparently as well, the merry atmosphere of the approaching feast. Ekigwe's mother ran out to know what the uproar was all about.

"Look at that big python on our wall fence," shouted

Ekigwe.

"Is that all?" was his mother's response. She then called her son.

"Ekigwe," called out his mother

"Go and tell Ikem to go to Adagbe shrine and fetch the shrine keeper." Ikem left the firewood he was splitting and went to the shrine.

It seemed like a needed break for Ikem whose muscle biceps were being stretched to the limits from hours of hitting the iron axe on the hard mahogany stem. Sweat was dripping from his body as if he just emerged from swimming in the village stream. If the python had appeared on Nweke's part of the compound wall fence, no one would have bothered it because Nweke would simply have ignored it. But the women knew that it was a great distraction and a disturbance to the kids.

Soon the shrine keeper was there and addressed the python.

"Father, don't mind them. They are little children and don't understand that you only came to greet them," declared the shrine keeper addressing the python with affectionate smiles. The children, eyes widened and glittering, backed off shrieking in disgust. They would glance at the keeper, take off their eyes for some seconds and would glance again.

The keeper then stretched forth his two hands to the python with the words, "Father, let's go home please."

The python responded and coiled around his hands and neck to the utter disgust of Nweke's children. The children squealed and continued casting glances of unease at the python and its keeper.

This had become a regular spectacle for Nweke's

household, causing his wives and children to form a habit of scanning their eyes on their walls every so often.

The Opoto usually lasted for one native week and a day which was five days in total. The last day of Opoto would witness a festival, a great gathering of masquerades and dance groups at the main market square, Oye. All groups performed at the village square in Oye before the chiefs and elders of Akpu till dusk. It was the climax of a merriment of unparalleled dimension for both the old and young of Akpu and the neighboring villages who also brought guest performances and masquerades.

In the midst of all this, Nweke's mood had changed from pensive to ominous. Within the market week before the Opoto, Nweke's mood had so changed that it prompted his senior wife, Mgbogafor to ask him if all was well.

"Nna anyi, o dikwa nma?" Nweke simply nodded his head yes. But Mgbogafor suspected that all wasn't well.

It was a full moon and from his obi, Nweke could hear the happy voices and laughter of his wives and children from the wives' compound. The wives' compound was separated from the obi by a mud wall. The mud wall had look-through round peepholes at specific intervals.

Nweke's wives were oblivious of the agony of their husband and of the gathering storm.

Nweke's youngest wife, Okpanma, was a reservoir of folk tales. For this, all the children loved her so much. Every moonlight night, the children only ate at their mothers' huts, after which Okpanma became their mother till they retired to bed. Okpanma told the children many beautiful Ibo folklores. But the story that touched them most was the story of a young orphan girl who lived with a wicked auntie and her two daughters. Each time the children gathered around Okpanma under the moonlight for her folklores, they would unanimously request the orphan girl's story before they would listen to other folklores. They didn't seem to get tired of hearing this story even though it brought them to tears each time they heard it.

This orphan girl's auntie treated her daughters like princesses but treated the orphan girl wickedly and like a beast of burden. She would send the girl to fetch water from a distant stream before dawn, when even adults were afraid of evil spirits in the dark. The orphan girl, upon return from several trips to the stream with an oversized pot on her head, too big for her age, was sent to the bush to fetch firewood. It was always past noon before this girl ate some food. On the contrary, the auntie's daughters did no work but were pampered greatly. Every time the auntie came back from the market, she would give the goodies she brought, like Elele (cooked bean cake), akara (fried bean cake), utu (a very sweet type of Ibo berry) and udala (Ibo apple) to her daughters and nothing to the orphan girl. Crying in agony had become routine for the orphan girl.

One day, the auntie came back from the market and gave some very sweet udala she bought to her daughters. As the daughters ate the udala and laughed and giggled, the orphan girl sobbed in agony and sorrow of heart. Instead of her weeping attracting the pity of the auntie, it attracted scolding and beating. The auntie told the orphan girl to go and pick up the udala peelings, which her daughters recklessly littered all over the compound swept clean by the orphan girl. The girl picked up the udala peelings and the seeds.

One day, the orphan girl had an idea. She thought, "I can plant my own apple tree so that I will always have my own apple."

She then secretly went to a place outside their compound and planted the udala seed.

Every day, she went to sing a song of her wishes to the seed she planted.

The children would join Okpanma as she sang the orphan girls song,

Udala m pue, nda (my udala germinate, nda)
Pue pue pue, nda (germinate, germinate, germinate, nda)

Pue lu nwa enwenne, nda (germinate for the motherless child, nda)
Pue lu nwa enwenna, nda (germinate for the fatherless child, nda)

-Chorus-
Enuwa bu olili, nda (The world is only for a visit, nda)
Onye nosia o'naba, nda (One goes home after the visit, nda)

After several visits to the planted seed, one day, she visited, and to her delight and joy, the udala germinated and sprouted from the soil. So she changed her song thus:

Udala m too, nda (my udala grow, nda)
Too too too, nda (grow grow grow, nda)

Toolu nwa enwenne, nda (grow for the motherless child, nda)
Toolu nwa enwenna, nda (grow for the fatherless child, nda)

-Chorus-
Enuwa bu olili, nda (The world is only for a visit, nda)
Onye nosia o'naba, nda (One goes home after the visit, nda)

After some months of continuous visits and singing,

the udala grew into a big tree. The girl was happy and full of hope. So she again changed her song thus:

Udala m mia, nda (My udala produce, nda)
Mia mia mia, nda (Produce produce produce, nda)

Mialu nwa enwenne, nda (Produce for the motherless child, nda)
Mialu nwa enwenna, nda (Produce for the fatherless child, nda)

　-Chorus-
Enuwa bu olili, nda (The world is only for a visit, nda)
Onye nosia o'naba, nda (One goes home after the visit, nda)

After more months of going to sing to the udala tree, it started showing signs of bringing forth fruit. The orphan girl changed her song again to:

Udala m kaa, nda (My udala mature, nda)
Kaa kaa kaa, nda (mature mature mature, nda)

Kaalu nwa enwenne, nda (mature for the motherless child, nda)
Kaalu nwa enwenna, nda (mature for the fatherless child, nda)

　-Chorus-
Enuwa bu olili, nda (The world is only for a visit, nda)
Onye nosia o'naba nda (One goes home after the visit, nda)

Again, weeks passed and the fruits matured. The girl changed her song again:

Udala m chaa, nda (My udala ripe, nda)
Chaa chaa chaa, nda (Ripe ripe ripe, nda)

Chaalu nwa enwenne, nda (Ripe for the motherless child, nda)
Chaalu nwa enwenna, nda (Ripe for the fatherless child, nda)

-*Chorus*-
Enuwa bu olili, nda (The world is only for a visit, nda)
Onye nosia o'naba,nda (One goes home after the visit, nda)

The orphan girl didn't have much longer to wait. She came back to sing for another few days and to her great surprise and joy, about a dozen ripe udala were on the tree. Then she went into the last lap of her dream:

Udala m da, nda (my udala fall, nda)
Daa daa daa, nda (fall fall fall, nda)

Daalu nwa enwenne, nda (fall for the motherless child, nda)
Daalu nwa enwenna, nda (fall for the fatherless child, nda)

-*Chorus*-
Enuwa bu olili, nda (The world is only for a visit, nda)
Onye nosia o'naba, nda (One goes home after the visit, nda)

Immediately, about six udala fell down. She was ecstatic and overtaken with joy. When she got home, the aunt and the daughters were very perplexed as the orphan girl couldn't hide her joy. One day, the wicked auntie told her daughters to secretly follow the orphan as she went to the stream because she always came back very happy unlike before. The girls kept a safe distance as they followed the orphan girl. The orphan girl, as usual, branched to the udala tree and began to sing:

Udala m daa, nda (My udala fall, nda)
Daa daa daa, nda (Fall fall fall, nda)

Daalu nwa enwenne, nda (Fall for the motherless, nda)
Daalu nwa enwenna, nda (Fall for the fatherless, nda)

-Chorus-
Enuwa bu olili, nda (The world is only a visit, nda)
Onye nosia o'naba, nda (One goes home after the visit, nda)

Immediately plenty of udala fell. As the orphan girl picked the udala, the girls ran home and narrated the story to their mother. So their mother told them to go to the udala tree and sing the orphan's song when the girl was at home doing her many chores. The girls reached the udala tree and sang until their voices cracked but not one udala fell down. The tree knew that they were not the orphan girl or even orphans at all, and so held back the udala. The girls furiously went home dejected, cursing and swearing, "We will cut down that cursed udala tree which refused to fall for my beautiful daughters," blurted out their mother furiously. "And I will deal with this wicked orphan." Nweke's children were very sad at the end of the orphan girl's story and most of them wiped tears out of their eyes.

But Okpanma always compensated the children with the following story which made them very happy. The children never got tired of any story they loved. It was the story of a rich family who had a very poor family as neighbors. The rich family was very pompous and mocked and looked down on their poor neighbors. One day, the mother of the poor family sent their daughter to a distant farmland to work on the farm and bring home some yams and cocoyam. This farm work was paid for with some yams and cocoyam according to the work you put in. To get to this distant farm, you had to pass seven streams and seven wildernesses. And they only survived with this kind of food for work.

On her way, the poor girl met an old fragile, gaunt and

haggard-looking woman. This old woman asked her for a drink of some of her water. The poor girl quickly gave her water from her gourd and even offered her some roasted yam. The old woman thanked her and told her to listen to some instructions for the things she was bound to encounter on her journey. Unknown to the poor girl, she had encountered a spirit in the form of an old woman. The woman told her that she would hear some crackling sound like the sound of rock in an empty container. Then she would also hear a dull sound like the sound of oranges in a container.

The old woman told her to move away from the dull sound and move toward the crackling sound. As she came closer to the crackling sound, she would find a pot of clay completely sealed. She should carry that pot and turn back towards home and call the family together and break the pot in the presence of the family. The poor girl thanked her and promised to do as she had advised. After a good distance, the poor girl heard the dull sound. She started to move away from the dull sound which was getting louder and louder. As she ran away from it, she started hearing the crackling sound. As she came to the source of the crackling sound, she saw a pot that was dirty and covered with sand and dry leaves. She carried this pot and turned back to go home, abandoning her trip to the farm as instructed by the old woman.

When she got home, the mother asked her for the food she brought and queried why she came home so fast. The poor girl explained and asked the mother to call the family. The mother was furious at her daughter for coming home without any food for them to eat. Nevertheless, she called the family. The family gathered, and as everybody was complaining about the poor girl's strange behavior and abandonment of her trip to the farm, she broke the pot on the ground in front of everybody. What happened was both shocking and amazing. Gold, silver and other precious stones filled everywhere. The poor family erupted in celebrations that attracted the attention and curiosity of their rich neighbors, who were now poor in comparison. Their rich neighbors became replete with jealousy and mocked and questioned how it came about that the former wretched people had suddenly become so rich that they were no match to their poor neighbors in wealth.

"Didn't I tell you that this woman and her daughter were witches?" gossiped the former rich neighbor. "Or how could they get so rich overnight?" Very soon, they heard the rags to riches story of their neighbor.

The dust hadn't settled on the celebrations when the former rich woman screamed at her daughter, "What are you still doing here eating and getting fat while your counterpart from these wretched people travelled far to bring her family untold riches?"

"You God-forsaken girl, tomorrow morning get up and go to that distant farm and bring greater riches than what that witch girl brought for her wretched family."

Early in the morning, the daughter of the former rich woman set out to the distant farm. On the way, she met the same frail old woman. The old woman said, "My daughter, kindly give me some water to drink. I am so thirsty."

Before she finished talking, the girl shouted at her, "You wretched old witch, don't come near me because you stink. If I am even going to give you water, how will you drink from my gourd with your dirty and smelly mouth?"

The woman nevertheless gave her instructions concerning the good and bad spirits along the way. Before she could finish, the arrogant girl pushed her out of the way and continued on her journey.

After what seemed to the girl like an eternity, she was tired of walking under the scorching sun. She complained that the farm was too far. She was now very hungry and weak and cursed out her mother for sending her on the endless journey. She contemplated going back home, but going back was now as far as going forward on the journey. But as she meditated on what to do, she heard the dull sound of the evil spirit. This rejuvenated her spirit, but instead of running out of the way, the girl continued until she saw the pot and collected it from the dull and evil spirit. She hurried home rejoicing. The mother had gathered the family together even before her daughter came home in anticipation of the great wealth. She asked her to break the pot of goodies. They were full of expectation as the girl broke the pot. Immediately, a debilitating foul odor came out first, followed by various plagues and diseases. Her nose was badly disfigured causing her to talk like a masquerade. Their family was a disaster and became a pariah in the town.

Nweke's children were very happy children. In the evenings before they retired to their various mothers' huts for dinner, you could hear the clatter of their voices as they sang their habitual and popular play dance games which they danced, holding hands and forming a big circle.

Akpakolo, kpankolo
Akpakolo, kpankolo

Udu m oo, ogene
Udu m oo, ogene
Onye omalu, I ya ya ya ya, I yaa (repeat)

CHAPTER FOUR

While all the happiness and excitement went on in Nweke's compound and in Akpu Town, Nweke had indeed turned into a noiseless time bomb waiting for the set time to explode. Then one fateful midday, on Oye market day and the last Oye market day before the feast of Opoto, most people had either gone to Oye market or gone to the farms to finish the harvest of yams and cocoyams in preparation for the coming great Opoto feast. There was an eerie atmosphere of silence in Nweke's obi. The ominous quiet was often punctuated by the cry of a particular bird disliked by many people. This bird was fond of crying out at the desolate still of the midday (mgbachi ututu) when Akpu men and women had gone to the farms and the quietness everywhere seemed pregnant with an evil expectation. The village madman translated the bird's song thus:

"Ugani kpoo, kpoo, kpoo", meaning "Let there be famine, famine, famine!" Most Akpu people considered the cry of that bird as an evil omen.

"Is anybody seriously sick?" they would ask. The connotation of that question is that if anyone was seriously sick and that bird started to sing, that sick person was not expected to survive.

Ekigwe often wondered why that bird was so wicked. "Does this wicked bird want all the people in Akpu to die from hunger?" he thought.

"No wonder why Okpolo was so poor that his visit to my father always coincided with mealtime. And I hear that he hasn't made cooking fire for some time. The ash in his fireplace is said to be perpetually so cold that nobody should bother to go to his house to borrow hot charcoal."

"I will make sure that I kill that bird with my catapult," Ekigwe resolved.

Nweke was tending his yams in the barn. He could care less about the bird's cry. He had weightier issues threatening to rip him apart. Nweke could no longer contain his own emotions which were stretching to explosion point.

Suddenly, Nweke burst out into one screeching cry of agony, the type of long cry heard in the village when a family lost a dear one after which the general cries would follow. Then like a man possessed, Nweke got up and ran toward his weather-beaten Okochi, his Ikenga (personal god). Okochi was majestically seated on its equally wooden and artistically crafted stool, obviously oblivious of the approaching storm. The chicken blood that Okochi was recently bathed in was yet to fully dry up, and looked so untidy upon the old blood which had blackened.

As if his Ikenga wasn't yet bloodied enough, Nweke grabbed it by its legs and furiously ran toward the stump of a felled iroko tree about a hundred yards outside his compound.

At the screeching cry of Nweke, men and women of his

clan and surroundings ran toward Nweke's compound in fearful expectation thinking that the unthinkable had happened. Had someone died just a day or two to the great Opoto feast to cast a dark cloud upon the air of merriment in Akpu village? Most of them had their hands on their heads in a melancholy surrender. But what Nweke's brethren and neighbors saw was worse than the death of a relation. They saw Nweke racing down the village pathway carrying his personal god, and a vicious expression on his face. It was obvious that Nweke had a sinister plan against his personal god, Ikenga. It was a sight never before witnessed in Akpu village. It took half a dozen young men to hold Nweke down and rescue the hapless god from Nweke's grip. Nweke's kinsmen arrived just in time to stop him and avoid an abomination of unparalleled proportions right in the full glare of all the ancestral spirits, visible and invisible, who had assembled for the great Opoto. Had Nweke succeeded, not only his family would have been wiped out but his entire clan. The gods would not have kept quiet at the evil perpetuated against one of their own and even in complete disregard of their presence. Nweke wanted to smash the wooden head of Okochi against the felled iroko tree stump because he was sitting idly by and watching while Ekigwe dreamed of joining the Efulefus. Nweke planned to burn the broken pieces of his god after smashing it.

"Was it that Okochi didn't have enough power to prevent Ekigwe from such evil thought or that I have committed any abomination or offense?" Nweke reasoned aloud.

Nweke was uncontrollable and in between sobs, queried what had been his sin. He asked his brethren whether they were not witnesses to the number of chickens and goats that he sacrificed to Okochi, his Ikenga. During one Opoto, Nweke even sacrificed a big cow to his Chi. After eating that cow, the village gave him the title of Ogbuefi (killer of cows) as his Ozo title name. But Ekigwe had always disagreed with his father concerning his touted sacrifices to his personal god. Some time ago, Ekigwe commented regarding his father's tendency for distrust, especially distrust of Okochi, his personal god,

"No wonder why Okochi is mad and cannot be trusted. After all, when my father sacrifices a chicken to Okochi, all that Okochi manages to get is the blood. My father eats the chicken!"

Ekigwe continued, "Even the chicken blood is not put in Okochi's mouth. It is poured all over Okochi, like a mockery, making him look so dirty."

Still, in between sobs, Nweke asked his brethren whether they didn't know why his former senior wife Mgbogafor, was childless.

"Did I not throw away the abomination she bore into the Evil Forest to assuage the anger of Okochi and the gods? And then I chased Mgbogo out of my house?"

"So where have I wronged Okochi?" continued Nweke refusing to be consoled.

This confession caused many people gathered, including Nweke's family, to stop their ears and open their mouths aghast. Not that killing of twins was news to them, but they didn't know that Nweke ever had twins let alone killed them and drove their mother away for that reason. Besides, the killing of twins was already outlawed by the colonial government, although many remote villages still secretly practiced it. Quite a good number of Akpu people disapproved of killing twins. But everyone wanted to be politically correct. Everyone wanted to be seen as the most fervent in observing the tradition of Akpu village. To Nweke's family, the gods had momentarily driven him insane because they neither met Mgbogafor nor heard of her. Nweke told nobody except his closest friend Akilika, but after the fact.

"I thought that the killing of twins has been banned?" asked one woman to another.

"Better keep that thought to yourself before your mouth leads you to a three-way path," replied the other woman. The dangers of breaking the village tradition were more real than breaking the laws of the colonial government. The enforcers of colonial government laws were too distant to be feared. The police were located only at provincial headquarters and appeared less frequently in the village than the masquerades. Therefore in Akpu Town, the fear of masquerades was the beginning of wisdom.

"What else does Okochi want from me?" Nweke soliloquized.

"Tufiakwa," shrugged Akilika.

"Thank the gods we stopped him just in time. Had he succeeded, the next thing would have been suicide, another calamity. And he would have died and left the clan to bear the horrible consequences of his abomination," reasoned Akilika.

Suicide in Igbo culture is an abomination. If anyone hanged himself, usually the most common form of suicide, no native was allowed to touch the corpse. A stranger from another village was usually invited to cut the rope and take the corpse to bury. The family could not mourn that suicide victim openly or officially, but sacrifices were made for cleansing. Any native that touched that corpse became contaminated and an abomination also.

In the evening, Akilika was at his friend Nweke's obi as usual, but to console him.

"Ogbuefi," started Akilika. "It is me, Opulozo, your friend."

Still too laden with emotion, Nweke simply nodded his head in acknowledgment, inhaling his snuff.

A few days later, the long-awaited feast of Opoto finally arrived. Nweke was recovering from his dangerous mood, but he was still a shadow of himself. The goat was slaughtered the night before the first day of Opoto. The last bleating of the goat was desparate and agonizing.

Uncharacteristically, Nweke thought about the futile cry of agony from the slaughtered goat and recollected his own cry of a different kind of agony.

But Ekigwe and some of the kids were almost in tears as they watched a man brutally slit the neck of their friend with a razor-sharp knife. He mercilessly severed the goat's head from its body. Two other men took away the body to a corner where it was carefully burnt to remove the hair. Thereafter, they slit open the belly to remove the intestines and other internal organs in readiness for sharing the meat. The head was also roasted and was handed over to the most senior wife. She came with a basket and collected the head of the goat. She moved briskly to the wives' compound where she made the popular goat head sauce delicacy with it.

The following afternoon, Ekigwe and the other kids

were licking their fingers as they enjoyed the stewed rice and goat meat. Children are truly amazing. Needless to say, they couldn't connect the tasty goat meat to the goat they pitied and fed so diligently only a few days ago and even shed tears while the goat bleated in agony.

Many years back, Nweke's first wife Mgbogafor was pregnant. Her delivery was due, so she was taken to the traditional midwife of the village. After preparations, the midwife took Mgbogafor into the hut for the delivery. Nweke's mother was with Mgbogafor at the traditional midwife's hut but stayed outside. After a while, came this sad commentary from inside the hut.

"What a misfortune," declared the midwife, an elderly man well known in the village for the delivery of babies.

As soon as Nweke's mother heard the midwife's comment, she blurted out "Toaa, abomination has occurred (Toaa, alu emee!)." She excused herself from the midwife immediately and rushed to Nweke's compound.

"Nweke," she called her son.

Nweke rushed out of his hut in obi, as he noticed the urgency in her voice.

"Nne, odikwa nma (Mother, is it well)?"

"Nwa'm, alu emee (My son, abomination has occurred)."

"Is Mgbogafor alive?" inquired Nweke.

"It would have been better if she wasn't," was the harsh response of Nweke's mother.

"Why Mother?" asked Nweke, refusing to believe what he obviously thought.

"Because this abomination wouldn't have occurred."

"Mother, please tell me what has happened?" pleaded

Nweke.

"She gave birth to twins, boy and girl."

"True?" asked Nweke.

"Go and see with your eyes," charged Nweke's mother.

"Toaa!" screamed Nweke.

"Alu emee (Abomination has occurred)!" he continued.

"My son, what shall we do now about it?" asked Nweke's mother.

"Let me get to the midwife first," declared Nweke.

At the midwife's place, Mgbogafor tearfully pleaded with her husband to spare the lives of the twins. But Nweke, a fanatic devotee of tradition, dispassionately wrapped the twin babies in palm fronds, put them in clay pots and stopping his mouth with palm leaves, marched briskly and fiercely without any emotions to an Evil Forest, not talking to anybody along the way. Of course, anyone that saw Nweke and his mood and movement understood enough not to ask questions. But if you asked questions, what mouth would he use to answer you, seeing his mouth was sealed with a palm frond?

He got there in half an hour, left the babies in the Evil Forest and came home with the same fierce mood and pace, the palm frond still in the grip of his lips.

Mgbogafor's plea to Nweke to spare the babies not only fell on deaf ears but also incurred the wrath of Nweke.

"Woman, your abomination wasn't enough. Instead of remorse, you had the audacity to ask that I allow your abomination to stay," came the vicious rebuke from Nweke to his wife.

"The dog that the gods want to destroy, the gods first make him lose the smell and aroma of faeces," Nweke continued to rebuke his wife. The food for dogs in Akpu was human faeces, especially children's. The dogs enjoyed faeces so much they could kill for it.

"I told you that Mgbogafor behaved like an osu, an outcast," Nweke's mother reminded him.

"You have seen the product of her first pregnancy," she continued.

"So are you still waiting for the gods to tell you?" asked Nweke's mother.

"However, you don't throw away the pot with the sour soup" she advised. But Nweke's mother had already done the damage. To suggest that Nweke should not throw away Mgbogafor with the twins is 'medicine after death.' She had already poisoned Nweke's mind against Mgbogafor.

Nweke's mother had been against her son taking Mgbogafor as a wife.

"Have you not heard that in their family, the women don't give birth to the male child?" Nweke's mother had queried.

"You want to bring that curse into our family?" continued his mother.

Nevertheless, Nweke persisted and married Mgbogafor. The Ibo placed a great premium on male fruits. If a woman gave birth to only girls, the husband was bound to take another wife in order to get a son. It was immaterial whether the man was impotent or not. The woman was always guilty of childlessness.

"Is it not the same curse still following Mgbogafor?" complained Nweke's mother.

"Otherwise, what is the difference between having only female children and having twins?"

"Except that this is even worse because it is an

abomination," concluded the woman, answering her own question.

The following morning after Nweke's dastardly act of throwing away the twins into the Evil Forest, he woke up in his obi in a mournful mood. Mgbogafor on her part was in her hut sobbing and mourning for her twins. To Mgbogafor, the world had ended. She was just existing.

The labor of nine months had gone up in the smoke of a man's fury.

"Who will console me?" she asked herself.

"The man I should run to for consolation is the very source of my agony," she continued sobbing.

As Mgbogafor stared emptily into the morning sky, she heard the song of a familiar bird which sang its routine melody. Normally Mgbogafor would hum along with the bird. But this time Mgbogor was not impressed at all.

"Why should this bird be singing as usual as if everything is normal?" she asked.

"Doesn't this mindless bird know that the world has ended?" continued the lamenting Mgbogor.

"Even birds can be so wicked and mock you."

The loss of Mgbogor's twins was the end of the world. But Mgbogor in her emotion did not realize that the world ended only for her. The birds would wake up every morning and would sing for joy.

Later that night, the full moon was out. Mgbogor's neighbor could be heard singing, oblivious of what happened to Mgbogafor.

"Some are crying while some are rejoicing. Such is life."

"But things can change for either, for no condition is permanent," her neighbor continued with her song.

Looking at the full moon, Mgbogor sadly commented,

"Even if humans have no sympathy, what about the moon?"

"Oh, what a wicked world!" she concluded.

Thereafter, Nweke persecuted Mgbogafor ceaselessly without a cause. Nothing Mgbogafor ever did was right in Nweke's sight. Finally, he drove her away, demanding a refund of the bride price from her family. Mgbogafor's family took her back from Nweke, but vengeance was lurking in their hearts.

Nweke promptly married Uduaku whom he had been eyeing for some time anyway. Nweke loved Uduaku, and not long after, she gave birth to a baby girl. Even though a boy was always preferable, Nweke was relieved and saw the birth of his daughter as a good sign. It's not the abominable twins. He named her Adaobi (first daughter of the family). But Nweke's mother named the baby Nkiruka (the future is more important), apparently in anticipation that the future holds the promise of a son. Uduaku followed it with the birth of a baby boy. Nweke heaved a sigh of relief and sacrificed a goat to the gods. Nweke so desperately wanted a baby boy, but not the type Mgbogafor gave birth to.

On the eighth day, which was two market weeks, it was time for the baby boy's naming ceremony and circumcision according to Igbo tradition. Nweke made a great feast for his clan. He slaughtered chickens and goats and palm wine was flowing freely. He named the boy Ekigwe, happy that he and his son shared the same market day of birth, 'Eke,' and he added multiplication of children to his son's name. But despite the posturing about the birth of Ekigwe, all did not seem to be well with Nweke. He did not have a clean conscience because when he threw away his twins, he had murdered sleep.

The killing of Mgbogafor's twins and her sacking caused a great enmity between Nweke and his ex-in-laws.

The young men of Mgbogafor's family vowed to take Nweke's life. One morning, Adaobi woke up with a nightmare. She woke up crying. When she was asked why she cried, Adaobi said that somebody cut off her father's head. Uduaku went in a frenzy to tell Nweke what her daughter said. Nweke simply smiled and told Uduaku there was no problem. But not all smiles are a reflection of happiness. Some smiles are just a baring of the teeth. For Nweke had not had peace since he threw away his twins and followed it with driving away Mgbogafor. He had even been having nightmares himself.

One evening, Nweke was in his obi with Akilika his friend, sniffing the snuff as usual.

Nweke told Akilika about the threats from his in-laws and the dream of Adaobi.

"Ogbuefi," Akilika called his friend.

"Opulozo," answered Ogbuefi.

Akilika continued, "You are a warrior and one of the great Ozo titled men of Akpu.

Dreams and nightmares can't scare you. But you have to make the sacrifice so that the guilt will be upon the gods."

"What do you mean?" Nweke asked Akilika.

"You have to meet Uguru, the witch doctor. He will tell you what to do. After you have done it, he will sacrifice a chick unto the gods to seal it. Then let us see what your in-laws can do."

"Besides, I hold the Mace (Ofo na Ogu) against my in-laws," declared Nweke even though his conscience said the contrary.

"The gods will confirm my ofo when I meet Uguru," continued Nweke. Akilika had nothing more to say concerning Nweke's insistence on his innocence. After all, just tomorrow the truth will be under the searchlight.

The next day, Nweke went to Uguru. As soon as Uguru sighted Nweke approaching his shrine, he exclaimed.

"Is that not Ogbuefi I am seeing?"

"It is me Ogbuefi," Nweke responded.

"You are the great seer who sees the moon in broad daylight," continued Nweke.

"Hoaa! What is bigger than the pigmy cricket has entered the cricket hole," thundered Uguru.

"But that thing cannot be greater than the great Uguru," replied Nweke.

Uguru shrugged, paced a few steps backwards, then forward and came to an abrupt stop banging his belled staff to the earth. Nweke kept a respectable distance. With the gesture of his hand and without further comment, Uguru ushered Nweke to a raffia mat to sit down. Uguru listened as Nweke narrated his mission. Afterwards, Uguru did his incantations and threw his beads. Then he said to Nweke, "Ogbuefi!"

"Oke Mmanwu n'afu ndi nmuo, anam anu ka I nekwu" answered Nweke.

"A white hen, two chicks, an alligator, a female monkey and a he-goat that has not mated," commanded the witch doctor.

Then Nweke thought, "Only Uguru knows the

relationship between a monkey, a he-goat and Mgbogafor. My own is to build the mud wall, after I finish, let it fall on whoever it pleases." Nweke left the witch doctor, his legs feeling too light to carry him.

Two market weeks later, Nweke delivered these items to Uguru. Without a word, Uguru gestured him to a stool and took most of the items to the back of his shrine. Nweke could hear the bleating of another goat which was probably brought by another Uguru client. After some incantations, Uguru told Nweke he should go and await word from him.

Uguru the Witch Doctor looked unkempt and ragged like his hut and immediate surroundings. His goatskin bag had lost all its hair as if glued over with layers of sticky dirt. Yet the confidence he exuded made dirt look very precious and honorable. You begin to wonder how a man who could not take care of himself or his surroundings was capable of taking care of your needs. So what attracted people to him? On the contrary, a witch doctor who looks clean would be missing the mystery and the fear of the bizarre associated with witch doctors and probably lose his clientele.

The next morning, Ekigwe's attention was attracted by the chant of a witch doctor along the village pathway. The witch doctor had in his hand a small chick which was desperately crying in agony, probably because the man was waving the little chick in the air, ringing a bell and calling out the gods to come and take and eat.

"N'enya lie, eeli," cried the witch doctor looking up repeatedly in obvious expectation.

Behold, it was Uguru the witch doctor calling on the

gods to come and collect Nweke's sacrifice. Ekigwe had seen this type of show by a native doctor before and it always filled him with wonder. Ekigwe watched Uguru from a safe corner and saw a bird circling so far up in the sky that he couldn't tell what type of bird it was. As Uguru repeated his calls, 'N'enya lie," the bird steadily descended lower and lower until it was circling just above the trees. The native doctor continued his chant until the bird finally perched on the iroko tree.

Uguru continued urging the gods to come and eat the sacrifice.

"N'enya lie, eeli."

It was now clear that the bird was a vulture. It descended lower to a palm tree. As Uguru continued his tireless call, the vulture circled very low and then landed on the pathway, carried the crying chick and flew away, vanishing into the vast sky. As the vulture swooped down on the chick, chickens in the surrounding area scuttled for safety chirping kuh-kuh-kuh kack, there's danger. Then Uguru changed his incantation and went his way, leaving watching Ekigwe to wonder why.

Ekigwe was both perplexed and unhappy at the treatment meted out to the little chick, whose cry touched him. He remembered how his mother would scream at the diving kite as it tried to snatch a little chick from its mother hen. But instead, the witch doctor had become the kite and was inviting a big bird to dinner over the innocent chick.

Some days later, Nweke went back to Uguru as appointed. Uguru told Nweke to go and bring back Mgbogafor to his home. Uguru told him that the gods had accepted his sacrifice and his plea.

"But the gods have ordered you to go to your in-laws and appease them and beg them to allow you to take back your wife," Uguru directed Nweke.

"What?" exclaimed Nweke audibly. He was filled with indignation.

"Did you forget that this woman gave birth to abominable twins?" Nweke reminded Uguru.

"Taa! Don't utter that word again," Uguru stopped Nweke.

"Are you asking me or are you asking the gods if they have forgotten what abomination?" queried Uguru angrily.

"Have you become wiser than the gods who gave her the twins? If the twins were abominable, is your wife abominable?" continued Uguru ranting.

"A man stepped on a millipede. The offended millipede did not complain. Instead, the offending man screamed and leaped up in agony," Uguru continued sarcastically with a grin.

"It is not for you to challenge the gods lest they consume you."

"The twins are abominable, not your wife. Your wife will give you a child when it pleases the gods," continued Uguru with a note of finality.

"Go home and do what the gods have directed you to do," commanded the witch doctor.

Nweke walked home dejected. How could he, Ogbuefi, concede to going back to his in-laws who had insulted him? How would he ask to take Mgbogafor again? And worse, what was he going to tell Uduaku. Nweke did not tell Uduaku he had a wife called Mgbogafor before her or that he ever threw away his twins. Uduaku's young children also did not know that their father threw away any twins. When a woman gave birth to twins, the twins were quickly and secretly disposed of and relatives usually thought that the woman miscarried. Only the parents and the native midwife, usually a man, knew what happened.

That evening, Nweke did not waste time to go to his friend Akilika to tell him the result of his meeting with the witch doctor. Nweke had a sad countenance as he entered Akilika's compound.

"Ogbuefi," Akilika called Nweke.

Nweke did not answer.

"Odikwa nma?" asked Akilika.

"Is it well?"

Nweke simply nodded.

"What did the great Uguru tell you?" Akilika probed further.

Nweke was still too heavy-laden to talk. Akilika knew that his friend was not a man of many words, especially when he was sad. Akilika ushered Nweke into his obi and brought out a kola nut and a gourd of palm wine. Both men reached in their goatskin bags for their snuff-boxes.

Snuff was the soothing balm of men.

"Did Uguru say you should kill a cow?" Akilika asked jokingly. This broke the ice as Nweke now spoke.

"You know I would prefer to kill ten cows than bring Mgbogor back," Nweke sighed.

Akilika knew that Nweke's pride had been hurt.

"You are behaving as if it's only your pride that has been hurt. Am I excluded from the journey to your in-laws?" This commitment by Akilika pleased Nweke

91

because he realized that Akilika would go with him and share in the embarrassment. Then Nweke and Akilika discussed and fixed a date for the trip to Mgbogafor's people.

Nweke got up early on the appointed day and went to his friend Akilika to remind him of their trip. Nweke and Akilika carried a keg of strong palm wine and went to the in-laws. When they arrived at the in-laws' place, some young men were very aggressive and asked what they were looking for in a place they called abominable. One of the young men said that Nweke and his companion should leave before he committed murder. The other young man cynically commented with the popular proverb, "After the swarming termite finishes flying about, it sheds its wings and falls for the frogs to eat." Nweke was back to where he started. Nweke was the swarming termite and Mgbogafor the frog.

It took the intervention of some elders to cool things down. An elderly uncle of Mgbogafor warned the hot-headed young man who talked about committing murder, "I know that we have been hurt, but we will give the young man a second chance to behave like an Ozo titled man."

"Can a man give birth to a son before of his father?" the uncle asked rhetorically in reference to the lack of wisdom shown by the overzealous young man in defying the elders.

"You either calm down or leave the compound now," ordered Mgbogafor's uncle.

Finally, peace reigned and Mgbogafor's uncle ordered the young men to give them a seat.

Then he addressed the visitors.

"We are all ears."

"So tell us the purpose of your visit."

Then standing up, Nweke spoke, "My in-laws, I bring greetings to you. When a child does wrong, you use one hand to whip him and the other hand to pacify him. I thank you for giving me and my brother, an audience. I have erred but I have come to retrace my steps and take my wife back. I ask for your forgiveness. The gods have shown me that Mgbogafor is innocent. I am all ears to hear what you require me to do before I can take my wife back. I will do as you please." Nweke bowed to the elders and sat down.

Then some elders got up, excused themselves and went out to consult. When they came back, they told Nweke that they had heard him but that he should go home and come back on an appointed date. The in-laws said they needed to confirm from their daughter if she still wanted the marriage before they could give Nweke an answer. Nweke and Akilika thanked them and left.

On their way home, Nweke felt great relief. He thanked Akilika for standing by him and accompanying him to his in-laws. Akilika told Nweke that it was a situation like this that proved great friends.

"Don't forget that we entered into a blood covenant," Akilika reminded him.

The Igbo people have a culture of entering into a blood covenant. The covenanting people are bound by the covenant not to do any harm to each other and not to keep quiet upon seeing the other threatened in any way. One is bound to protect the other party to the covenant. As they continued on their long trek home, Nweke spoke,

"Opulozo."

"Ogbuefi," answered Akilika.

"But what is my crime that my in-laws were so incensed against me to the extent that the young man threatened to kill me?"

"Ogbuefi, what is important is not what the young men threatened to do but the attitude of the elders and their intervention. Young men are emotional and overzealous. If your sister was returned to your family in that manner when you were young, somebody's head would have collected sand in your compound. And certainly worse if it were your daughter, Adaobi."

"What manner are you talking about?" asked Nweke as if he had become suddenly ignorant of his own extreme behaviors.

Akilika wasted no time to answer him, "We have a proverb that says, 'With a gentle tongue, the snail moves through thorns,'" replied Akilika.

"When you returned Mgbogafor to her people, you told them that you married their daughter to give you a son and not to give you an abomination."

"Was that a gentle tongue or an acidic tongue?" continued Akilika.

"Even the oracle rebuked you," Akilika concluded.

Nweke said nothing but simply nodded in apparent agreement. After that, they continued their trek home without much discussion.

On the appointed date, Nweke accompanied by Akilika went back to the in-laws. Two young men accompanied them for the purpose of carrying the palm wine and some big yam tubers. This time, Mgbogafor's people treated them to a light reception during which Nweke paid back the dowry. After the reception, Nweke pledged to his in-laws that he would take good care of Mgbogafor. She bade goodbye to her family and accompanied her husband for the second marriage journey. Mgbogafor came back to some prepared merriment. It was when Nweke came back with Mgbogafor that Uduaku knew that Nweke had married before. Men didn't have to explain their actions to women in Akpu.

CHAPTER FIVE

The feast of Opoto had come and gone. It was now planting season. The rainy season had arrived although Akpu village had witnessed only her first rains. At this time, the yams were more for planting than for eating. So it was the season of Ugani (food scarcity). It was also the new school season.

The near calamity that befell Nweke's family and clan as a result of his attempt to kill his personal god had died down and Nweke had slowly recovered to accept the realities of the day.

"These Christians have turned the world upside down," Nweke told his friend Akilika.

"Ogbuefi, there is nothing the eye can see that will make it bleed," responded Akilika.

Nwaforcha, Nweke's nephew, was the only man in Akpu village that commanded Nweke's absolute respect. Nwaforcha was a prosperous and respected trader who lived in a distant city across the river Niger. He was educated up to standard six but couldn't go further even though he was very intelligent. So Nwaforcha was sad because there was nobody to sponsor him to the famous secondary school, CMS Grammar School, which he passed its entrance examination. Nwaforcha, therefore, developed a passion for sponsoring young people to acquire the white man's Christian education. Although a young man, Nwaforcha was well-known and respected in Akpu village and even beyond. He invested heavily in the education of all brilliant youth in Akpu and surrounding villages as if to make up for his lost opportunity in education.

Nwaforcha was one of the earliest victims of the clash between Akpu tradition and the coming of the white man to the country and their Christians to Akpu village. Many years ago when Nwaforcha was still about twelve years old, it was discovered by his family that he visited the Efulefus. His family didn't take kindly to this development and feared the abomination that his continued visit would result for the family. Nwaforcha was warned by his father to end any form of contact with the Christians, and they started to watch him. But Nwaforcha was caught red-handed and the report went straight to his father. He was then promptly thrown out as an outcast and rejected by his family.

"Agbalu uzo owele mgba, o diechi (A stitch in time saves nine)," remarked his father. The young boy pleaded and wept to be forgiven but his tearful pleas fell on deaf ears. His mother's subtle pleas were also rejected. The overzealous young men in his clan, with the full consent of his father, tied him and cast him outside the borders of the village at midnight as an evil son. He was left at the mercy of wild animals.

The biggest problem for Nwaforcha was not that he

was tied, neither was it wild animals. His greatest problem was darkness and the night. One of the things that Nwaforcha dreaded most as he was growing up was to run errands for his father at night. Ibo folklore dwelt a lot on spirits of the dead. There was a very thin line separating the people from their dead ancestors. Nwaforcha, like a lot of Akpu kids, grew up with fairy tales of spirits of the dead. After all, masquerades are the spirits of the people's dead ancestors. So, as soon as Nwaforcha stepped out of his hut and compound at night, he became enveloped with debilitating fear. Every object Nwaforcha saw at night became elongated and had a human shape. Apparently, dead people grew taller after they die. To worsen matters, Nwaforcha was dumped on a road near a burial ground. As soon as Nwaforcha was dropped there, he felt that a host of dead people were curious about who their unexpected new neighbor was and had their gaze focused on him. Nwaforcha closed his eyes in fear. As soon as he closed his eyes, Nwaforcha saw uncountable images of dead people seated on their graves and all of them peered steadily on him. Paralyzed with fear, Nwaforcha considered himself already in the land of the dead. Suddenly Nwaforcha heard rumbling footsteps against the dry leaves by the bush path.

"Oh, they have decided to come and take me to their land of the dead!" he concluded and opened his eyes in terror.

Nwaforcha saw a profile of a real human and thought it was a ghost indeed coming for him. He gave out a scream of agony to the extent that the man leaped in surprise. This man was not the type to fear ghosts. He walked regularly on the burial ground at night as he went after dangerous wild animals. He didn't fear wild animals but wild animals feared him. During every Opoto feast, the last day's great gathering at the village square always featured a procession of great hunters with Ogbuagu at the lead. Each hunter decorated himself with the heads of the most dangerous animals he had killed. Ogbuagu (killer of tigers) always had the heads the most feared wild animals like tiger, lion or buffalo. A young man who was his aide usually carried these relics and followed him. His Dane gun was decorated with the skins of his victim animals as he stepped in rhythm with the drums intoxicated by the instigation of the oja, the famous Ibo flute. But he carried the Odu-okike (elephant tusk) from the elephant he personally killed. He would dance to the beat of the drums and the oja flute.

As the man, Ogbuagu, regained his composure, he went after the person that gave out the scream to know what he was doing there. Nwaforcha desperately shouted "Noooo" as the hunter came closer to him. Nwaforcha thought that one of the dead people actually came out of the grave to grab him. He was in effect refusing to follow the dead and was wriggling like one trying to free himself from a deadly stranglehold.

"This man must have become newly mad," the hunter thought.

But on closer look, he saw that it was a boy and he was tied up.

"Who must have done this wicked act," the hunter soliloquized.

"Whose son are you?" the hunter asked the boy as he untied him.

He didn't answer but just starred at the hunter in

99

apparent terror. Then the boy came out from the trance and regained himself as he realized the hunter was a real human trying to help him. Still, the boy didn't want this man to return him to his father who wanted him dead. Only the Christians were his best chance of staying alive.

"Please take me to the Evil Forest," Nwaforcha pleaded.

"What do you want in the Evil Forest?" asked the hunter totally surprised and still struggling to make sense out of the strange situation.

"He wants to go from frying pan to fire," the hunter thought to himself.

"To the Efulefu people," Nwaforcha continued to plead.

"Now it is making sense to me why this boy requested that I take him to the Evil Forest," reasoned the hunter. The Evil Forest was the abode of the Christians or the Efulefu. They cleared a portion of the Evil Forest and built their Church there.

"Let's go," the hunter told Nwaforcha, and they set out.

In less than an hour, the hunter and Nwaforcha were at the entrance to the Christian Missionary Society house. The hunter left Nwaforcha at the Mission gate and directed him to go inside. Nwaforcha bowed down in greeting and thanked the hunter profusely. The Mission compound was dark and had an eerie silence enveloping it. This had Nwaforcha unsettled but nothing could compare with his recent deadly experience near the Burial Ground. Nwaforcha groped his way to the Mission House and sat down at the doorway. The shrubs this time didn't look like overly tall humans. Soon Nwaforcha slept off and did not dream about any ghosts.

After the third cockcrow, Nwaforcha was woken up by a tap on the shoulder. It was the Missionary Catechist.

"Wake up boy. The day is breaking," the Catechist told Nwaforcha, repeatedly tapping on his shoulder to rouse him from sleep. Nwaforcha rubbed his eyes with the back of his left hand as if to wipe away the sleep. He then bowed his head and greeted the Catechist.

"Did you pass the night here?" the Catechist asked Nwaforcha.

"Yes sir," replied Nwaforcha.

"Wait here for me. I'll be back soon."

"Yes sir." A few minutes later, Nwaforcha was startled as he heard the sound, Gommmmmmm, gommmmmm, gommmmmmm.

Apparently, the Catechist had woken up to ring the first church bells for the morning. After the third church bells, it was time for morning devotion.

The Catechist then came back to Nwaforcha.

"When did you come here?" continued the Catechist.

"Late in the night."

"Is your father aware of your whereabouts?"

"No sir."

"Then why did you leave your father's house to come here?"

Nwaforcha then proceeded to tell the Catechist his gory tale and pleaded with him not to return him to his father's house. Of course, the Catechist was already familiar with the brutal treatment meted out to admirers of the Christians. He also realized the implication to both himself and Nwaforcha of returning him to his father and assured Nwaforcha that the Church would help him. But the Catechist had to consult with the Parish Priest first.

The Catechist met with the Parish Priest that morning and relayed to him the story of Nwaforcha.

After hearing Nwaforcha's predicament, the Parish Priest directed that Nwaforcha live with the Catechist until the Church assigned a teacher to raise him up. The Christians had no problem taking him in. After all, they knew so well the problems and frustrations of Christian converts in Akpu village and the surrounding districts.

Nwaforcha was baptized and given the name Nathaniel. He was not kept long in Akpu village to avoid the family realizing that the Church had come to his rescue and the associated problems.

Nwaforcha's mother suffered disgrace in the village. For a long time, she was the subject of gossips among women. They gossiped that she couldn't raise her son properly which was why he became so wayward that he hung around the Efulefu rather than help in his father's farm work. No wonder that he became an outcast and nobody knew if he was dead or alive. Most times in Akpu, women are blamed for the failures of their sons. But when these sons succeed, men are given the credit. Life became tasteless and an agony for Nwaforcha's mother and in a short period left her a mere shadow of the elegant woman she once was. Nevertheless, Nwaforcha's mother refused to give up hope that one day she would reunite with her son.

The church quickly assigned Nwaforcha to a teacher in a nearby Mission School as both a houseboy and family member. Every time the teacher was reposted from village to village, he took the young Nwaforcha with him. Nwaforcha enrolled in school and was very intelligent. He was also very good at football and was on the school's football team.

Nwaforcha quickly adjusted to his new environment. His school was located in a Supervising Mission which was headed by a white Priest. This was the most exciting aspect of Nwaforcha's new life. Nwaforcha had never come close to a white man in his life. He only saw white men when they were inside the car driving past him, and even that was once in a blue moon. But now every day he woke up in the morning, and as he went about his compound sweeping chores, his eyes would occasionally glance towards the white man's house peradventure he came out of his house.

One day, as the school children came out on break, Nwaforcha had a double blessing. The white Priest just alighted from his car parked on the school premises. He was visiting the Headmaster. Nwaforcha and the other schoolboys bowed in greeting. This was Nwaforcha's first close contact with a white man. The Priest replied to the children, "Good morning children," to their wild excitement. Nwaforcha noticed that the white Priest "spoke through his nose" like birds, an opinion shared by other school children and, privately, by even some teachers. Secondly, while the white Priest was with the Headmaster, the school children gathered around his shining black Morris Minor car in admiration. The body of the car was like a mirror and reflected the children's images, but the images were very dwarfed to the children's amazement and amusement.

"Hey look at Aforcha. He's so short," excitedly exclaimed one of the kids with a giggle.

"He's also even shorter than me," responded Nwaforcha also giggling.

That was Nwaforcha's first time to come near a car and

the first time for most of the other kids.

The following year was so far the most eventful in Nwaforcha's life. Nwaforcha went with his teacher to a distant posting across the River Niger to the island township of Burutu. Burutu was an island in the Atlantic Ocean off the Nigerian South-Western coast and was the major trading outpost of the British colonialists.

Nwaforcha, helped by another schoolboy, carried the teacher's iron box and his own bag to the motor garage where, with his teacher, they boarded a wooden-bodied lorry to the Onitsha township wharf. This was Nwaforcha's first visit to a township that had electric lights and all.

As their lorry passed the center of the bustling township of Onitsha, Nwaforcha's attention was attracted and consumed by the inevitable staccato noises of the open Tincan Quarters where hundreds of metal tradesmen beat aluminum sheets into various shapes of boxes, buckets, pots and other utensils. That noise was a trademark of Onitsha Township. The utensils made here were transported and marketed all over the country and even beyond. Nwaforcha was so fascinated and amazed by the emerging world that he felt that he was yet to fully appreciate what the future held in store for him.

At the wharf, Nwaforcha and his teacher were to board a steamship, called Erico to Warri where the ship would pick more passengers before she continued her sail to Burutu. Nwaforcha was shocked to see a house on the water as he looked at Erico swaying its waist as if responding to a rhythmic sound of music coming from the massive water below. Soon it was time to board Erico and people lined up after their boxes were loaded into the bowels of the ship. As Nwaforcha walked into the ship, he felt the gentle sway of the ship so he held fast to the ropes to keep him from slipping into the ominous looking and unpredictable water below. Nwaforcha watched other passengers to know if they felt what he felt. A few minutes later, Nwaforcha was startled when Erico blasted what appeared to be her horns, signaling it was pulling out of the wharf. Birds perched on trees around the wharf scuttled away in caution, equally startled by the blast of the ship's horns.

As the ship passed through the creeks, Nwaforcha's excitement knew no bounds as he watched the surrounding villages recede one after the other. The journey was like a fairy trip to Nwaforcha, who had never ridden in a car until that day, and now on a ship. Suddenly, the ship stopped at what seemed to be in the midst of nowhere. Nwaforcha's dream ride had suddenly paused. He thought that the ship stopped because it developed a problem.

"I don't know how to swim. So what will I do with this massive expanse of water if this ship spoils?" thought Nwaforcha to himself, beginning to feel nervous. What calmed Nwaforcha's nerves was the calm composure of his Master and Teacher. While Nwaforcha was still trying to figure out what was going on, some people were disembarking at what was a bus stop of some sort. Nwaforcha just couldn't comprehend a bus stop right in the middle of a sea. He waited to see the end of this drama. It was as if he was dreaming because the ship stopped in the middle of the water and there was no land in sight. At these stops, people disembarked from the ship into little canoes which promptly disappeared into the vast water. The canoes first appeared as dots emerging from the skyline until they transformed into little canoes coming to pick passengers from the "bus stop" and then headed back to a collection of wooden houses that stood upon stilts in swamps called villages. As the ship's journey progressed, Nwaforcha sighted some of the villages where the small shuttle boats could have come from. Nwaforcha was both amazed and frightened at the thought of living in one of these villages. He fervently hoped that his final destination was not like those villages.

After a day's journey, they finally arrived at the port of Burutu. Nwaforcha was to live with his teacher in this town for a long time. On this island, you could almost see the vast Atlantic Ocean from any location and that was not only truly amazing but sometimes frightening to Nwaforcha who had never seen a river. His village had only streams. His imagination about water was always running wild. Nwaforcha enrolled in the school where his Master was a teacher. He made many friends and it wasn't long before Nwaforcha knew every nook and cranny of Burutu. He even learned how to swim and could swim like a fish.

After his standard six and the elementary school certificate, in which he excelled, Nwaforcha was employed as a tally clerk in the biggest trading company of the colonialists in West Africa, the United Africa Company with its headquarters in Burutu. Because of this company, the UAC, there were hundreds of white people and even their families in this island town. The white colonists loved Nwaforcha for his accuracy and dedication to work. He was put on a fast track for promotion and was soon promoted to a senior tally clerk, a big position for an African. Soon Nwaforcha bought a bicycle, a luxury reserved for whites and a few privileged Africans. Nwaforcha had now grown into a prosperous young man but had not visited his village since he was thrown out of his family as a boy and moved from place to place with a teacher.

Nwaforcha's Master was now the Headmaster of the CMS school in Burutu. He regarded Nwaforcha as his own son and was his bank. Nwaforcha kept all his money with him and not a penny of Nwaforcha's money was ever lost.

While in Burutu, one thing struck the imagination of Nwaforcha. He noticed that white people not only loved to eat chicken, but also its eggs. Therefore, chicken was very expensive in Burutu. Back home in Akpu, eggs were for hatching into chickens only, not to be eaten as food.

So Nwaforcha kept wondering how they got chicken in Burutu when they ate all the eggs.

Nwaforcha was due for his annual leave. He planned to visit his village, for his heart yearned for his family, especially his mother and siblings. Soon it was time for him to proceed on his annual leave. In preparation for this visit, he bought fancy gifts for his parents and family as a whole. On his list, were items like singlet and torchlights for his father and uncles, wrappers for his mother and aunties and handkerchiefs. Nwaforcha also bought a tilly-lamp and a gramophone. He was fully prepared for this trip.

Above all, Nwaforcha took with him, a sizable value of ego oyibo (white man's money), which was in coins. Akpu village money was cowries (seashells). Many villages had never seen or used the white man's money. A penny was equivalent to bags or pots of cowries (Akpa ego).

So Nwaforcha went to the wharf and joined Erico, for the long all-day journey to Onitsha. Nwaforcha was back to the meandering of Erico through the creeks and massive expanse of water. The stilted swampy villages were a familiar sight to Nwaforcha. He was no longer frightened by water. Besides, he was now a man and could also swim very well. At Onitsha, Nwaforcha spent the night at the wharf, and very early in the morning, he took the lorry called Onyemaechi (Who knows tomorrow), to the nearest motor station to his village.

From there, Nwaforcha arrived at Akpu village and his father's compound. Nwaforcha left home as a boy but returned as a man.

Nwaforcha was not recognized by his family, who gathered around his shiny bicycle to admire it. There were a few rickety bicycles in Akpu village but that was the first time a brand new Raleigh bicycle would be seen in Akpu village. Nwaforcha embraced his mother and told the bewildered woman that he was Nwaforcha, her son.

"My own long lost Nwaforcha?" his frail-looking mother probed.

"Yes, your son Nwaforcha. I am finally back."

His mother, who was opposed to making her son a castaway but was overruled by her husband and his brothers, wept uncontrollably for joy. She screamed, "Akpu people come and join me to see what I am seeing ooooh," in-between tears.

Nwaforcha's father was speechless seeing his outcast son return so prosperous. He was very quiet and subdued

108

in obvious guilty conscience. He realized that in the new world, power and wealth rested with those who left Akpu gods and tradition to join the Christian God and the white man's tradition.

Upon realizing his father's mood, Nwaforcha called his father apart and had a private heart to heart discussion with him. Nwaforcha told his father that he didn't fault him at all because he did everything he did according to Akpu tradition. He told his father that it was God's plan for him to be thrown out so that he would go to the Christians and the white man and acquire some knowledge and wisdom and bring its fruit to his father's house and the entire village.

"Father, it wasn't your fault at all that I left the family. God allowed it so that he will use it to save Akpu from darkness and poverty." His father wouldn't fault that because he was already seeing the signs.

"If it was anybody's fault, the fault belonged to Akpu traditions," concluded Nwaforcha.

Nwaforcha's father was very happy to hear his son exonerate him of guilt.

Nwaforcha's brothers and sisters surrounded him, stared at him in bewilderment and asked endless questions about his life in exile. Soon the news of Nwaforcha's triumphant return spread all over Akpu Town. People came from all the surrounding clans to see for themselves.

One man said, "Afulu m kwe (I saw and I believed)." Nwaforcha received a hero's welcome and became the toast of Akpu Town.

Soon it was night time and the reality of Nwaforcha's return hit home. Nwaforcha brought out the tilly-lamp, whose light shines brighter than a thousand palm oil lamps. Even the kerosene lantern was reserved for the privileged in Akpu village but it was a candle light in comparison to the tilly lamp which actually shined brighter than most electric bulbs except fluorescent bulbs with a high voltage. The tilly lamp was the first of its kind in Akpu. Nobody in Akpu village had ever heard about a tilly lamp, let alone seen one.

"Did you call it 'ntili' (Igbo word for shatter), my son?" asked his mother.

"No Mother, it is tilly lamp," Nwaforcha corrected needlessly because his mother still pronounced it as ntili.

"It is indeed ntili, because it has shattered all the darkness in this surrounding," concluded his mother. A big crowd gathered instantly in Nwaforcha's father's compound to see what shined so brightly as if the moon was brought down to the village, a pure wonder in Akpu village. Nighttime was never the same again in Akpu Town, which used to be complete darkness, and people went to bed early like chickens. But this night, people still milled around Okeke's compound when the first cockscrow was heard. In fact, early risers who went to distant farms rose at the first cockscrow.

"Aforcha, please you must put off this ntili so that people will go back to their homes. I have never heard of people being awake in this town till the first cockscrow." But deep inside, she was having a great time. Her home had become the Mecca of the village.

"Let the whole Akpu Town relocate to this compound," mocked Nwaforcha's mother.

"I was mocked because my son went to the Christians and was called an outcast. Now the Christian God gave him the light and wealth which Akpu gods can't give. We are free from this great darkness!"

"And let all those who mocked me that I didn't have a son come and see. Indeed, light is attractive" continued his mother.

Then she started singing and dancing: "Ubiam ka n'ikpu, mmem (Poverty comes from the womb)."

"Ubiam ka n'ikpu, mmem."

This means that your womb is the guarantee of your poverty when it doesn't bear you children. Likewise, it was also the guarantee of your wealth through children.

"Nwa ka ego (Child is greater than money)!" exclaimed Nwaforcha's mother.

"My outcast son has brought light and wonder to Akpu Town. Let gossippers come out and gossip about the wonder," she continued, remembering the gossip about her outcast and probably dead son and the mockery and disgrace she endured.

Because of the light from the tilly lamp, people around Nwaforcha's compound rarely went to bed until Nwaforcha decided to shut down the tilly lamp. Families far from Nwaforcha's compound could see the reflection of the tilly lamp's bright light on trees. During moonlight nights, the tilly lamp relegated the brightness of the moonlight. It was a refreshing and welcome light in Akpu's darkness.

On the following Sunday, something happened that completely overshadowed the wonder of the tilly lamp. Nwaforcha set up the gramophone soon after he returned from the Church. This latest development raised a big question and controversy in the village. Who exactly was singing those melodious songs? Different people had varying answers to this question. Most people kept their thoughts to themselves but a few vocal villagers said that those singers were the white man's ancestral spirits speaking.

"Don't you know that they are the white man's masquerades, but are still in spirit form and lodged in that gramophone which was why nobody could see them with the ordinary eye like Akpu's own masquerades," proferred a wannabe oyibo. Nwaforcha's uncle, Obi, suggested that the singers were tiny pigmies crowded into that machine crying in agony. Okeke was happy that his son had forgiven him but was still subdued and just observing everybody. He felt that Nwaforcha had brought home something bigger than him and his Ikenga. And he began to wonder, "What do we really know about who should be an outcast and who shouldn't? Are we not simply being driven by our fears and our selfish desires?" Nwaforcha's father, Okeke who had been quiet since the return of his son, cautioned Obi to ask Nwaforcha whatever he didn't know lest he made a fool of himself.

"Onye ajuju a digh efu uzo (He who asks questions does not miss his way)," he advised. But even Nwaforcha found it difficult to explain the gramophone concept to them because some of the villagers kept peering into it peradventure they could spot the singers. Some villagers were convinced that Nwaforcha had brought white man's witchcraft to Akpu and only he would understand what those witches were singing.

What made the gramophone a complete enigma to Nwaforcha's uncle, and to many in Akpu, was that it had a neck which was so flexible that each time Nwaforcha wanted it to sing, all he had to do was just to bend its neck and point its mouth down to the rotating plate.

"You are still wondering who is singing?" Emeka, a neighbor asked Obi.

"Are you so backward? Can't you see its neck?" queried Emeka mockingly.

"Watch your foul mouth and don't insult me. Have you ever seen an Akpu man with this type of neck? You illiterate?"

"Ewu Lokoja (Goat from Lokoja)," Emeka fired back angrily.

To prevent a fight, Nwaforcha's father intervened with this advice to Emeka, "Mouth does not pay a visit to another mouth unarmed."

Every day was now a day of merriment in Nwaforcha's compound as people trouped in and out. Some of Okeke's friends commented sarcastically, "Nwaforcha is no longer an outcast. He's now Okeke's son."

"Ego n'ekwu (Money talks)!" concluded Emeka.

"Tell me, who will cast Nwaforcha out now for going to the Christians?" continued Emeka.

"And will Akpu Ukwu (god of Akpu village) have given Nwaforcha the great wealth he now has if he didn't go to the Christian God?"

"Is it not better to be a rich outcast than to remain in Akpu poor and in darkness?" asked Emeka. Emeka had escorted Nwaforcha to the Church in the morning to Nwaforcha's delight. Obi commented that Emeka was not the only wannabe Christian, but that the others didn't summon the courage to show up. There was a bitter war going on between the gods of Akpu and the angels of the Christian God. The prize was the souls of the villagers of

Akpu.

"Akpu hasn't seen anything yet. Who knows what my son Aforcha will bring out next?

Just keep bringing them out, my son. There's no fear," declared Nwaforcha's mother gleefully.

The time for Nwaforcha to travel back to Burutu was fast approaching. Nwarforcha had developed a great business acumen. He once sent one of his younger brothers to buy him a live chicken for a Sunday lunch of rice and stew. He was surprised when his younger brother told him how much he bought the chicken for. Nwaforcha discovered that one chicken in Burutu could buy ten chickens in his village. He was quick to see the economic impact of this in his life and quickly seized the moment. Thus the beginning of the chicken trade and the turning point in Nwaforcha's fortunes. For the balance of his leave, Nwaforcha spent it buying chicken in Akpu and surrounding villages. One of his uncles wondered what he would do with so many chickens.

Nwaforcha told his uncle that chicken was the white man's food.

"I said it! Now it is making sense" concluded Nwaforcha's uncle.

"That is why these white people in Nwaforcha's gramophone spoke like birds."

"The truth is slowly coming out. They have eaten too many chickens and are sounding like chickens. Can't you see that they sound almost like our masquerades?" Nwaforcha was greatly amused. He was having fun. Nwaforcha went back to Burutu with a large consignment of chickens.

Within a week of Nwaforcha's arrival in Burutu, he had sold all the chicken to the white people who ate a lot of chicken and eggs. He earned a profit equivalent to his six months' salary. Nwaforcha was speechless. He had never handled that kind of money in his life. Nwaforcha started to plan for resignation and full-time business.

But Nwaforcha always wondered how people who ate all the eggs of chickens could still have chicken to eat in due course since there wouldn't be eggs left to hatch into chickens. He reasoned that the white men must have thus exhausted all the eggs in their country and didn't have any more chicken, hence they desperately sought after every chicken in Burutu. Nwaforcha reasoned that it was all to his benefit anyway because he would have made all the money he needed before they finished all the chickens in the country.

In Akpu, egg was a rare delicacy reserved only for the adults. Only eggs which the hens failed to hatch were ever eaten. And only adults indulged in this "sweet mouth." Anyway, there were usually not enough unhatched eggs to go around. So only adults ate the eggs. Giving eggs to children was thought to be unnecessarily spoiling them and leading them to steal. Nwaforcha remembered when he was little and he and his siblings saw their mother chewing something. They asked their mother what she was chewing. Their mother quickly closed one eye and told them she was chewing one of her eyes. Every attempt by Nwaforcha and his siblings to close one eye failed. So they concluded she was indeed chewing one eye. But their mother was eating egg!

Before long, Nwaforcha resigned his job at UAC to the

displeasure of the white bosses who loved his work ethic. He embarked on the chicken trade full-time. Nwaforcha went back to the village to buy more chicken. He made sure he took with him more gifts for the villagers. This time, most discussions in the village centered on Nwaforcha, his gifts, chickens or white people. Nwaforcha bought so much chicken that Akpu village did not have enough chickens to meet his demands. Eke market became dedicated to the chicken trade, and Akpu people called it the Chicken Market. Many young men in Akpu became involved in the chicken trade and so traveled to distant towns and villages in search of chicken. These young men became equally enriched relatively. Similarly, other towns and villages brought chicken to sell in Eke Chicken Market in Akpu village.

Very soon, Akpu Town became very prosperous because of the chicken trade. The story of the chicken trade became the story of Nwaforcha, the outcast, even beyond the shores of Akpu, and many young men left their unprofitable businesses and skills to rear chicken. It became a common saying that the outcast had brought more blessings to the people than the preferred sons. The age-grade of Nwaforcha, the 'Akpokue Dike,' age-grade were so proud of him that they gave him the name "Nwakaibie (The child that is greater than other children)." The euphoria surrounding Nwaforcha was electric far beyond the borders of Akpu Town. A new masquerade dance group launched recently by a neighboring village came to Nwaforcha's compound to perform in his honor. Nwaforcha's compound was filled to the brim and so many more people were outside. The masquerade dance group had police, also a masquerade, which controlled the crowd and kept the peace. Their performance was so good that Nwaforcha gave them a goat and some money. Immediately, the masquerade daughter sprang to her feet and did a fast routine of beautiful dance steps in appreciation of Nwaforcha's gifts. She danced in jubilation towards where Nwaforcha was seated ending her dance at Nwaforcha's feet. Her father then called out in greeting and gratitude, "Nwaforcha de."

"Mmuo na nma," replied Nwaforcha.

"Nwaforcha ekene m gi ooo. Dije daalu," continued the father masquerade to thank Nwaforcha.

Nwaforcha became so rich that he could afford to buy a lorry, the first of many in his first major investment, the road transport business. He named his transport business Oranyeaka (with the help of the people). Oranyeaka transport started with only one lorry. This lorry had wooden benches arranged in rows. The lorry transported passengers and their goods between major cities in the region through mostly dirt and dusty roads. The passengers were seated on the rows of benches, whereas their goods were arranged beneath the benches. The loads of the passengers were so tightly packed beneath the benches that there was barely room for the passengers' legs and feet. It was usually a bumpy and dusty ride as most roads were not paved, but that did not diminish the usefulness of the lorry. The leaves of most trees along the few motorable roads were coated with brown dust. It was the dusty evidence of prosperity.

The lorry often came to Nwaforcha's compound in Akpu village. Each time the lorry arrived at Nwaforcha's compound, the driver proudly blew the horn and revved the engine in some kind of announcement that Oranyeaka was in town. This usually caused the young men to shout the name of the lorry and always said, "Fire on! We hear you."

The lorry had beautiful paintings and designs on its wooden body. On one side of the lorry was the beautiful and colorful drawing of a picture, supposedly of the Virgin Mary carrying Baby Jesus. Under the picture were artistically designed letters: S. M. O. G. (Save Me Oh God).

Obviously, the driver or the artist was asking to be saved from road accidents or from the darkness and the evil spirits of Akpu Town. The imagination of people was of an ever-presence of evil spirits especially at nights in Akpu. The lorry never lacked company once parked in Nwaforcha's compound, as it was the favorite destination of Akpu young boys. They rubbed their palms on the body as if to feel it and smell the scent of success.

The imprint of the lorry's tires on the main dirt road of Akpu village often remained on the road for over a week until it rained, as no other vehicles came to Akpu village save Oranyeaka. And when the people saw the fresh tire imprints on the road they immediately remarked that Oranyeaka was in town.

"Great Machine," they exclaimed. Every time the driver parked the lorry, the conductor would jump down acrobatically from the rear of the lorry and place a heavy wooden rectangular wedge behind the tire to prevent the lorry from rolling backwards. To start the lorry, the conductor would use a long iron rod bent ninety degrees towards one end to make room for handling. Then the Conductor would put one end of the rod into a hole that led into the engine and vigorously and swiftly turn the rod clockwise to cause the engine to rotate. Only a strong man could turn the rod to start the engine. Often the rod was turned several times before the engine could respond.

As soon as the lorry moved, the conductor would grab the wedge and throw it back into the rear of the lorry ready for the next stop. Everything was done with fanfare and sometimes, the conductor would hang precariously outside the side of the lorry, holding on with one hand and throwing one leg in the air. The conductor was a star of some sort in Akpu.

Nwaforcha also teamed up with his former teacher and master to establish a secondary school in the city which was by the River Niger. He had a passion for the education of the youth, probably to make up for his own lost opportunity by giving others the opportunity.

Despite the success of Nwaforcha through the white man's Christianity, the power of the ancestral spirits still loomed very large in the psyche of Akpu villagers. The reason was partly because the fear of the ancestral spirits was still very real in the psyche of Akpu people and so was the desire to belong, as well as the perks of the rich Akpu tradition. There was therefore a dilemma, a big conflict of choice between the spoils of wealth from the white man's Christian tradition and the rich experience of Akpu's esoteric culture. Nwaforcha's success was to Akpu people at best an enticing, inevitable and necessary evil. It was a dangerous enticement to "evil" which the white man craftily calculated to destroy the tradition of Akpu Town. The calamity of it was that men of Akpu village were fast falling into the trap, but Nweke was convinced that the ancestral spirits and the gods of their forefathers were bound to fight back.

CHAPTER SIX

Nweke paused from sorting the yam seedlings to listen to the sound of the approaching boots. In Akpu Town, only Nwaforcha could have shoes sounding like those. Ekigwe quickly came to Nweke's mind. Nweke's family, especially Adaobi, had spoken in favor of Ekigwe joining the Christians and going to school. They dreamt of Ekigwe one day becoming prosperous like Nwaforcha. So of course, Nweke knew the consequences of Nwaforcha's visit. He knew that Nwaforcha was the only man he had absolute respect for and couldn't say no to.

Soon Nwaforcha walked into the Obi and greeted Nweke, "Ogbuefi, I greet you."

"Nwakaibie," Nweke responded.

Nweke exchanged pleasantries with Nwaforcha even though hurting inside and in a suppressed mood. While they exchanged pleasantries, Ekigwe came into the obi from the wives' compound to greet Nwaforcha. Ekigwe was prodded by Adaobi and his mother to go and greet Nwaforcha. Ekigwe's sister and the women peeped anxiously through the look-through holes in the wall to see what would happen. Nwaforcha remarked about the rapid growth of Ekigwe,

"Is this the small Ekigwe of yesterday?" exclaimed Nwaforcha, visibly amazed.

"Yes he keeps shooting up like a palm tree," acknowledged Nweke about Ekigwe's growth. But Nweke had a veiled apprehension over the intent of Nwaforcha's observation.

Predictably, Nwaforcha dropped the bomb!

"Ogbuefi," Nwaforcha called Nweke.

"Nwakaibie," answered Nweke, afraid and nervous.

"Has Ekigwe started primary school?"

Nweke quietly shook his head in the negative, looking very dejected and defeated. At this point, Nwaforcha commanded Ekigwe to put his right hand over his head and attempt to touch his left ear. There were no Birth Certificates then. The school authorities used your ability to use your right hand to touch your left ear and vice versa to determine if you are of school age. Ekigwe effortlessly touched his left ear to the shock of Nwaforcha.

"Tooaa!" screamed Nwaforcha.

"What a waste!" lamented Nwaforcha in a loud voice.

"A potential Sergeant is being wasted."

In those days, the rank of Police Sergeant was reserved only for the white colonial masters.

Only a select few of fortunate Africans dreamt of ever attaining the rank of Sergeant.

There was a Police Sergeant in the neighboring town. The Sergeant was so celebrated that the famous young women dance group based their best song on praising his achievements:

"Controversial Sergim, Edimondu the son of Nwando, we salute you.............."

"He has brought white man's money in abundance for he said we should enjoy life. We salute you. We celebrate you."

These young ladies once performed this song and dance at Nwaforcha's compound at night under the glitter of the tilly lamp. They also sang a tune that celebrated Nwaforcha's accomplishments. They sang that Nwaforcha, alias Nwakaibie, had turned the lowly chicken into an elephant with his outstanding wisdom. That because of Nwaforcha's exploits a mere chicken has become a passport to riches.

"No wonder he is called Nwakaibie" they sang. Nwaforcha gave the dance group a goat and some oyibo money. That night Nwaforcha resolved that Akpu village must produce her own sergeant. And Ekigwe was on his mind.

Nwaforcha turned to Nweke and queried why Ekigwe hadn't enrolled in school. Nweke said nothing. Nwaforcha then instructed Nweke to make sure Ekigwe enrolled in school come following Monday. Nwaforcha told Nweke that if school fees were a problem, he should come and collect the money before he went back to Burutu.

Ekigwe's sisters, who were watching through the peephole, erupted in jubilation and dancing. The delay of the destiny of Ekigwe and Nweke's family had come to an end.

There was a Christian primary school at Oro Village about an hour's trek from Nweke's compound. Ekigwe started school in Oro CMS Primary School on Monday. Every day, instead of going to the farm with Nweke his father and his wives and children, Ekigwe went to school. As for Ekigwe's older sister, Adaobi, school was not on the itinerary at all. It was unheard of to send a female to school. Not even Nwaforcha's intervention could accomplish that feat. Women were considered other people's kindred and property because they'd soon get married and belong to other families and even to other villages. It was therefore pointless and a waste to spend scarce cowries and coins sending them to school.

On the contrary, women were supposed to bring wealth to their families through their labor and their dowries. That is why some women were named Obute Aku (bringer of wealth), especially if the family's fortunes turned for the better immediately after their birth. Of course, only a bumper harvest of yams could achieve this. Only utterly foolish men would even imagine sending their daughters to school.

Nweke considered his son Ekigwe as something he had lost to the white man's culture. He took solace in his second son Umeh who unlike Ekigwe not only dedicated himself to his father's farming but was even hostile to the Christians and the white man's culture. As far as Nweke was concerned, Ekigwe was dead and Umeh had become his firstborn son.

"One mother may give birth to children, but it's not the same god that creates the children," Nweke sighed. But Ekigwe was the toast of his mother and his sisters. Even the other wives of Nweke did not subscribe to his attitude toward Christians and his traditional fanaticism. But the women dare not show their resentment toward Nweke's fanatic stand on Akpu's traditions.

Ekigwe's mother wouldn't dare show that she supported Ekigwe's going to school. Women had absolutely no say or input into the direction of the family.

Their role ended with working the farm and cooking food for the family. They didn't enter the man's compound (Obi) except on invitation or to sweep it.

However, women were respected and honored in Akpu within their expected roles in society. Some women excelled in trading at Akpu markets and markets of neighboring villages. A woman called Afuekwe made one of the best ogili in the market. Ogili is an indispensable spice used for cooking the best soup in Akpu, the onugbu (bitter leaf) soup. In Akpu markets, nobody bought from other ogili sellers until Afuekwe finished selling all her ogili. Afuekwe was well known in Akpu and beyond for her ogili. She was honored with the 'Iyom' title, the female equivalent of the Ozo title. In Akpu tradition, women like Afuekwe commanded the respect of both men and women, and her opinion was sought in important matters concerning the town but not in masquerade cult matters at all. Masquerade or Ancestral Spirit matters were strictly for men.

In the evening, Akilika visited Nweke as usual. Nweke narrated the afternoon visit of Nwaforcha and the inevitable result of that visit – tthat Ekigwe would start school and join the Christians. Akilika blew hot and cold. His response to Nweke was very philosophical. In between inhalation of snuffs, Akilika cleared his throat characteristically and consoled Nweke thus:

"Ogbuefi," he started.

"Opulozo" Nweke answered him.

"Let the white man relieve us of all our weak and troublesome sons. Let them be the white man's burden."

"But peradventure any good comes from there, we thank the gods. Look at Nwaforcha. He was cast away by his family. He learnt the white man's tricks, maybe even their witchcraft. He served their God and came back to Akpu wiser and very wealthy. Who can stand before him today in our surrounding towns? After all, you still have a son, Umeh." This idea was fast becoming the thinking of men of Akpu village. Let the white men relieve us of all our lackluster children. "Echi di ime (Tomorrow is pregnant)."

"If they turn out good at last, it's still to our benefit." Thus Akilika concluded his advice to Nweke concerning Ekigwe.

CHAPTER SEVEN

On the following Monday, Ekigwe started school at the Primary School set up by the Christians at the Evil Forest. Ekigwe's mother Uduaku armed him with a black wooden slate and white, blue and red chalks for writing on the slate. A discarded beer bottle was thoroughly washed and filled with water for Ekigwe's drinking. Ekigwe loved the chalk color combination and often smelled the chalk for its aroma, an aroma of success and prosperity. Ekigwe going to school was a great victory for his sister Adaobi and his mother as well as other wives because Ekigwe had set a precedent. It was left to see if Nweke cared about precedence.

Ekigwe did very well in school. But Ekigwe's intellect brought him more troubles than honors. He learned a,b,c,d to z in no time and was able to recite and write it on his black slate to the delight and amazement of his mother and sisters. Ekigwe's mother and especially his sister, Adaobi, dreamed of Ekigwe being educated and able to bring home the trappings of Western civilization just like Nwaforcha. But his father was not interested. Ekigwe enjoyed school and always turned his empty bottle of water into a flute each time he was on his way home from school. The afternoon scorching sun didn't seem to bother him even though he often had blisters on his feet from the hot sand. Like all kids, he went to school barefoot. But Ekigwe didn't like what went on among many school kids on their way home from school. The children from the Anglican or CMS (Church Missionary Society) School and those from RCM (Roman Catholic Mission) School were always engaged in a shouting match. The RCM kids would scream at the CMS kids, "CMS Oku nmo, udaa. Kwa ututu kwa uzo nni, udaa", meaning "CMS hell fire, udaa. Only good at eating very early morning food, udaa."

Whereas CMS kids would return, "Faada, oli akwa okutu," meaning "Reverend Father, consumer of chicken eggs......"

Only white people were Reverend Fathers at that time. These hateful chants continued on village roads until the children branched into their various homes. This Church antagonism was not limited to school kids. The CMS and the RCM were practically at war with each other in Akpu. Ekigwe who belonged to RCM didn't join other kids in these hateful chants because he thought it was contrary to the religious teachings in the school.

One day Ekigwe was beaten by CMS kids on his way back from school. He came home with torn school uniforms. Uduaku, Ekigwe's mother went to complain to Nweke in the obi.

Nweke asked Uduaku whether she expected him to go and fight the "Efulefu fight" (fight of the lost) for her Efulefu son.

When Akilika paid his usual evening banter visit, Nweke wasted no time to tell him in between tobacco snuff inhalations how his wife wanted him to leave his barn and join the Efulefu fight. Akilika was surprised.

"Fight over what?" asked Akilika casually.

"Ekigwe was involved in the Efulefu children fight."

"You know that every day they are coming back from school, the favorite pastime of those kids is to curse each other. Their parents are not spared."

"And his mother came to disturb my work. Did I not tell you not to underestimate the patience of the gods? Their eyes may not move, but they are not sleeping. Sometimes we foolishly regard the patience of the gods as weakness. Can't you see that the gods have caused the 'Christian gods' to start fighting themselves? So that they kill themselves and we do nothing, just watch."

"Ogbuefi, I never thought of it that way. Your words are loaded with wisdom," agreed Akilika.

The majority of Akpu Town was CMS, probably because they settled in Akpu before the RCM arrived with their "Onyeocha" Reverend Father. But the RCM were very aggressive in spreading their doctrine in Akpu. They would visit the native midwives and baptize the newborn babies with the permission of the parents of the babies and gave the baby a Catholic name. One woman gave birth to a baby girl at the native midwife's place. The RCM promptly baptized the baby with the name, Francesca. But the family, unable to deal with the pronunciation, called her Furanci. These parents didn't even understand the meaning of baptism or what the RCM did other than that the RCM had initiated them into RCM membership. So most of these so-called converts still continued with their heathen practices, masquerade cult and Ozo titleship. Of course, the RCM didn't mind so long as they increased their ranks and got more 'converts.'

Indeed, the RCM first and later the CMS incorporated the Ozo title rather than lose their members because the Church forbade heathen titles. So the Church initiated the Church Ozo (Ozo Uka) to accommodate the Ozo titled men. The Church also found ways to accommodate other practices like polygamy, which were normally contrary to the church doctrines all to increase their numbers. The CMS and the RCM churches were constantly engaged in unhealthy competition.

The rivalry of both missions was not restricted to the school kids. The elders of both churches were at loggerheads. Only the Akpu heathen culture inevitably united them as Akpu village tradition did not recognize or spare CMS or RCM members. Most of these elders were having the best of both worlds, enjoying the spoils of heathen tradition as well as the trappings of Christian Western civilization. They still visited witch doctors secretly and wore amulets around their waists even while in church. But on Sundays, they put on a different garb, the garb of holiness and they would be ready to swear that they had nothing to do with heathen practices. Old habits die hard. One of the respected elders in the RCM Church was to do the funeral ceremony of his late older brother. A week before the funeral, he consulted the witch doctor who was a Rain Maker to prevent rain from falling throughout that day and night so as to avoid spoiling the occasion. When the news spilled out, some members of the Church confronted him and accused him of indulging in a heathen practice.

"All I did was prevent rain from marring the funeral ceremony of my beloved brother," he countered. He was very livid and challenged them, "Let any one of you pull down his trousers and prove that he's not wearing an amulet." The men quietly dispersed.

"Look at the hypocrites," he scoffed.

CHAPTER EIGHT

Two things scared the living daylight out of Ekigwe. The cow and the flogging masquerade. The flogging masquerade wasn't much of a problem to Ekigwe because masquerades only came out during village feasts. Even during the village feasts, masquerades appeared late in the mornings. Because of the long distance to school, Ekigwe usually left for school very early in the morning, well before masquerades start to appear. In the afternoons, school teachers usually escorted the school children home after school during every feast.

However, Ekigwe had a certain stray cow to contend with in the mornings while on his way to school. This cow belonged to the god of a shrine called Udo in Oro village. The cow roamed the village freely like an outlaw eating people's farm crops with impunity. Nobody dared touch a cow belonging to Udo. Nobody was going to fight you. But you'd have Udo itself to contend with. The road to the stream unfortunately passed through the Udo Shrine vicinity. All the people who passed this road always held tight to their belongings because if anything dropped from your hand while you were passing the road by Udo Shrine, you wouldn't pick it up. If you were so foolhardy to pick it up, the consequence was that your nose became so disfigured that you spoke like a masquerade.

Ekigwe feared cows more than he feared masquerades because a masquerade could at worst flog you and leave you bruised. But Ekigwe had a certain deadly imagination of an encounter with a cow. Ekigwe believed that unlike the masquerade, a cow not only could pierce you with his horns but could also stamp out all the food you had eaten, including stamping the very life out of you.

This Udo cow was fond of lying down at a road junction along Ekigwe's path to school every morning. One day, Ekigwe saw the cow at this junction. The cow simply laid down on the road, chewing away. Ekigwe reasoned that the cow laid in ambush for him, "I said it. I know it's waiting for me to come and go to school."

It was obvious that this cow was in no hurry to get up and move away. Ekigwe stood at a safe distance that would give him enough room to run should the cow decide to go for him. He waited for almost an hour before an elderly wine tapper returning with his wine kegs asked him, "Look here, boy. You are late to school. What are you standing here doing?" Immediately, the palm wine tapper noticed the cow and grinned, "Come with me and pass. The cow is not after you. It is minding its business." He then led him past the cow. While the wine tapper walked with Ekigwe past the cow, Ekigwe walked on the opposite side of the man and had his eyes fixated on the cow. After he passed the cow, Ekigwe wondered why the cow didn't even bother to look at him. Ekigwe had escaped the deadly encounter with the cow but not the lesser trouble of lateness to the school. The headmaster flogged Ekigwe for lateness before he was allowed to his class. For Ekigwe, it was far better to receive six strokes of the cane than to die in the hands of a cow.

The Christians usually baptized the converts with an English (Oyibo) name. Christopher, the son of the village Catechist was one of such. The school children called him Okili, an Ibo acronym for Christopher. Okili was Ekigwe's only friend in the school. He always gave Ekigwe some hot akara balls every afternoon break. Okili's mother was well known for the delicious akara, the bean cake that she fried and sold every day at the nearby Oye market. Every break time, hordes of school children followed Okili around the school playground begging him for some of the akara balls that his mother gave him as lunch snacks. Okili would only give the akara to Ekigwe. But there was no way the akara could go around the crowd of school kids going after Okili. Okili was apprehensive at break times because of this. One break time, while the children chased Okili round the school's large open field chanting, "Okili please give me some akara."

Okili told them to wait. The children waited expectantly while Okili opened the package of smoking hot akara balls. Okili gave some akara balls to Ekigwe. He then spat his saliva severally on the remaining akara balls and offered them to anyone who wanted among the waiting kids.

"Who would like to eat Okili's spit with his ugly looking brown teeth?" complained a school kid. The school children sighed and dispersed in disappointment. Okili proceeded to eat his akara in peace.

CHAPTER NINE

About half a mile from Ekigwe's compound on his route to school, there was an udala (local apple) tree at a crossroads. Under the shade of this tree sat a certain neighborhood imbecile from dawn to dusk every day. His name was Nkwo Okpokpo Isi (Nkwo the big head). He kept watch over the udala tree, an assignment he created for himself. Children love udala and always looked at ripe udala on the tree with a longing. All the children in the village knew Nkwo the big head. Children dreaded this man so much that when they passed this udala tree, they would look the other way lest they attracted his attention and then a possible accusation that they were staring at him. For some reason, Nkwo the big head always felt that people stared at him. If any school child thus attracted his attention, he would get up and follow the child. The child would normally run to school or run home. Nkwo was never in a hurry. He would simply trot at his own calculated pace till he reached the school and reported the child. If the child was going home after school, Nkwo would trot patiently till he got to the kid's home and made his complaint. He seemed to know every kid.

In Akpu Town, it was forbidden to pluck udala and many other fruits from the tree. People were expected to patiently wait for fruits to ripe and fall down before they were picked by a fortunate passerby. That was why some people visit fruit trees very early in the morning to be the first to get to the fruits that fell when men were asleep in the night. In Akpu, it was common to see a fetish or charm tied around a tree of value. This fetish usually wards off intruders because the people believed that those charms were capable of inflicting terrible diseases and even death to unauthorized individuals.

One morning, as Ekigwe trekked to school, he got to the udala tree and was attracted by so many ripe fruits on the tree. Ekigwe did not see Nkwo who probably went aside to the nearby bush to use the open toilet. Ekigwe brought out his catapult and shot at the tree to cause some ripe udala fruits to fall. This attracted Nkwo's attention from where he stooped and emptied his bowels in the bush. Nkwo sprang from the bush like a hen whose chicks were under attack.

Ekigwe, on sighting Nkwo, ran off to school frightened to his marrow. Ekigwe got to the class panting and praying in vain that Nkwo gave up on his pursuit. Meanwhile, Nkwo reached the school and reported to the Headmaster in his incoherent speech, "A school kid had plucked the udala from the tree and ran away." The Headmaster assigned a teacher to take Nkwo round the classes to identify the erring child. In the next twenty minutes, Ekigwe had barely regained his breath when to his horror, Nkwo, accompanied by a teacher, entered his class. The two teachers had a brief talk after which they asked Nkwo to look and see if the boy was in that class. Nkwo scouted the class with his queer eyes which always frightened kids, and pointed his finger in Ekigwe's direction with the words "that one." Ekigwe, paralysed with fear, sprang to his feet at the teacher's thunderous command. Ekigwe was led away to the Headmaster's office for an obvious date with the whip. Satisfied, Nkwo left and trotted back to the udala tree to wait for another offending kid.

Ekigwe was very intelligent and excelled in school to the delight of the teachers. Every time his teacher asked a question in class only Ekigwe could give the right answer. Soon Ekigwe's classmates became envious of him. But Ekigwe had yet other sins. One day during breaktime, Ekigwe was out playing with other kids at the school's football field. An argument arose because the Queen was scheduled to visit the country on her way to a tour of the British Empire. A portrait of the queen was circulated in the school and the kids thought she was so beautiful. It got to a point where a kid suggested that the queen was so beautiful she probably didn't fart or use the toilet. The other kids readily agreed with that suggestion.

"She is always seated on that throne except when she is on tour like now. So how can she use the toilet or poop?" continued the wisecrack.

However, Ekigwe differed saying she was a human being like them.

"Didn't our teacher tell us that all human beings use the toilet and poop?" insisted Ekigwe.

"He always thinks that he is the smartest one in the class," remarked a kid.

"Yes, even the smartest in the school just because the teachers like him and so score him high marks," added another kid. The kids were about to beat Ekigwe up, but he smartly left them before it got to that.

Another sin of Ekigwe was that only he enjoyed Okili's bean cake (akara) balls. A particular boy in Ekigwe's class called Chukwuma turned himself into a thorn in the flesh of Ekigwe. Chukwuma was very good at wrestling. He always used the technique called "iluege" to throw any schoolboy down in no time. Chukwuma and his gang of friends were in the habit of testing every new kid in the school. If the new kid proved to be strong and fearless, Chukwuma and his friends would want him to join their group. But if the new kid showed weakness and was afraid, the gang would put him on their blacklist and try to make his life miserable. Every break time, Chukwuma and a few friends would target Ekigwe. One day, Chukwuma's gang challenged Ekigwe to a wrestling match. It was either Ekigwe accepted the challenge or Chukwuma wrestled him by force while his friends watched and applauded. One day, Chukwuma not only floored Ekigwe but also deliberately put sand in his mouth to the applause of Chukwuma's friends. After break, the teacher asked Ekigwe why he was so dirty. Ekigwe narrated his encounter with Chukwuma. Chukwuma was summoned by the teacher and later sent to the Headmaster. Some of Chukwuma's friends testified against him and he was found guilty. Chukwuma was given twelve strokes of the whip by the Headmaster and warned to steer clear of Ekigwe. This signaled the beginning of Ekigwe's problems in the Oro School and in Akpu Town.

Chukwuma got home that day and told his older brother Isike how a certain troublesome boy caused the Headmaster to give him twelve strokes of the cane. Chukwuma's elder brother usually was an ancestral spirit that wore the Ekwulo flogging masquerade. Isike told Chukwuma to relax.

"Have you forgotten that Akpu Ukwu (Great Akpu) feast is around the corner?" he consoled Chukwuma with a mischievous grin. Akpu-Ukwu celebrated the Python, the god of Akpu Town. If a python strayed into your compound, it came to pay you a visit. So you respectfully received it or called the keeper of its shrine to come and carry it back to its shrine. Quite often, people used the masquerade to settle scores in Akpu. Flogging masquerades would lay an ambush for their victims and flog them until they bled. Then the masquerade would vanish. Usually, nobody dared identify these masquerades even if they knew the man inside the masquerade. So, masquerades did not only entertain, but sometimes they were used for vendetta.

Soon it was Akpu Ukwu feast, and Ekigwe did not know what lay ahead for him. Ekigwe didn't know there was a sinister plan by Chukwuma for his brother's masquerade to ambush him.

Chukwuma had already boasted to his group of friends in school that during the coming Akpu Ukwu, Ekigwe "will see" — that meant that Ekigwe was going to pay for his sins.

So on this fateful morning, Ekigwe was walking to school. He didn't have the cow to contend with. But something bigger than the cow, the spirit of the ancestors in the person of Chukwuma's brother, was lying in ambush for him.

Usually, masquerades didn't appear early in the morning but late morning. But mischievous masquerades, especially those targeting young ladies on their way to or from the stream usually did appear early. Young ladies like beautiful Okpanma who turned down some young men's advances recently became such a target. Okpanma broke her precious water pot during such an attack as she returned from the stream walking elegantly with the water pot craftily balanced on her head. Okpanma's beauty and gait were very hard for the men to resist but she wouldn't reciprocate to the frustration of many Akpu men.

As Ekigwe walked to school, suddenly a masquerade ran out from the bush, "Ekigwe de," greeted the masquerade quite unnecessarily. Before Ekigwe could even understand what was happening, the masquerade had descended on him with many strokes of his canes and disappeared back into the bush leaving Ekigwe writhing in pain. Ekigwe later gathered himself and his books together and reported the incident at school. Chukwuma was among the first to comment, "It served that brat well. I hope it taught him some lessons." But although Chukwuma and his friends were jealous of Ekigwe for his superior academic performance and his monopoly of Okili's akara balls, some of Chukwuma's friends thought the punishment meted out to Ekigwe was excessive and unjust. So one of Chukwuma's friends went ahead to tell Ekigwe that it was Chukwuma who arranged his brother's masquerade to attack him. Chukwuma did not realize that it didn't please some of his friends when he gleefully told them how Ekigwe was thrashed by his brother's masquerade.

Ekigwe unwisely reported this to his teacher who in turn reported it to the Headmaster. The report was tantamount to revealing the identity of the man behind the mask, or unmasking the masquerade, the most serious abomination in Akpu village. Akpu village called it "killing the masquerade or the ancestral spirit." To kill a human being was bad enough. To kill again an ancestor long dead is a different matter.

Chukwuma was summoned by the headmaster and subsequently expelled from the school. Chukwuma's dismissal from school was not as important as the reason for his expulsion.

Chukwuma's expulsion was evidence of an abomination against the Akpu people. The reason for expelling Chukwuma from school could only mean one thing, that somebody had killed the masquerade, a sacrilege of the highest order in Akpu, and even the entire region.

CHAPTER TEN

Even the killing of the sacred python or the sacred tortoise, both forbidden in Akpu village, was not as abominable as the unmasking (killing) of a masquerade. How could you bring back and identify the spirit of a dead ancestor? If you killed any snake of the sacred species, even by mistake, you would have to organize a funeral ceremony as if a prominent human being died.

You'd still perform other cleansing rites to cleanse your family as well as the village of the abomination.

Therefore to unmask or "kill" a masquerade was an abomination of untold proportions. Of course, to kill the spirit of an ancestor that was already dead was no small accomplishment and an unkind reward for their effort in coming from the dead to visit their people.

So when Chukwuma was suspended from school, his father wasn't troubled at all by Chukwuma's inability to continue his Christian education as much as he was troubled that a grave abomination had occurred against Akpu Town.

Chukwuma narrated to his father the reason for his suspension from school. His father exclaimed that the last had not been heard of the evil consequences of the white man's visit to Akpu Town.

"Ihe ehi huru gbalaga oso ka okuku huru n'atu onu (fools rush where angels fear to tread)," Chukwuma's father remarked with a sinister grin.

Ekigwe was at home in his mother's hut, oblivious of what was germinating in Akpu village as a result of the evil seed sown by Chukwuma.

That night the Town Crier was heard beating his ogene (gong) with a deliberate cadence.

Gom gom gom, gom gom gom, rang the ogene, interrupting the serenity of the night as well as many fairy tales in families.

This cadence usually sent the message of trouble to Akpu village even before the crier spoke a word. Then came the terrible announcement.

"No man or woman should be seen on the road this night because the ancestral spirits are out in a rage. They have lost one of their own. I have spoken as I was sent."

The topic of discussion throughout Akpu village that night was what could have caused the ancestral spirits to seize the night? It was an unusual occurrence.

Akilika visited Nweke that night.

"Ogbuefi" Akilika called Nweke.

"Opulozo," Nweke answered.

"Did you hear the Town Crier?" Akilika asked Nweke.

"Of course I did," responded Nweke.

"I wonder what has happened," continued Nweke, not realizing that whatever happened was about his own family, his son Ekigwe.

"One thing is clear," declared Akilika.

"Where a child points his finger crying, if his mother is not there, his father is surely there. Tomorrow morning we will surely hear something." With those words, Akilika retired to his house leaving Nweke to wonder what had happened in Akpu village.

Nweke woke up in the morning and went to the farm. But he didn't stay long on the farm because he didn't have peace of mind. He thought that strange things had been happening in Akpu village since the advent of the Christians. The news of the unmasking or "killing" of the masquerade spread like wildfire throughout Akpu village. But it wasn't clear who did it.

Nweke's youngest wife, Okpanma went to the hut of Uduaku for banter about the Town Crier's announcement.

"Good morning Nne Ekigwe," greeted Okpanma.

"I slept well my children's mother," replied Uduaku.

"Did you hear the Town Crier last night?" continued Okpanma.

"No. I went to bed early last night. What did he say?"

"That an ancestral spirit has been killed," replied Okpanma.

"Akpu ukwu gbata osoooo!" Uduaku exclaimed.

"Come again my second," requested Uduaku.

"Did I hear you right?" she continued, obviously alarmed.

"We have to talk carefully because you know it's strictly a man's business," cautioned Uduaku.

Later that night, by midnight, the guttural voices of hundreds of ancestral spirits filled the town. The ancestral spirits were lamenting and mourning the death of one of their own. The mysterious noise filled the whole town for two nights. But the third night, the noise was steadily moving toward Nweke's compound.

As soon as the news filtered to the mother of Ekigwe and to his sister, Adaobi, Adaobi hurriedly smuggled Ekigwe through the back village pathway under cover of darkness to the Christians for refuge. Only Adaobi and her mother knew Ekigwe's whereabouts. They kept it away from Ekigwe's half-brother, Umeh, because they knew that Umeh hated Ekigwe. Umeh felt that Ekigwe was pompous because he went to school and felt too big to go to the farm like everyone else.

"Ekigwe ate in this family. He's sheltered under our roof but wouldn't contribute anything because he wouldn't follow our father to the farm," complained Umeh.

Umeh seemed to savor anything that brought Ekigwe into disrepute. One of the problems of polygamy is the rampant quarrelsomeness common with children of polygamous wives. It seemed to emanate from a fight of supremacy among the wives. But Umeh's hatred for Ekigwe seemed to transcend that.

The Christians hid Ekigwe and arranged to smuggle him to a Christian community in a distant village where ultra-conservative Akpu traditional chieftains had no influence.

By this time Nweke had known that Ekigwe "killed" the masquerade. Nweke told his Umunna (clan) that the moon had appeared in broad daylight.

"The unthinkable has happened," Nweke lamented.

Nweke's compound as well as his neighbors' had no peace that night and the next four nights. The spirits cried in various tones and cadences and called for restitution. The ancestral spirits operated only at night and vanished before dawn. The traditional mourning period for dead spirits was seven market weeks. One week is four market nights - Oye, Afor, Nkwor and Eke.

Nweke knew fully the consequence of Ekigwe's offense. He said concerning Ekigwe, "Is he not the evil child that entered his mother's womb through the back door?" Nweke lamented that Ekigwe won't rest until he destroyed his family completely.

On the first night of the ancestral spirits visit, Nweke screamed and demanded for Ekigwe's head but the mother told him that Ekigwe's whereabouts were unknown. Nweke commanded her to fish him out so that he would answer the spirits of the ancestors. Nweke said that Ekigwe should not only answer the ancestral spirits but he should indeed join them in the spirit world. To that Ekigwe's mother said, "Tufiakwa, the gods forbid."

The traditional funeral rites of a dead ancestral spirit were more complex and expensive than the funeral rites of a dead titled chief, and Nweke was expected to bear all the costs.

The morning after the first night of the ancestral spirits' mourning, Akilika was now getting weary of the chain of events in Nweke's family. Akilika had developed cold feet after the first near-tragic event in which Nweke wanted to teach his god a lesson because Akilika had a guilty conscience. It was Akilika that informed Nweke of Ekigwe's supposed romance with the Efulefus (Christians), which led Nweke to that unfortunate attempt to kill his own god.

But Akilika felt that he had no hand in this more disastrous event. He had no hand in Ekigwe going to school which resulted in the current dilemma. Akilika simply came to console and encourage his friend Nweke.

He knew that Nweke's problem was not the ability to afford the costs of a funeral for a dead ancestral spirit and the associated cleansing, but how to produce Ekigwe, who would bear the brunt of the cleansing procedure.

Nweke told Akilika, "My eyes have seen my ears."

"Every night is now a nightmare for me," Nweke lamented.

"What is bigger than the cricket has entered the cricket's hole," he continued.

Akilika told Nweke, "No matter how heavy a rainfall is, it will fizzle out."

"Ogbuefi, you're a great man who has encountered greater things in life and you handled them. This one will not be an exception" he concluded.

"Opulozor alu emee," Nweke continued with his lamentation.

"Know one thing, that nothing the eye can see that will cause it to bleed," Akilika consoled Nweke. Akilika assured Nweke that he would go to the custodians of the masquerade cult and ask them on Nweke's behalf what needed to be done and what was expected of him. Nweke was too devastated to meet with them himself.

"Every dog feeds on excrement, but when a dog eats the excrement and carries it about on its mouth, people are bound to say, hey look at a dog that eats excrement," Akilika said this as he left Nweke to return to his house in reference to Ekigwe's talkativeness in revealing the man behind the mask. Most adults in Akpu know that it's men inside every masquerade. But when you open your mouth too wide to say so, everybody will pretend they don't know and scream "Abomination!" Ekigwe certainly opened his mouth too wide.

Meanwhile, the Christians had sent Ekigwe to a teacher in a distant town called Achara to continue his school.

But Nweke was told that he either produced Ekigwe for the cleansing process or he would do the cleansing on his son's behalf. The cleansing included dancing to the drums of the spirits naked in the village's market square. Nweke told Akilika that he would rather die than abide by that demand of the Mmanwu (masquerade) cult. The next market week witnessed a tense standoff between Nweke and the masquerade cult. Masquerades started to keep nightly mourning vigil again all around Nweke's compound, this time leaving no room for people to leave the compound or come in.

After seven market weeks of siege, it was announced that Nweke and his household became ostracized in Akpu village. Not even his son's mentor, Nwaforcha, could save him because fighting the masquerade cult was akin to fighting ghosts and nobody dared fight ghosts and win. Killing an ancestral spirit was one aspect of Akpu's tradition that any wise Akpu person wouldn't like to interfere in or intercede in for anybody.

Nweke's anger started shifting momentarily from his son and the Christians to the traditions of his people. Nweke felt that the very tradition which he had fanatically protected and defended was now turning around to make him a victim. Nweke now saw his people's traditions, especially the masquerade cult, as very brutal and unreasonable. A labyrinth of thoughts consumed Nweke. He remembered how his father's gods were unable to stop the Christians from surviving in the Evil Forest, let alone kill them. Indeed the Christians waxed stronger every day and were steadily growing in number. They were entrenching in the Evil Forest and had even changed the roof of their church from thatch to zinc and were clearing more Evil Forest around them to expand the school. Then his own personal god did not fare any better. It was becoming increasingly doubtful if the village gods were stronger than the Christian God.

As Nweke pondered on these events and his next move, news filtered to Akilika that the masquerade cult of Akpu was planning to burn down his friend's house on the next Nkwo market night, three nights away. Akilika informed his friend Nweke and begged him to succumb to the demands of the masquerade cult and survive. The masquerade cult was synonymous with the law and the tradition in Akpu village. It was a source of fun and fear, excitement and expectation, protection and intimidation, provision and procreation in Akpu village.

Nweke spurned Akilika's advice and decided to confront the masquerade cult violence for violence. He sharpened his machetes and loaded his Dane guns, determined to challenge his people's culture and take a last desperate stand in self-defense. Nweke's eldest daughter Adaobi had been watching the unfolding drama with great apprehension. Akilika's wife had informed Nweke's wives of the plans of the masquerade cult to burn down the compound but the wives were afraid of Nweke and felt helpless because Nweke was obviously a bomb waiting to explode. Nobody wanted to detonate the bomb on herself.

Early in the morning of Oye market day, two days to the d-day, Adaobi ran to her paternal grandmother's (Ochie) family in the neighboring village of Offia to tell them of the impending doom facing her father, her brother and her entire family in a matter of two days.

CHAPTER ELEVEN

In Igboland, the fear of ancestral spirits was the beginning of wisdom. The following morning, Offia Village sent some men to persuade Nweke to run for his life and also move his family to Offia. Nweke bluntly refused to take refuge in Offia. The men from Offia overpowered Nweke and forcefully took him to his mother's family as well as all his household. Nweke's mother's family, helped by Offia Village, built huts for Nweke's family in Offia Village. Men took turns to watch over Nweke lest he tried to do "what the earth forbids," until Nweke's nerves calmed down and Nweke started to accept the new realities of his life and environment.

On Nkwo night, the masquerade cult kept their date with Nweke. They visited Nweke's compound but found nobody there. Disappointed, they destroyed Nweke's compound and left it in ashes. It was a heap of rubble. Akilika came to his friend's compound the next morning. He paced about in mourning and wonder and lamented, "Toaah! The stubborn fly follows the corpse to the grave and is also buried." Other neighbors also paced about sighing and wondering, some of them in tears. Some neighbors placed both hands on their heads as they starred at the rubble that used to be the home of one of Akpu's finest.

Months passed and years passed and no word was heard of Ekigwe. Although Nweke consoled himself with his second son Umeh, he often felt that subsequent events had vindicated his son Ekigwe's stand in abandoning his people's tradition, and his father's gods for the Christian God. Nweke saw Ekigwe in himself, but pride and guilt had taken hold of him. Nweke had tasted the wickedness of his town's tradition and even the powerlessness of their gods as well as his personal god. He thought that his god was only good at eating up all his chickens and had never risen to the occasion when it mattered most. Nevertheless, Nweke could not go beyond his thoughts because he was in a dilemma. Shame would not let him turn to the Christians and he wouldn't want to stir up the hornet's nest again in Offia which was also very traditional.

"Maybe Offia's gods would prove to be more powerful and reliable than Akpu's gods," Nweke consoled himself. But only time would tell.

There was apprehension in the family about the whereabouts of Ekigwe and his fate. Only Adaobi and the women knew how he escaped and where he escaped to. Adaobi did not even know that Ekigwe had been moved elsewhere. She was in constant sadness over her brother's fate but she was afraid to go to Akpu Village Christians to inquire about the whereabouts of Ekigwe because her family was considered banished from Akpu. Although the family worried about Ekigwe, his brother Umeh had no sympathy toward him. He told the family that Ekigwe had caused enough problems for the family which should keep the family fully occupied. He wondered aloud why the family would still worry about Ekigwe's whereabouts. He said that Ekigwe's absence was better for the family than his presence.

After Ekigwe escaped to the Christians from the masquerade cult, he was sent to live with a teacher in a distant village Christian school located in Achara town where he continued his education. Two other boys who were older than Ekigwe joined Ekigwe as houseboys to the Teacher.

The presence of the two older boys proved to be another Achilles heel for Ekigwe. He was a fragile-looking teenager, slim and of average height though still growing. His countenance appeared intimidated, probably from his experience at the Akpu Elementary School and coupled with frightening ancestral spirit encounters. Nevertheless, his fragile looks belied his intelligence and resilience. In contrast, one of the two older boys was short and of stocky build with a mean face that makes one wonder if he had ever been happy once in his life. The oldest among them was also the tallest and heavyset. Both Ekigwe and the other short boy knew their oldest colleague well enough not to be deceived by his smiles. His smiles were sinister and he did the meanest things when he was smiling.

Ekigwe's weakest point was that he was a slow eater. His mates were guzzlers who ate blazing hot food very fast. While Ekigwe blew air on his scoop with his mouth to cool it down, the other boys would eat the hot food fast and occasionally even open their mouths to let off steam. The big boys made sure the food was dished steaming hot.

"Please let the food be a bit cooler before we eat it," pleaded Ekigwe once.

"When did you become the Master to issue orders around here?" the oldest boy snarled at Ekigwe. Ekigwe was frightened and held his peace.

Ekigwe was thus always left hungry. He therefore requested that the food be shared into three equal portions every time they had food to eat. But the two bigger boys bluntly refused Ekigwe's request, asking why they had to dirty three or six plates when they could easily dirty only one or two plates depending on what they were eating. Even Ekigwe's offer to wash all dishes was turned down by the big boys.

"Are you saying that our hands are so dirty you couldn't eat with us from the same bowl? Who do you even think you are?" queried one of the big boys. But they only wanted to eat the greater portion of the food every time to ensure they had enough. Their master the Teacher gave strict instructions on the measure of the food to be cooked, especially rice or beans, which had a measuring cup. But the Teacher expected the boys to share the food into three equal parts before they started to eat. But he was not there to know if his instructions were followed and Ekigwe was understandably too scared to report.

One afternoon, the boys had a lunch of foo foo and okra soup to eat. Normally, the boys would finish eating the foo foo before they shared the meat or fish in the okra soup. That afternoon, as soon as the boys finished washing their hands and sat around the two dishes, the biggest boy dipped his hand into the soup and took out the only piece of meat. He gave the other boy a little piece and put the rest in his mouth. Ekigwe protested and went to report to their master, the Teacher. The Teacher gave the biggest boy six strokes of the whip that afternoon. Thereafter, the biggest boy twisted Ekigwe's ears as he warned Ekigwe and told him that any weekend the teacher traveled, he had better travel with him because he would see hell. The two bigger boys threatened to beat up Ekigwe if he ever again raised such an issue before their master, the Teacher. So out of fear Ekigwe kept mute and suffered in silence. Ekigwe was hungry every day and still had to be sent to fetch firewood alone. Ekigwe alone did the work meant for the three servants. It became another Animal Farm situation between the three boys.

Every mealtime, the two big boys made sure the food was served steaming hot. The story was the same every day.

To worsen matters for Ekigwe, the two big boys were performing poorly in school, whereas Ekigwe excelled in his studies. The Teacher always spoke harshly to the two bigger boys comparing them to Ekigwe and often calling them "big for nothing" and "coconut heads."

But the Teacher did not notice that Ekigwe wasn't happy and was becoming emaciated. Sometimes Ekigwe longed for his mother and her food.

One day, the boys called Ekigwe to come and eat. Ekigwe declined in protest.

"He is starting a hunger strike," remarked the younger of the big boys both laughing.

"Ewu nwuru n'oba ji obughi aguru gburu ya," responded the biggest boy, meaning that "the goat that died in a barn of yams did not die of hunger." Yam was the favorite food of goats.

There was a toilet at the fringes of the Teacher's compound which the boys called latrine. There was a small, thatched shithouse housing the toilet. It was a pit toilet dug so deep that if anything, including a human being, fell into it, there was no need to look for it because it would have been buried deep inside poop and maggots. A wooden structure was built around the hole leading into the pit designed to help users properly direct their poop. People squat on this structure and directed their poop at the entrance of the pit toilet. There was a wooden cover to the pit hole probably to keep the stench away and also to ward off flies and cockroaches. One evening, the second big boy used the pit toilet. Even though the boy's face was usually a picture of disgust, you could notice that his poop stunk so much that it was repulsive to him. Despite the shithouse standing at the fringes of the compound, the stench was all over the compound. The Teacher emerged from the house to use the toilet. The stench hit the Teacher on the face like extreme winter hits the face as one emerges from a warm house. The frown and disgust the Teacher wore on his face told the whole story about his mood. Then the Teacher called out the biggest boy, "Sir," he answered.

"Who used this toilet?"

"Ekigwe sir," lied the biggest boy against Ekigwe.

"Where is Ekigwe?" howled the Teacher. Ekigwe heard the Teacher and came to answer. As soon as the Teacher saw Ekigwe, he commanded, "Lock him inside that toilet for one hour."

"Yes sir," answered the biggest boy. Then he grabbed the terrified Ekigwe who didn't even understand what was going on. He pushed dumbfounded Ekigwe into the shithouse and locked the wooden door. He sighed as he told his colleague who actually produced the foul bomb, "The Teacher should have said, 'Push the idiot into the shithole,'" and they had a good laugh.

Hours later, Ekigwe was heard screaming and banging on the shithouse door. The two big boys had even forgotten Ekigwe inside the shithouse until they heard his screams and the banging. They would have ignored Ekigwe but were afraid that the Teacher would hear his banging. So they reluctantly unlocked him.

Ekigwe emerged from the shithouse hours later sweating profusely and very sad. Ekigwe never understood his crime!

It was Saturday morning and the Teacher had traveled on Friday to his village for the weekend. He was going to supervise the mud bungalow he was putting up in his town. He planned to roof his bungalow with the novel aluminum roofing sheets, quite an accomplishment at that time. Except for one thing, this Saturday morning was like any other weekend, laid back and there was no hurry to get to school on time. An owl was perched on the roof of the mud house crying incessantly. Nobody could claim to know what the owl was saying but every attempt to drive the bird away failed as the bird appeared to be unperturbed by the stones the boys threw at it. Instead, the bird continued with its pattern of song suggesting it had a message it must deliver. Fear gripped the boys because owls were associated with superstitious evil omens. So what message could it deliver save evil messages?

"I have never seen an owl in this compound, let alone see it perched on our house," commented the younger of the two big boys, his mean-looking face giving a more ominous meaning to his comment.

"That is very true," agreed the biggest boy.

"We have to do something about it," continued the biggest boy.

"If a chicken wakes up early in the morning and starts to pursue you, better run with all your strength because the chicken may have developed teeth during the night," concluded the biggest boy. He was making reference to the unusual and mysterious visit of the owl to their house and worse, the daring refusal of the owl to leave. The biggest boy was inferring that there must be danger which they had yet to identify. But Ekigwe was unconcerned and said nothing. To Ekigwe, his issues were far bigger than the gathering of a hundred owls.

Soon, there arose for Ekigwe the last straw that broke the camel's back. Later that morning, the Teacher's mistress came to visit the Teacher. The visit diverted the boys' attention from the bird. "Please tell the Teacher that I am here," demanded the Mistress. But as the Teacher had travelled to his village for the weekend, "When the cat is away, the rats rule the house." The boys did not immediately respond to the Mistress's request, as the two big boys were busy discussing strategy as soon as they set eyes on the Mistress. So the Mistress asked the boys for the Teacher again.

"Please I said you should tell the Teacher that I am here," she stressed.

"The Teacher is not at home," answered the oldest boy.

"Where is he?"

"He went out this morning."

"To?"

"He traveled to the village."

"Can I wait for him?" she asked, looking disturbed.

Apparently, she had great expectations for today and

the hope looked like it was about to be dashed.

"You don't seem happy. Any problem?" asked the biggest boy.

"No, there's no problem. It's just that I didn't have any other plan today. I had expected to spend the day here with him," she said, looking really sad and disappointed. The oldest boy noticed her disappointment and wasted no time in taking advantage of the situation.

"That's not a problem. We can take good care of you, Miss," assured the oldest boy, smiling mischievously. He then led her into the house and gave her a seat.

"What do I get you to drink?" offered the houseboy.

"We have Krola and we also have Heineken beer."

"I would like Heineken beer," she said, feeling more relaxed and started thinking, "Yeah, it's like he'll really take care of me."

"Good, I think you'll need it," commented the houseboy again grinning mischievously. The girl understood him clearly but feigned ignorance. Deep inside, she was very happy at the prospect of this unexpected younger blood treat.

"Wow! It's really true what they say that every disappointment is a blessing. I can't wait for this blessing," she excitedly reasoned.

Soon the boy came back with the beer, served her and engaged her further in a conversation.

The oldest houseboy told her that the Teacher had traveled and won't be back for two days. He told her she might as well relax and have fun.

Although she was privately elated at the prospect of experiencing three young boys, she pretended she didn't have any interest beyond the drink. The biggest houseboy was bad enough he understood every pretension of the Mistress.

"Relax and have what type of fun?" she asked, frowning.

Yet the boy not leaving anything to chance thought that she probably could have felt insulted and might report to the teacher. So he quickly added, "Sorry for any misunderstanding, please. I meant that you should relax for the food to be ready because I have asked my second to prepare food for you. Do you have a preference?"

"I'm ok with the beer," she said now, sounding urgent. The boy fearing he was about to lose her became a bit jittery and doubled back to find out what he was doing wrong in chatting her up.

"I won't tell Teacher that you came to see him. As far as the Teacher is concerned, you didn't come here. Is that a deal?"

"Perfect," replied the girl, now looking more relaxed and happy.

"I wanted to go because while I was burning with desire, you were busy talking about food and I thought you were not interested. I didn't come here to eat food. If I wanted food, I'd eat in my house," concluded the girl.

So the houseboy plotted for them to eat the sweet food which she brought for the master. He engaged the lady in a conversation and convinced her to have sex with all the boys on the Teacher's bed. Actually, the lady needed no convincing. She badly wanted it. The wannabe master then came to Ekigwe and the other houseboy excitedly telling them the coup de tat he had plotted. The second houseboy was excited, but Ekigwe was terrified because he had never had such an experience or even dreamt of it, let alone his master's Mistress. An Igbo proverb said that nobody in his right mind puts a goat in his barn to guard over his yams. Certainly, the Teacher had unwittingly kept goats to guard over his yam.

The boys went to the lady in turns on the master's bed. When it was Ekigwe's turn, the last guy, he refused to go. The other two boys threatened Ekigwe with fire and brimstone unless he went to the lady. They feared Ekigwe could report to the master unless he participated. So Ekigwe out of fear reluctantly entered the master's bedroom and stood there. The lady told Ekigwe to lie on the bed. Ekigwe obeyed, simply lying on his side. Surprised, the lady teased Ekigwe.

"Is this how you usually did it?"

"With your clothes on?" continued the lady.

Ekigwe timidly nodded, "Yes," to the lady's great amusement.

Then the lady went ahead, undressed Ekigwe and guided him through the process. Fulfilled and happy, the lady bade the boys farewell and left. As she went, the lady was so overwhelmed by lying with three boys that she didn't know when she exclaimed to herself the Igbo proverb, "Hmmmm, obu otua ka ife nlacha n'esi ami." It is equivalent to saying, "When it rains, it pours!" in reference to the number of young boys she laid with and implying that it was after all not such a disappointment that she missed the Teacher, her regular customer. Then, not long after, the lady left, "Chei," came a scream by the second big boy from the Teacher's room.

"What is the matter?" queried the biggest boy fearfully.

"Please come and see oo!" he replied.

The boys discovered that the lady had spotted blood on the master's immaculate white bed sheet. The two big boys became frantic and were running helter-skelter looking for bleach. In the frenzy, one of the boys found a bottle of bleach, grabbed it and effectively spilled it on the bedsheet even beyond the stain. It now turned into an ugly mess. All efforts to remove it proved abortive and even made it look worse. The two older boys were seized with fear of their master who brooked no nonsense. Therefore they conspired to tell the master that Ekigwe wounded himself and in the process of applying the iodine located in the Teacher's bedroom, he stained the master's white bed sheet.

"No wonder," exclaimed the second big boy.

"No wonder what?" asked the biggest boy.

"Have you forgotten the visit of that wicked owl early in the morning?" he reminded the biggest boy.

"Cheiiiii that is very true ooo!" acknowledged the biggest boy.

"I knew that the evil bird was up to something and now we know the clandestine reason for its visit," he concluded.

When the Teacher came back, the two big boys rushed to him to make the report. Ekigwe tried to defend himself, but the Teacher was so furious that he didn't wait to hear from Ekigwe. He brutally whipped Ekigwe inflicting several injuries upon an already weakened boy.

Ekigwe was emotionally devastated. He felt that everything in the world was against him. His father was against him. His town, Akpu was against him. His mother and his sisters were nowhere within reach, and now even the Church represented by his master was also against him. Of what use was his life, he reasoned. It was better for him that he was dead, he concluded.

CHAPTER TWELVE

Next Saturday morning, the Teacher was out and Ekigwe's two big colleagues were playing the draft game and making noise as usual. Ekigwe wrote two suicide notes, one for his mates and one for his Teacher. He dropped the suicide note for his mates on the bed in their room and dropped his Teacher's note also on the Teacher's bed. He then took his Teacher's rope and sneaked out headed for the Evil Forest in Achara town. He wrote in the suicide notes that he had gone to the Evil Forest to hang himself. He narrated how his mates starved him in the Teacher's house as well as how they used him as a beast of burden to do the work meant for the three of them while they ate up all the food and then played games. He also narrated the story of the Teacher's Mistress and how he was raped and the soiled bedsheet. He wrote how the Teacher after being deceived by his two colleagues whipped him mercilessly, refusing to hear his side of the story.

By the time Ekigwe's mates saw their own note after their noisy draft session they considered it too late to look for Ekigwe and prevent his suicide. They considered

Ekigwe already dead. Besides, who dared go near the Evil Forest anyway let alone at night. Ekigwe's mates did not know that he left a separate note for their master.

A cold sweat descended on both boys immediately and they became very frantic. They nervously planned what they would tell the Teacher in order to exonerate themselves from blame. They planned to tell the Teacher that Ekigwe was homesick and had complained he was exiled from his family. But if they told the Teacher this, how did they know that he went to commit suicide except they showed the Teacher the suicide note? This would make them liars because he clearly stated his reason for suicide. Therefore the boys resolved to tell the Teacher they were suspecting suicide because he had repeatedly talked about it.

As they were still nervously deliberating about it, the bicycle bell rang, and rang again and again causing more panic as they thought the Teacher rang the bell repeatedly because he already had wind of the story.

The Teacher saw only the two big boys and instinctively asked, "Where is Ekigwe?"

"Ohhh this is a confirmation he has heard about the suicide," concluded the biggest boy.

"It's true. We're finished!" agreed the other boy.

"What are the two of you murmuring there? I said, where is Ekigwe?" repeated the Teacher angrily.

They were now fully convinced that the Teacher knew about the Ekigwe suicide development.

The two boys were so paralyzed with fear that they became incoherent and began to stammer. The younger of the two boys said that Ekigwe went to fetch firewood. On hearing his mate, the older boy was weakened and knew the game was up. He didn't answer the Teacher's question but simply stared in terror into the darkening night. The Teacher immediately smelled a rat and, raising his voice asked, "Is that why you're so frightened? Where is Ekigwe, you good for nothing morons?" As they stared at the Teacher in obvious fear and terror, the Teacher knew that something sinister had happened.

The Teacher stormed into his bedroom in a rage to fetch his whips. As he entered the bedroom, his copy of the suicide note was on the bed staring him in the face. Startled that a note was on his bed, he picked it up. Behold, it was a suicide note from Ekigwe. His jaw dropped and his hands were shaking as he read the suicide note. Unfortunately for the boys, Ekigwe wrote "Teacher's copy" on the note, meaning that there was another copy.

"Who has the other copy," the Teacher wondered. "The police, the school, or the boys? But the boys were with Ekigwe so he could have told them verbally unless the two boys went out." These thoughts ran wild in his mind. The Teacher couldn't even think of whipping the boys again because the note made his hands limp. Many other thoughts ran through the Teacher's mind. What would the church do concerning him, now that the boy entrusted in his hands was dead? Not only dead but dead by suicide, an abomination in the land?

"Where are the other copies? With the school? With the police? With who? Ohhh with who?" continued the Teacher to talk to himself as if he were going mental. The Teacher could not reason well any longer. If he could, he would have realized that Ekigwe didn't know anything about the police station. He would report to the police but then what about the embarrassing mention of his mistress in the note? It was already late at night and everything had to wait until the next morning. How could he sleep with the fate of the boy put in his care unknown? The Teacher wished all of it was simply a bad dream and somebody would soon wake him up. Nobody dared go to the Evil Forest in the day, much less at night. And there was no transportation anywhere at night to the police post very far away at the provincial headquarters. Even the frightful ride of the bicycle would take all night and day to get to the provincial headquarters.

The Teacher could not sleep that night and each time he dozed off, he saw terrible scenes. The night was worse than a nightmare. He hoped Ekigwe changed his mind and would soon return that morning. By midday, Ekigwe was nowhere to be found. The Teacher locked the boys in their room and traveled to the police post to report Ekigwe's disappearance.

After the long ride in an overloaded lorry, he got to the police station weak and devastated. Since the news about Ekigwe, he had no appetite so he had not eaten. Yet from where the lorry dropped the Teacher, he had to trek two miles to the police station. He got to the police station, looking ruffled, dusty and exhausted.

"Good afternoon sir," the Teacher greeted the mean-looking Police Constable seated behind a wooden counter.

"Yes, what can I do for you?"

"I....I...I.I," stammered the Teacher nervously.

"I...I what?" charged the Constable angrily.

At the raised voice of the Constable, the Station Sergeant walked out of his office.

"Sergeant, sir," yelled out the Constable, saluting.

The Sergeant received the salute.

"What's this man doing here?" queried the Sergeant.

"Sir, he came here to say, 'I..I..I.'"

"Constable John."

"Sir."

"Allow him to say what he did," ordered the Sergeant.

"Yes, sir," saluted the Constable.

The Teacher told them his houseboy left the house and hadn't returned for two days, and his mates said he went to the Evil Forest to commit suicide.

"So you murdered your boy and used him for ritual and you came here to tell us 'I...I...I, he committed suicide'?" thundered the Constable.

"I can see that you are tired of being a miserable teacher right? You now want to be a millionaire, so you used your boy for a ritual?" The Teacher wanted to talk but the officer handed him a dirty slap.

"You'll take us to that Evil Forest and show us where his body is dangling," declared the Sergeant.

"Constable," shouted the Sergeant, "Lock this man in the guardroom until he is ready to sing."

"Yes, sir," replied the Constable.

The Constable marched the Teacher along a dark hallway, pushing him sometimes. They got to a brown metal door and stopped. The Teacher was now shivering with fear, not knowing what to expect. The Constable selected a long and worn-out metal key from his bunch, put it in the brown metal door keyhole and opened a rough chapter to the Teacher. The Constable pushed the Teacher into the room and slammed the rusty metal door behind the Teacher, leaving him at the mercy of some hardened inmates. It was a narrow smelly cell filled with other criminals, some shirtless.

Immediately, the Teacher saw what seemed like a million eyes staring menacingly at him. Within seconds, one of the inmates who appeared to be the chief spokesman of the cell introduced the Teacher to the boss of the cell, a sturdy, dark-skinned, short man. He had his head shaved to the skin showing the rough contour of his skull full of scars. He was heavily bearded and a frown was better than his sinister smile. The boss gave him the rules of the cell, first of which was to hand over any valuables, including his watch and shirt to the boss. The inmates called the boss "Snake." The Teacher trembled when one of the inmates called the boss "Snake."

"If a snake does not swallow its neighbor, how does it grow fat?" came the boss's acknowledgment with a sinister grin.

The Teacher turned this statement over in his mind several times in fear.

"Who will he swallow?"

"Does this mean they'll kill me this night?" reasoned the Teacher, paralyzed with horrible expectation.

He was allowed to have on only his underpants and singlet. Later the police brought some food to the Teacher that night, but another inmate snatched the food from the Teacher.

"Are you mad?" queried the inmate.

"The boss never belle full and you want to chop?" he continued. The inmate was saying in the local English dialect that the Teacher was crazy to presume he would eat before the Boss filled his belly with food.

"Sorry sir," answered the Teacher, trembling.

That night was another nightmare, a compounding

nightmare. The Teacher did not sleep throughout the night for fear of what could happen to him at night. In the morning, there was a crackling sound in the keyhole. The door swung open. The Teacher thought they were bringing in another criminal into the overcrowded room, but the Constable ordered him to follow him. It was a great relief for the Teacher when the police came to take him in the morning. The "snake" did not swallow him after all. He only swallowed his food.

While the Teacher's boys were locked up in their room, they traded the blame over their treatment of Ekigwe. Besides, the older boy chided the younger one concerning his sloppy answer to the Teacher that Ekigwe went to fetch firewood.

"Your answer betrayed us," complained the big boy.

"But we already messed up by treating Ekigwe like a slave because you knew he was like an orphan. My slip of tongue did nothing to change the teacher's mind because he already knew that Ekigwe committed suicide. Didn't you see the note from Ekigwe that he was reading? So why are you blaming me? Are you not the oldest amongst us? Instead of you admitting your failure to provide leadership, you are here accusing me. I only obeyed you to starve Ekigwe so that you have enough food to satisfy your greed. And are you not the one who arranged for us to sleep with Oga's Mistress? And you even forced Ekigwe into it?" This speech shot the older boy like a poisoned arrow in the heart. But the older boy wasn't the talking type. He simply asked his younger colleague, "Have you finished rambling?" And immediately followed it with a dirty slap and another slap. The younger boy did not fight back because he knew that only two of them were in that room as well as in the house, and the guy could even kill him. There was no escape route from the room and the small wooden window had two iron bars across so that nobody could pass through it.

Fearful thoughts ran through the younger boy's mind as he bore the pain from the slaps, "I think I should just pipe low in order to stay alive while I am trapped with this wicked boy. Since there is no means of escape from this room, the only way to stop a fight is that one person died and he is stronger than me, and more wicked," he reasoned. He tried to assuage his fears by reasoning, "Well he won't kill me because if he does, he can't escape and it will be obvious that he killed me."

"I hope he understands that. But he is so wicked, he may not think about that until he has killed me," came another thought.

"Oh, God! The Teacher is wasting so much time to come back," he continued to lament in his mind.

They went without food that night and every little noise they heard alerted them because they thought the teacher was back and about to release them from the house arrest. At past midnight, the bigger boy screamed, and the other boy leaped up in terror and, panting, asked what the matter was. The big boy had a nightmare. In his dream, a man was pursuing him with a machete to kill him. After he told his colleague his nightmare, his answer was, "It was the spirit of dead Ekigwe after you. He will continue to come after you till he is pacified."

"It was not Ekigwe but an older man," corrected the big boy.

"Of course, he would come with a different face and body so that you won't know it's him."

"Oh we are finished," declared the big boy.

"I'm not among, I slept peacefully." corrected the younger boy.

"Why is he after only me? Was it not both of us that mistreated him?" insisted the big boy.

"Ekigwe knows his enemies," remarked the younger boy and continued, "Well, you know you are the leader. And he's no more the Ekigwe that you knew. He is now a ghost and he knows who did what. Maybe after he kills you, he'll come after me. But for now, he's after the leader."

Now panicking greatly, the big boy asked him, "What are we going to do to stop Ekigwe from killing somebody?"

The younger boy thought in his heart, "Big for nothing wicked boy." But he dared not say it out loud. The big boy would kill him, as there was no escape route out of that room.

"When we are released from this room, you should tell the teacher to allow you to visit the witch doctor. He should have a solution," suggested the younger boy.

"You think so?"

"Yes. The witch doctor talks with ghosts and he's probably already talking to Ekigwe's ghost."

"So Ekigwe is now a ghost and stronger than us?" the older boy remarked to himself apprehensively as if it were just dawning on him.

"Sadly yes. But the witch doctor will help us find out what Ekigwe's ghost wants as appeasement. The only problem is he may want a human head."

"Whose head?" shouted the older boy.

"How can I know?" answered the younger boy very fearfully.

"But I heard you can pay the witch doctor to get the

head by himself."

The big boy was indeed already thinking about his mate's head, and the younger boy noticed a vicious glance from him. This sent shivers down his spine that he started to wonder if he should have held his tongue. The big boy was a bit comforted by the idea that the witch doctor could find a head by himself and added to the relief of the younger boy, "What the witch doctor will need from us is money, and the teacher will help us pay him."

"I think so," answered the younger boy happily.

As he mused over his chances of survival with the wicked older colleague, there was a crackling sound like that of a key at the door. The door opened, letting in the Teacher in handcuffs. Two policemen also entered the room. The boys were happy to be released but horrified to see their Teacher in handcuffs, certainly a bad omen. The boys didn't know that they simply exchanged their small prison for another, albeit bigger, prison.

CHAPTER THIRTEEN

Meanwhile, Ekigwe arrived at the Evil Forest. Ekigwe was not frightened by the Evil Forest. He did not care that whoever entered the Evil Forest died after one market week. After all, he came there to die. He would long be dead before one market week. But a few yards into the Evil Forest Ekigwe was startled by something he sighted. He moved nearer and to his shock, it was a man with a swollen stomach. The man was abandoned in the Evil Forest by his family because he had a swollen stomach. It was considered a taboo in Achara town. In Achara town, any man with a swollen stomach was considered an evil man who developed a swollen stomach due to his evil deeds, and like twins, he was only good for the Evil Forest and should not dwell among normal beings. Ekigwe saw the plate of food and the water left at the man's side, a sort of last supper. The man pleaded with Ekigwe to help him and not let him die. Ekigwe was filled with compassion for the man and momentarily forgot his own ordeal and mission.

Then Ekigwe thought, "How can a dying man help another dying man?"

Ekigwe thought it strange and odd that an elderly man who had lived most of his life and being in that miserable condition still wanted to live.

"Is life this desirable?" Ekigwe thought almost audibly.

"What is it that makes this old man still want to live?" Ekigwe wondered.

Ekigwe briefly went into a meditation.

"Here I am with a rope because my father, my village, the Teacher and the Church abandoned me. This man's whole family, including his children, and even his village abandoned him in this hopeless forest. He's very sick and miserable. Yet he's still yearning to live! But I am young, healthy and strong, but with a rope to end my life." Ekigwe came to himself as if an evil cloud was lifted up from him. He suddenly saw the many ugly happenings around him and realized that he was indeed in the dreaded Evil Forest.

Ekigwe, filled with shame and fear, immediately threw away his rope and took to his heels, running like one possessed. He occasionally looked back as he ran out of the Evil Forest, filled with all sorts of abominable sights to see if anyone was pursuing him. But Ekigwe didn't know where to go because he didn't want to go back to those other two bullies.

"If I don't end it now, where will I go from here?" he wondered.

Then Ekigwe remembered his friend at school, Udeh. He used to visit Udeh's house with him during breaks and eat with Udeh the lunch his mother prepared for him. Udeh's father, Nwankwo knew Ekigwe as his son's friend and encouraged their friendship because of Ekigwe's good conduct. He also heard of Ekigwe's excellent academic performance. Nwankwo often wished Udeh would excel in school like Ekigwe. Nwankwo once reasoned aloud almost in lamentation, "Those who are pampered are often less successful in life than those who suffer. Just look at Ekigwe whose family is nowhere to be found. Yet he's the best in his class. The ironies of life."

"Ukwa na amilu ndi na enweghi eze," he concluded. He said an Igbo proverb, that "the breadfruit yielded fruit in abundance for those who had no teeth."

Ekigwe was caught between the devilish Evil Forest and the deadly Teacher's house. Thoughts ran wild in Ekigwe's mind.

"I was with Udeh on Friday. I said nothing about this to him. I didn't even go to him in the morning or afternoon. And now at night I go and tell him what emergency?" Ekigwe continued, "I will give it a try. I will lose nothing. If I am refused, at worst I will climb a very tall tree and fall from it."

So, left with no option, Ekigwe reluctantly went to his friend that night. His hand felt limp as he went to knock on Udeh's wooden gate. Nevertheless, he picked up a stone and hit the gate repeatedly. He felt that they might have slept and he was simply disturbing the people's peace late in the night.

"What a nuisance I have become to humanity and to myself," lamented Ekigwe.

Then he walked away in anguish to go and do the unthinkable. As he staggered along away from Udeh's compound, he heard a sound from the direction of Udeh's house. He stopped to listen, and to his surprise, it was Udeh's father, "Who is it?" shouted Udeh's father.

"Father, it is Ekigwe, Udeh's friend."

"Did you say Ekigwe?" asked Udeh's father.

"Yes sir, Ekigwe. Is Udeh at home?" As he spoke, Udeh came out from the house and joined his father at the gate.

Udeh was very surprised to see Ekigwe, who rarely visited in daytime, much less at night.

"Is that you Ekigwe?" probed a surprised Udeh as he peered through the yellowish glow of the palm oil candlelight.

"Yes it is me, Ekigwe," he answered.

"What brought you here this night? Is everything okay with you?" Udeh continued to peer into Ekigwe's face with the dim, yellowish light of the palm oil lantern. The lantern was being seriously threatened by a light breeze.

"Not so much," replied Ekigwe wearily.

"Let's go into the house first, please," offered Udeh.

Ekigwe felt a sudden surge of vitality and life inside him as they walked into Udeh's house. He could even then feel the breeze caressing his face and neck instead of the frigid and still air just a few minutes ago. Inside the house, Udeh gestured at a seat for Ekigwe to seat down.

Now seated in the house, Ekigwe narrated his predicament to his friend. Udeh's shock was beyond words.

"I am amazed and disappointed that you never mentioned this problem to me. What is then the use of our friendship?" queried Udeh.

"Even if I can't help, at least it is said that two heads are better than one," continued a worried and sad Udeh.

"Then we put heads together like we're trying to do right now and find a solution. You did not need to go through all you've gone through so far."

"You are very correct about all you have said. You know that when you are facing the kind of troubles I was facing, you may not think right," answered Ekigwe.

"The truth is that I had lost hope in human beings," continued Ekigwe.

"And I said to myself that the scarcest thing in this world is human compassion," Ekigwe continued to explain.

"I am very sorry that I didn't think about telling you. At some point, I thought that I was alone in the world and nobody cared about what I was going through. But now I know that I am wrong."

Udeh was sad that his friend had to go through all that. Udeh in turn narrated the story to his father. Udeh's father noticed that Ekigwe was weak and hungry and called out to his wife, waking her from sleep, "Mgbeke."

"Nna anyi," answered Ude's mother from mkpuke.

"Odikwa nma," inquired Ude's mother.

"Ekigwe is in our house. Please get him some roasted yam and palm oil first. Then please prepare dinner for him," directed Udeh's father. After Ekigwe ate and rested, Nwankwo sent for him and asked Ekigwe.

"My son, why did you leave your teacher's house to come here this late?"

Ekigwe narrated his life story to his friend's father and pleaded that they don't take him back to the Teacher. He pleaded with them to trace his village and send him back to his mother. This was a very difficult task for Nwankwo. Nwankwo had never been to Akpu village. But Nwankwo had an idea. A teacher in a town neighboring Achara had once requested that Nwankwo give him Udeh to train. That meant that Udeh would be his house boy while going to school. Nwankwo refused to release Udeh because Udeh ran a lot of errands for his father and helped him on the farm, and Nwankwo had nobody else to do those errands for him. Nwankwo asked Ekigwe if he could live with a very good teacher in the town next to Achara. He told Ekigwe that he could always visit them in Achara when he needed to and that they also would visit him occasionally.

As far as Ekigwe was concerned, he needed no convincing. Anywhere but his former teacher and the two bullies was okay. So Ekigwe accepted and was very happy and relieved. For Ekigwe, it became like an Igbo proverb that said, "When the enemy keeps pursuing somebody, he will chase him into a good place." Two days later, Nwankwo, accompanied by Udeh took Ekigwe to another teacher in Ogwu village, next to Achara town.

The policemen had escorted Ekigwe's former teacher back to Achara town. The police and the Teacher went to the Teacher's house. The boys were unlocked but were handcuffed. Both the Teacher and the policemen were afraid to go to the dreaded Evil Forest to look for Ekigwe. They knew that no sane man entered the Evil Forest. Only the witch doctors and those who have collected the witch doctor's charms dared. Therefore they went to find a witch doctor in Achara town. They finally arrived at a popular witch doctor's shrine in Achara. After they told the witch doctor their mission, he shook his body, rattling the many strange things attached to his apparel.

"Have you decided to return to your Maker?" came the surprise question from the witch doctor.

"Or you have never known that the Evil Forest was a forbidden place for anyone to enter except when certain 'things' are done?"

Then the police pleaded with the witch doctor, "Please tell us these 'things' we are required to do first, Wise One.

We'll do them urgently."

The witch doctor listed the requirements they would provide so he could clear the way for them to enter and search the Evil Forest. He reminded them that if they didn't provide those items, they could still enter the Evil Forest at their own detriment.

"It was not called the Evil Forest in vain. That's the abode of evil spirits like the spirits of twins, lepers, people with swollen stomachs and the like," the witch doctor reminded them.

He told them to listen carefully so they wouldn't forget anything as he listed the following items which included: the skull of a vulture, two eggs of a python snake, a bald monkey, a bush rat and a white chicken. He told them to bring some amount of money also. The police excused themselves from the witch doctor and the teacher. Outside, the policemen wondered where they could get a vulture, let alone its skull. Even the python is dreaded, and if they knew where to find a python, who would dare touch its egg? The leader of the policemen, Sergeant Thomas, called out the Private, "Private Agu."

"Yes sir."

"You have three days to go to your village and provide these items," commanded the Sergeant.

"Sergeant sir, I would rather resign than go near a python's egg," replied Agu.

"Shut up!" thundered the Sergeant.

"Yes sir. But can I suggest something sir?" requested Agu.

"Suggest what?"

"Oga, that money which the witch doctor demanded, I will tell the teacher that the witch doctor demanded double. We will give half of it to the witch doctor and you will keep the other half for the funeral in case the python swallows any one of us," suggested Agu to please the Sergeant, who understood him very well.

"You are a very wise Constable. Request granted!" responded the Sergeant.

"Sir, my second suggestion is that we should tell the Teacher to suggest to the witch doctor that we pay him money to buy the items himself because the police are not allowed to touch certain things."

"Rojas!" the Sergeant consented.

So the Teacher proceeded to ask the witch doctor to accept money in lieu of those bizarre items. The police knew a lot about corruption and knew that the witch doctor simply padded the list with items the gods didn't demand. Of course, the witch doctor readily accepted their offer of money in place of monkey and the like. The police ordered the Teacher to provide the money to the witch doctor. The witch doctor told them to come back in a market week, the following four days.

On the appointed day, they now proceeded to the Evil Forest with the witch doctor in the lead. When they got to the Evil Forest, they found the man with the swollen stomach. The man was Ibe, the village wino. Ibe begged them to help him just as he had begged Ekigwe. He told them that he saw a boy pass by with a rope. Ibe was too sick and too weak to crack his jokes. It was obvious that he didn't have many more days to live.

Ibe, the village loafer and wino, was well known in Achara town as a drunk. He was seen anywhere there was a ceremony or merriment especially funeral ceremonies. He would eat anything that was served and drink palm wine until he was too tipsy to recognize the difference between palm wine and water. He would crack jokes and make people laugh uncontrollably. He never lacked funny things to say. Once at a child naming ceremony, an age-grade mate asked Ibe, "Ibe, so you are also here?"

"Why not?" replied Ibe, surprised at what he considered a foolish question pregnant with mischief.

"How could I leave an Ozo title ceremony and attend a witch doctor's ritual and incantations? Is that your mischievous prayer for me?"

Ibe's age-grade mates at the ceremony and other people cracked up.

Sometimes they called Ibe, "Kama nri gado n'ite....." Ibe would usually complete the statement for them thus, "Ka o dolu n'afo." They were literally saying, "instead of the food to be stored in the pot, let it be stored in the stomach." That was what they considered Ibe's philosophy.

Once Ibe had an encounter with Government Tax agents looking for tax evaders. Tax collectors visited Achara town to arrest able-bodied men who had not paid their taxes. This was a bi-annual ritual in the local government or anytime the local government needed money. And during this exercise, most able-bodied men in Achara went into hiding. No matter how drunk, Ibe also used to go into hiding each time he heard that local government tax collectors were in town.

But this time, Ibe didn't mind "leaving an Ozo title ceremony to go to the ceremony of witch doctors casting out melancholy spirits."

Ibe came out boldly hovering around while other men ran helter-skelter to avoid the local government tax agent's arrest. The tax collector's truck was parked by the roadside, with some arrested men already inside the truck. A surprised elderly man asked Ibe what he was still doing in the vicinity, or was he too drunk to notice the tax agents? Ibe smiled and replied, "There is no relationship between a vulture and a barber," to the man's amusement. A vulture didn't need a barber because it already had a bald head. Very soon, Ibe was to realize that he was the vulture and the tax agents the barbers. But the man concluded concerning Ibe's stubbornness, "The cricket killed by the bird called Okpoko was indeed killed by its ear." Okpoko was a very noisy bird.

However, the man still wondered what in the world gave Ibe this uncharacteristic boldness.

"Well, who knows. A monkey dancing in the bush must have somebody playing the music for him," concluded the man.

The tax agents ignored Ibe to his utter disgust and frustration. After hanging around for a while, Ibe asked the agents, "Do you all not have eyes to see me or you just don't know your job? Why have you not asked me for my tax receipt? In case you want to know, I have not paid my tax this year or even last year." A tax agent replied to Ibe, "Hey Mister, we are not looking for your type." Ibe felt both disappointed and insulted.

"What type are you looking for? You morons." The men ignored Ibe's question and insults. They knew that even if they offered Ibe for sale, nobody would buy.

"So even to go to prison is not an easy task," Ibe thought.

"Life is wicked," Ibe concluded and went home dejected. Ibe later became sick and developed a swollen stomach which was an abomination in Achara. Any man with a swollen stomach was taken to the Evil Forest to die just like twins. Lepers and sufferers of smallpox were taken to an outpost in the wilderness until they either recover or die. During this period, people avoided plucking leaves along the village pathway. Any busy fingers risked leprosy or smallpox.

CHAPTER FOURTEEN

Meanwhile, Ekigwe was adapting to his new life at the Ogwu Town Primary School.

Ekigwe had just one year to spend in this primary school before graduating. Ekigwe was very happy in Ogwu. For the first time in his life, Ekigwe was truly happy. His master treated him very well, and he was well received in the school among other pupils. What gave Ekigwe much joy was the promise of his friend's father, Nwankwo, to help him through the secondary school. To complete his joy, Ekigwe received a scholarship award from the state toward his secondary school due to his excellent performance.

The only dent in Ekigwe's joy was an occasional remembrance of his mother and his sister Adaobi. Ekigwe hoped to someday go in search of his town and family in Akpu Town.

Little did he know that his family no longer existed in Akpu Town, not long after his escape.

In no distant time, Ekigwe completed his primary school and enrolled in the State Government Secondary School on scholarship. During every break, Ekigwe travelled to his friend Udeh's house in Achara town. Udeh's father, Nwankwo was very proud of Ekigwe for his excellent school performance and his good behavior. Nwankwo took Ekigwe as his son.

Nwankwo knew that Ekigwe had a great future and was happy to be a part of it.

Nwankwo and Udeh proudly accompanied Ekigwe to the Government Secondary School at Ndiagu, to start a new stage of his life. Throughout his stay in secondary school, Ekigwe nursed the hope that one day he would unite with his family. He vowed to go in search of them as soon as he became a man and got a job.

Ekigwe justified his scholarship and after completing his secondary school education emerged with distinction in the Cambridge Examination.

Udeh visited home and his father had hardly welcomed him when he excitedly reported, "Nna, ima na Ekigwe a passiala cantab (Father, do you know that Ekigwe has passed Cantab)?" The Cambridge Examination was often called Cantab.

"Nwam, o gini bu Cantab (My child, what is Cantab)?" asked Nwankwo.

"Eh! You don't know Cantab?" queried Udeh in surprise.

"If I knew, my son would I ask?"

"Our people say that one who asks questions does not miss his way," remarked Nwankwo.

"Cantab is Cambridge, Papa."

"Oh, my son."

"You said Ekigwe has passed Cambridge?"

"Yes, Papa. With grade 1!"

"Hey! You mean it?" asked Nwankwo excitedly.

"I am not surprised at all. We have not heard the last about that boy," continued Nwankwo.

"So when is he coming back from school finally?"

"Definitely he will be back for Christmas."

"I thank the gods of our fathers," declared Nwankwo.

"I wish his parents were around to hear the great news."

"I'm sure one day they'll hear," assured Udeh.

"He plans to look for them as soon as he starts work and gets his first salary," Udeh told his father.

"Every man will want to have that boy as a son," said Nwankwo about Ekigwe.

Udeh stopped the conversation here before his father started wishing Ekigwe rather than Udeh was his son.

Udeh thought that his people, the Igbo, were too competitive and sometimes even mischievous. He remembered when some of his friends asked him if he had "crossed the bridge."

"What bridge?" Udeh asked.

"Lekwa nwantakili a amaghi ihe bu bridge." They laughed at Udeh, implying that this little boy didn't know what was the bridge.

"Have you passed Cambridge?" they now asked Udeh in plain language, laughing at Udeh more loudly as Udeh realized the meaning of "crossed the bridge," with an expression of surprise on his face.

"Some people fall into the river and get drowned in the process of crossing 'the bridge.'" Udeh commented, concerning a boy who committed suicide because he took the Cambridge examination three times but failed each time.

Ekigwe later came home to Udeh's house to announce

186

that he had been offered a job in the city with the Electricity Corporation of Nigeria in Enugu (ECN).

"When are you starting your new job?" asked Udeh.

"In January, after the New Year."

"Wonderful," exclaimed Udeh

"So you'd be around for the exciting nmanwu festival?"

"Yes," replied Ekigwe wearily.

"You don't seem to be excited," commented Udeh

"Well, I'm okay, just thinking." With this response, Udeh didn't want to probe further because he remembered Ekigwe's checkered history of travails with masquerades and tradition.

Such celebrations brought sad memories to Ekigwe and always dampened Ekigwe's spirits as he thought about his family, whose fate he didn't know.

"A person whose father was killed by a buffalo does not drink with a buffalo's horn," Udeh thought.

CHAPTER FIFTEEN

It was January 15, and Ekigwe reported in his new office in Enugu. Ekigwe was among the few Nigerians who had the Cambridge Certificate. He was given the position of Executive Officer Grade 3. It took little time before Ekigwe left a good impression on the Colonial Officer, an English man who wore his glasses rested down his nose and looked over the glasses at you.

Ekigwe wondered why he wouldn't look through his glasses. It was surprising to the staff that he liked Ekigwe and got along with him because most staff feared the Englishman. So within a year Ekigwe was already promoted to Executive Officer Grade 2 which some staff hadn't achieved in five years.

A young lady who worked in this office had taken notice of Ekigwe and developed a liking for him. But Ekigwe was shy and naive and wouldn't usually take notice of that. One day during lunch break, a very talkative colleague of Ekigwe approached Ekigwe.

"Ekigwe."

"Yes?" answered Ekigwe.

"My name is Jimmy."

"How are you doing?" asked Ekigwe surprised at the bold and direct approach of his colleague. "But Jimmy sounds like the name of a dog," commented Ekigwe, displaying uncharacteristic boldness and wit. In those days, a lot of dog owners called their dogs 'Jimmy,' to the extent that in many villages, Jimmy has become synonymous with dog.

Jimmy, who was usually very comical, laughed loudly.

"How is your girlfriend?" asked Jimmy. "Which girlfriend?" Ekigwe asked surprised.

"Why are you pretending?" asked Jimmy.

"I don't know what you are talking about," continued Ekigwe.

"If you don't have anything important to say, better keep quiet please," remarked Ekigwe.

"Ok, you don't know Ebele?" Jimmy asked Ekigwe mischievously.

"Please if this is one of your usual sinister jokes, stop it. I'm not in the mood."

"But I always see how she stares at you in the canteen. I think she loves you," continued Jimmy.

"Well, I'm not aware of that," snapped Ekigwe, who was not used to this type of discussion.

"Ok, by the time her belly bulges, not only will you be aware of it but the whole office will," declared Jimmy feigning very vindictive.

"Now I can see your dirty imaginations are at work," replied Ekigwe getting frustrated.

"Dirty imaginations?" asked Jimmy chuckling.

"Oh yes. And when you tell a thief to help you catch your chicken, he will shrug and say, 'Oh no, please. It will bite me,'" joked Jimmy. "But if you dare blink your eye, the chicken will disappear!" continued Jimmy.

"I believe you are referring to yourself," Ekigwe replied, getting weary.

"Have you not tuned her yet?" continued Jimmy.

Ekigwe had always heard boys talking about tuning girls, but he always wondered how they accomplished that trick. As far as Ekigwe was concerned, he could only tune a radio. Ekigwe would of course like to know how to tune girls, but he was too shy and timid to venture into that. He only knew how to read books. His friends sometimes called him a "Bookworm" or "Booker T."

So one lunchtime, his talkative friend, not done with his jest about Ebele, told Ekigwe he could show him how to tune Ebele and even kiss her.

Ekigwe agreed to be tutored on tuning but certainly not kissing. Ekigwe thought kissing was both disgusting and dangerous.

"I don't want to commit suicide, please," retorted Ekigwe.

"What?" screamed Jimmy.

"You heard me, joker," replied Ekigwe looking very serious.

"What is the connection between kissing and suicide for God's sake? All I said was that you'll enjoy kissing Ebele. I didn't say you should commit suicide, please," pleaded an embarrassed and confused Jimmy. Ekigwe's reaction definitely took Jimmy unawares and obviously beyond his comic abilities.

"You don't know the connection between kissing and suicide?" retorted Ekigwe. "Please tell me cause I don't know," replied Jimmy, looking serious for once.

"Well, I guess you didn't study Health Science in

school. Do you realize how many millions of germs you release into the atmosphere when you sneeze or yawn? That is why people have handkerchiefs all the time, so they can sneeze or yawn into it," lectured Ekigwe. Jimmy was completely dumbfounded that somebody could reason that way and held his peace.

"How could somebody actually kiss another person?" Ekigwe wondered with alarm. The dread of what his Health Science Teacher once taught about germs hadn't left Ekigwe. The teacher told them that when someone sneezed, millions of germs were released. Since then, Ekigwe covered his face with a handkerchief whenever somebody sneezed or yawned near him. To worsen matters, Ekigwe's Health Science teacher had a long neck and a lean face and always leaned forward looking like somebody just recovering from some sickness. As he gesticulated with his hands and face about the germs, it made germs appear more real and frightening to Ekigwe.

"No girl, no matter how beautiful, is going to release millions of germs into my mouth in the name of kissing," Ekigwe assured himself.

"I am not tired of life yet," Ekigwe told Jimmy with regard to kissing. Jimmy had recovered from his shock and laughed uncontrollably. Then he told Ekigwe.

"One day, you'll come back to thank me with a bottle of Snapp when you see how sweet kissing could be, especially kissing Ebele."

"So you've been kissing girls for real?" Ekigwe asked Jimmy in amazement.

"Of course," replied Jimmy. Now Ekigwe was beginning to be confused.

"If kissing was so dangerous and the mouth contained

millions of germs, how come Jimmy, my kissing teacher, is still alive?" Ekigwe had started warming up to Jimmy, and Jimmy had become the first friend of Ekigwe in the office and indeed the city. Jimmy and Ekigwe always went to eat lunch together, and sometimes Jimmy brought Ebele along. However, Ekigwe had not been able to look Ebele in the eye, let alone chat her up. The few times a conversation developed between Jimmy, Ekigwe and Ebele during dining, Ekigwe would look down unless he was looking at Jimmy. Jimmy convinced Ekigwe that if kissing Ebele was his only problem, then he had no problem.

"You have to walk before running. Once you tune Ebele and capture her, kissing will come naturally. Don't worry at all. I will show you the basic rudiments of tuning. I will not rest until you capture Ebele," declared Jimmy with confidence. Ekigwe didn't show much enthusiasm, but curiosity and excitement about making Ebele his girlfriend got the better of him.

Jimmy and Ekigwe finally agreed to meet immediately after work the next day for the first practical test. They would wait for Ebele to walk out of the office.

So after work the next day, both men were at the gate of the office and Jimmy tutored Ekigwe on what to do.

"Just wait here with me."

"Soon you'll see Ebele walking home."

"Walk fast and meet up with her."

"So what do I do when I meet up with her?" asked Ekigwe, very nervous.

"Just say 'good evening' and see what will happen."

Ekigwe marveled within himself, "So it's after all so easy. Just 'good evening,' and Ebele is my girlfriend. This Jimmy must have a magic wand."

A few minutes later, Ebele was out of the office on her way home.

"Ngwa, move fast and follow her," charged Jimmy the teacher.

Ekigwe sheepishly stepped up, caught up with Ebele and said, "Good morning, sorry good evening." Ekigwe was sweating and terribly embarrassed for stuttering. Ebele smiled mischievously. Before Ebele finished responding, Ekigwe was yards ahead of her. Noticing his mistake and that no magic happened, Ekigwe was frustrated, went round in a loop, and came back to Jimmy cursing.

"See what you've done to me? You have badly embarrassed me," complained Ekigwe angrily.

"Did you not greet her?" queried Jimmy.

"Yes I greeted her but nothing happened."

"Did she not respond?"

"Yes, she did, and so what?" complained a frustrated Ekigwe.

"Wow, she did?" exclaimed Jimmy.

"You should have picked it up from there," Jimmy remarked.

"Picked what up? You are very wicked," complained frustrated Ekigwe.

"You just wanted to embarrass me before Ebele."

"Is that how to tune a girl? You are a wicked man," continued Ekigwe, very angry that he disgraced himself.

"Don't worry," Jimmy said, trying to pacify Ekigwe.

"You'll do it better next time. This is just the first step. You've not done badly at all for a first attempt. Your next try will certainly be much better."

Ekigwe had thought that something magical would

happen the moment he said "Good evening" to Ebele. But Ebele simply replied, "Good evening." Maybe Ebele would have said more, but Ekigwe didn't wait to receive the feedback before fleeing. Ebele was actually puzzled at the speed with which Ekigwe passed after saying "Good evening."

But Ekigwe later mastered the art of 'tuning' and became quite comfortable at talking to Ebele.

It was the second year that Ekigwe had been with the Electricity Company. Ekigwe received mail inviting him for an interview for entry into the Army Cadet Officer's Course in England. He had sat through an examination in the middle of his second year at ECN. Ekigwe was planning to go back to Akpu village in search of his family after more than ten years. Instead, he found himself preparing to travel to England for the military school lasting four years.

Ekigwe had to resign his post at the ECN. There was an emotional reception in Ekigwe's honor at ECN. Ekigwe had started enjoying his stay at ECN, especially since he had become more comfortable in his relationship with Ebele. And now he had to leave. He promised Ebele he would not forget her and would look for her upon his return from England. At that time, there was no telephone, and mail took months to go overseas and back. Jimmy had become friends with Ekigwe. He cautioned Ekigwe about applying the tricks he taught him in England.

"White people are great kissers. If you go about kissing over there, I bet you'll come back with an Oyibo wife," Jimmy cautioned jokingly. Ekigwe laughed a lot and told Jimmy it would be Jimmy's fault if he came back with an Oyibo wife.

"After all, you're my kissing and tuning coach," joked

Ekigwe.

Ekigwe thought he would miss Jimmy's jokes a lot. Ekigwe promised he wouldn't disappoint Ebele by coming back with an Oyibo lady. Jimmy jokingly told Ekigwe he had nothing to worry about concerning Ebele.

"I will watch over Ebele till you return. And nobody will dare come near her," assured Jimmy.

Ekigwe saw his opportunity to pay Jimmy back in his own coins.

"Am I so foolish to give my yams to a goat to watch over?" replied Ekigwe, feigning seriousness. Of course, everybody knew what goats do to yams. The reception erupted in laughter. Jimmy was not the type to be dampened by "njakili" (acidic jokes). But he was surprised that Ekigwe rose to the occasion. Ekigwe's joke caught Jimmy off guard.

Every solid Ibo man was able to withstand "njakili." Anyone not able would be miserable in Iboland.

Back in Udeh's house at Achara, it was a mixed feeling. Udeh and his father were very sad to see Ekigwe go, but they were happy that Ekigwe had such an opportunity to go to the white man's country. He was bound to return a great man in this country, Nwankwo declared.

"Every person that has traveled to the white man's land in search of the 'golden fleece' always came back a great man ruling over the natives," he continued.

"Look at Engineer Amobi, Doctor Oye and Barrister Agunwa who drives the longest car in this region, all went to Oyibo land. And the list goes on," declared Nwankwo.

Ekigwe promised never to forget them. He said that they took him in when he had nowhere to go.

"You are the father that I can see, and Udeh has

become my brother," Ekigwe tearfully told Nwankwo and his son.

Udeh escorted Ekigwe to Lagos for his trip. They went to the wharf where Ekigwe boarded a big ship. Udeh entered the ship with Ekigwe and both of them were speechless because they never imagined that an upstairs house could sail on the water. The ship had rooms and beds like a house.

"I wish I could have a house like this on the land," Udeh told Ekigwe playfully.

"With God all things are possible," replied Ekigwe.

"Just like I am now travelling to England, something unimaginable a few years ago," continued Ekigwe.

Due to Ekigwe's life experience, he was often spiritual and philosophical.

Even though it was mid-afternoon, the sun had disappeared into the gathering clouds. It was getting so dark that it appeared like late evening. There was a mild rumbling of thunder intermittently.

"This rain will be very heavy," commented Udeh.

"It is very uncharacteristic at this time of the year," replied Ekigwe, both Udeh and Ekigwe having a steady gaze at the ominous thickening dark clouds. Just then the rain started in drizzles.

Udeh and Ekigwe hurried to take shelter under an uncompleted building.

"Chaiiii! It is the day that I went hunting that deer learnt how to climb trees," lamented Udeh on behalf of his adopted brother Ekigwe. Deer did not have the ability to climb trees. If deer suddenly learnt to climb trees, hunters would usually look for them on the ground, whereas the deer hide in the trees like birds. Udeh was lamenting about the possible consequence of such a heavy rain on the ship which was to take Ekigwe to England. Ekigwe assured Ude that just as he didn't worry about his house when it rained, the ship was protected from the rain. A few hours later, the rain stopped and the sun reappeared. With a sigh of relief, Udeh hugged Ekigwe and bade an emotion-filled farewell to him.

When Udeh came back to Achara, he told the story of the ship for weeks to everybody's amazement. Udeh said that the ship was magnificent and had the aroma of aristocracy and success all around it. To this, a neighbor, Eloka, said that it was not a surprise because only successful people like Ekigwe entered the ship.

"What will a failure like our age-mate Nnaka be finding in a ship when he can't even fill half of his barn with yams?"

"You're mad," Nnaka fired back at the neighbor Eloka.

"Tell us your age-mate that has not married and you are here opening your mouth that stinks. Yes, I haven't filled my barn but I feed my wife and children. You would have married if you had enough money for the bride price. Nevertheless, when you see a lady willing to marry you, come and I'll lend you the bride price," Nnaka concluded.

At this point, Eloka was filled with shame as everybody laughed at him. Udeh's uncle blamed Eloka and reminded him that he started it all, "Mouth does not travel to the house of another mouth empty-handed." He was essentially telling him that those who live in glass houses don't throw stones!

CHAPTER SIXTEEN

Meanwhile, Akpu village Christians welcomed a new Parish Priest. His name was Reverend Father John Odera Nwankwo. There was so much pomp that it was difficult to imagine that Akpu Town was celebrating the arrival of a Priest once a forbidden thing. To crown it, the Priest in question was once an abomination abandoned in the Evil Forest to die. Akpu Parish was Odera's first posting upon his return to Nigeria from Rome. The women's dance group, the young girls' dance group and drama, as well as the famous Atilogwu young men's dance group, took turns to entertain during the warm reception given the new Parish Priest. The church in Akpu had grown over the years and had become the headquarters of a Parish.

Years ago when Nweke, Ekigwe's father threw away his twin babies into the Evil Forest, the Christians rescued one of them, the twin boy. The twin girl had died before help arrived. The rescued twin boy was recorded as belonging to Nweke's wife, Mgbogafor, and named John Odera (Once destined). The Church gave Odera to a Christian family Oko and Mgbeke to raise. But the Church bore the expenses. The Church did not tell the adoptive parents about Odera's roots. Neither Nweke nor Mgbogafor knew that their twin son survived.

After his secondary school, Odera enrolled in a seminary. Upon completion of the seminary school, he was ordained a Priest. Subsequently, Odera was sent to Rome by the Church. When he returned to Nigeria, the Church posted him to Akpu to help build the growing Parish.

But Odera did not know that he had any links with a different family in Akpu, neither did he know he was a twin. But his lack of resemblance to his foster parents had been a subject of gossip and had entered his heart.

Odera settled down in Akpu which had become more receptive to Christians as many natives of Akpu had been converted. The people of Akpu did not know that the new Parish Priest was not a biological son of Oko and Mgbeke of Akpu. Neither did Oko and Mgbeke know the biological parents of Odera.

One day, Odera was reviewing the parish records and activities over the years. Odera picked up a dusty old notebook. The title of this notebook—'Twins Rescued From Ajofia The Evil Forest'—was what attracted Odera's attention. As Odera turned the pages of this notebook, he stumbled on something that startled him. The record of one John Odera who was a twin and thrown into the Evil Forest but was rescued by the Christians in Akpu. Odera was struck by the strange coincidence with his names and even his age because Odera was twenty-eight years old and the record in the parish showed that the twin was rescued twenty-eight years ago. Odera thought that the similarity was too much to be ignored. What set Odera thinking was when he remembered the gossip about his lack of any resemblance to his parents. Could there be something about himself that he didn't know? Odera, therefore, resolved to dig deep into the whereabouts of this rescued twin boy. He decided to look closer and investigate it. Odera wanted to know what became of this rescued twin and who his family was that did that despicable act. The only record Odera found was that the twin belonged to one Nweke and Mgbogafor of Akpu village. Of course, Nweke and Mgbogafor had long been exiled to Offia village.

From that time on, the passion to find out any links between him and that Odera twin consumed the Priest. As for Nweke and his family, they were now forgotten in Akpu village. Only the elderly with sharp memory remembered Nweke and his family. Nweke and his family were now effectively natives of Offia village, Nweke's mother's town. Odera made some preliminary inquiries about Nweke but didn't make much progress. Dozens of families answered Nweke in Akpu.

Years seemed to have healed the wounds of Nweke. He had settled in well in Offia and was becoming again the great farmer that he used to be in Akpu. Most young people didn't even know that Nweke was not originally from Offia. His old friends from Akpu exchanged visits with Nweke once in a while. Every time Nweke's friends visited him from Akpu, his conversation would not be complete without a mention of his travails in Akpu and the loss of his wayward son, Ekigwe. Akilika was the most frequent visitor to Nweke. But even Akilika visited once in a blue moon, as both Nweke and Akilika were getting advanced in age.

Nweke's daughter, Adaobi, had never given up on her brother, Ekigwe, with whom she was very close. Adaobi always eavesdropped on her father's conversations with

Akpu visitors peradventure she may get wind of Ekigwe's state. At every opportunity, she would ask her father's friends from Akpu if they had any news of Ekigwe. But how could they when they were heathens and had no relationship with the Christians? Indeed had Akilika been a Christian, he would have known much about Ekigwe by frequenting the school or Church.

One day, Adaobi overheard from her father's discussions with his Akpu visitors that the Efulefus (Christians) had a new priest in Akpu. Adaobi knew that only the Christians had the key to locating her brother's whereabouts. After all, she was instrumental in his escape to seek refuge with the Christians of Akpu village. For this reason, Adaobi had a guilty feeling which partly explained her determination to locate Ekigwe's whereabouts.

"Maybe if I didn't help him escape, we wouldn't be looking for him today," she had thought many times. Adaobi continued to reason, "I will go to the Akpu Church and ask them, 'Where is the boy I deposited with you all some years ago?' And they will not dare give me a 'we don't know' answer."

Adaobi was determined to visit the Akpu Parish even though she was not a Christian. Adaobi vowed that if converting to a Christian would help her locate her brother Ekigwe, it was worth the risk. Adaobi was encouraged to take that risk because she knew that her father had softened his zeal for the village gods following his ordeal in his fatherland Akpu. His father's gods had disappointed him to the point of his attempt to smoke the life out of his personal god and even take a daring stand with his Dane gun against the spirits of his forefathers, the masquerades. Only the timely intervention of his mother's kinsmen saved what would have been bloodshed and calamity. Nweke now turned to Offia gods to see if they were more reliable. He thought that any gods should be more reliable than Akpu gods. But he had now also softened his hatred for the Christians.

One Sunday morning, Adaobi intimated to her mother and the most senior wife of her father, Mgbogafor, about her plan to visit Akpu Town Church Parish. Later that morning, Nweke came from his obi and asked for Adaobi.

"Adaobi has gone to iyi stream to wash ukwa (breadfruit)," replied her mother. They knew that Nweke loved to eat ukwa.

"Very good," replied Nweke happily.

In Akpu, it was not a man's concern to see washed ukwa or unwashed one for that matter. His only concern was to be served cooked ukwa. Nweke was sure to later ask where the ukwa Adaobi went to wash in the stream was. But as part of Adaobi's plan, she had bought washed ukwa at the previous day's market, ready for cooking.

CHAPTER SEVENTEEN

Adaobi's gloomy state since she came back from Akpu could not be hidden. Her mother probed her ceaselessly about her sad countenance since she visited Akpu village. It was obvious to her mother that something terrible had happened to put Adaobi in a state of perpetual mourning. One day as Adaobi was being questioned about what troubled her, she burst out weeping uncontrollably. It then became clear that she had been hiding something very serious. Her mother called Mgbogafor to witness her state. Then Adaobi let the cat out of the bag, "It is Ekigwe," she sobbed.

"Which Ekigwe?" screamed her mother, her voice breaking into a shrill.

"My brother," replied Adaobi sobbing louder. By this time other wives had come out of their huts and rushed to Uduaku's hut to know what the fuss was all about.

"Please tell us, did you find Ekigwe?" Mgbogafor asked in a chorus with two other wives.

"Tell us!"

"They said he committed suicide." The women went into a screaming commotion.

Nweke's compound burst into a crying uproar. Nweke came in from his obi perplexed. Soon he understood what caused the commotion.

Then Nweke let out a typical scream of lamentation, "Toaa, alu emee!"

"What is my sin before the gods?" he asked nobody in particular. The thought immediately came into Nweke that he could be paying for the sin of that night when he beheaded the Okwe man, Anayo. But he quickly shrugged it off.

By this time, his mother's people were rushing into Nweke's compound and the women were joining in the crying uproar whereas the men gave out the manly shout of "alu." Nweke went back to his obi and let out steam on his snuff joined by other men whereas the women moaned uncontrollably. Nweke was already used to calamities and misfortunes.

The rest of the day and night was weeping and mourning in Nweke's compound. By morning, Nweke's compound was full of people who came in to condole Nweke and his family.

After the traditional days of mourning were completed, Uduaku called her daughter Adaobi into the hut.

"My daughter, what about this Priest who told you that Ekigwe committed suicide?"

"Did he tell you where Ekigwe was buried?" Adaobi shook her head sadly and said, "No mother."

"You must go back and ask him where Ekigwe was buried so we can collect him and bury him here." Uduaku was only being sentimental because tradition does not allow natives to even bring down from the tree the corpse of a suicide victim, let alone bury him. Only strangers could touch the corpse of a suicide victim.

As for his father Nweke, he didn't ask any further questions concerning Ekigwe's place of suicide or his grave because he knew that suicide was an abomination. Moreover, Nweke was laboring under a heavy weight of guilt concerning Ekigwe. He felt that he contributed to Ekigwe's suicide, but he kept that to himself. Nweke often felt that abomination had become a recurring decimal in his life and family. To make matters worse, Nweke felt that he had a hand in this abomination cycle. He again remembered the man he beheaded in Okwe town and the twins he wasted at the Evil Forest. He remembered Ekigwe. He had a melancholy conclusion that his sins were visiting him.

With many unanswered questions hanging on Adaobi's neck, she decided to go back to the Akpu Parish Priest for answers. So Uduaku and Adaobi agreed that Adaobi would travel back to the Parish Priest. This was to be kept out of the ears of Nweke because it would mean trouble. It was even a foolish adventure because even if Ekigwe committed suicide in Nweke's compound, neither Nweke nor any other person was allowed to touch his corpse.

So the following morning, Adaobi set out to Akpu to meet the Parish Priest. When Adaobi arrived at the Parish, she was told the Parish Priest was in a meeting with some parishioners. Adaobi was given a seat and she patiently waited for the Priest.

The Parish Priest was happy to receive Adaobi. He had not finished his investigation about his links to Nweke and his family, and he badly wanted to meet Nweke and Mgbogafor personally.

"How is your father?" asked the Parish Priest.

"He is very well," replied Adaobi.

"So what brought you here today?" asked the Parish Priest.

Adaobi told him they wanted to know the details of Ekigwe's suicide.

"Where did Ekigwe commit the suicide?"

"Did he leave a suicide note?"

"Or did you find out why he committed suicide?"

"It was in a distant town called Achara," replied the Priest. "That was where the Akpu Parish then sent him to live with a teacher while attending primary school."

"Why did Ekigwe commit suicide?" repeated emotional Adaobi.

"That part was not very clear, but it was said that he was maltreated in the teacher's house by his fellow and bigger house boys," answered the Priest. This filled Adaobi with sorrow and she burst into tears again.

"My brother had nobody to protect him," she sobbed.

"If I didn't smuggle him out that night, maybe he would have suffered but still be alive and our family would have remained in our village Akpu," Adaobi who perpetually lived in guilt and wouldn't stop blaming herself lamented within herself.

The Parish Priest consoled Adaobi and promised to find out further details about Ekigwe's suicide. Adaobi pleaded with the Priest to help her locate Achara town and the primary school. The Priest promised to do his best but told Adaobi to give him some time. Both finally agreed on a date for Adaobi to return to the Priest for the trip to Achara.

CHAPTER EIGHTEEN

Meanwhile, the Priest embarked alone on a trip to Achara before the appointed date. He believed that any fruitful result from his search for Ekigwe's resting place would enhance his chances of fulfilling his own burning desire to unravel the connection if any with the rescued twin of Akpu Church records and also a possible link to Nweke and his family.

So Odera the Parish Priest prepared and set out to Achara town. The journey to Achara town was a rigorous half-day toil. Odera set out very early in the morning and rode his bicycle through the mostly bumpy dirt road. He set out by 6 am so that he would cover most of the distance before the scorching sun became too hot. Odera could have arrived at Achara by midday, but an unexpected obstacle awaited him midway to Achara. A very windy rain a few days earlier had felled a giant iroko tree across the narrow road, rendering it impassable. The detour passed through a deep and frightening stream. This stream had no bridge save for a tree felled across the stream, which allowed people to walk across, balancing themselves on the tree trunk, a make-believe bridge.

"Should I go back to Akpu or risk taking my bicycle across this risky tree trunk?" reasoned Odera, thoroughly frightened and frustrated. He had a long look at the uncertain water down below, wondering how deep it was. Odera remembered that he had never swum in his life, and if he slipped and the water was deep, he would be drowned. Odera was at the point of giving up and returning to Akpu when he sighted a farmer approaching with his hoe flung across his shoulder. Odera waited patiently for the farmer and rehearsed in his mind how he would ask him for help. Soon the man approached, and before Odera uttered a word, the man addressed him in Igbo.

"I greet you, Sir. I hope you are not contemplating suicide by crossing with your bicycle at this point?"

"Tufiakwa," responded Odera dissociating himself from the stranger's despicable suicide suggestion. The man continued, "A man got drowned yesterday as he attempted to cross this stream here. But I will take you to a shallow point where you can cross safely." Father Odera had mixed feelings.

"Is this man an angel sent by God to rescue me?" pondered Odera.

"Or is this a clandestine ploy to get me drowned so as to steal my bicycle?" Odera continued thinking.

Then Odera had a defiant feeling and decided to follow this man to a shallow point of the stream and cross.

The crossing was so easy and uneventful that Odera wondered why the community left people to suffer and even drown rather than clearly show the safe way to cross. Odera offered the stranger some money to show his gratitude but the man refused the money and told Odera that he expected that the day he may be stranded, he would expect someone to come to his rescue without waiting for money. Odera was amazed at the man's kindness. He thanked the man profusely and continued on his journey. To Odera, the rest of the journey was easy and uneventful, especially considering the traumatic experience he had in that place. He arrived at Achara in the late afternoon and asked his way to the Parish.

Odera stood at the gate of the Parish looking for somebody to direct him to the Priest's residence. He scouted the vicinity and the Church premises and noticed that it was bigger and more established than Akpu Parish. Soon he beckoned at a man in the Church compound who came and showed him the residence of the Parish Priest.

The Achara Parish Priest received Odera and was very happy to host another Parish Priest. It was very refreshing for Odera to finally arrive at a house where he could freshen up and relax.

"I am Reverend Father Odera," the Akpu Priest introduced himself.

"I oversee the Parish in Akpu Town to the glory of God," continued Father Odera.

"I am Jude. Please welcome to our Parish," replied Achara Parish Priest.

"You should have a bath and freshen up for dinner," continued Father Jude. Father Jude ordered his housekeeper to set up a bucket of water at the outside bathroom for the visiting priest. Soon Odera finished bathing and was in his pyjamas ready for dinner.

Odera and his host ate a dinner of pounded yam and bitter leaf soup prepared by one of the parishioners for the more senior Achara Parish Priest, Reverend Father Jude

Okafor.

"This is one of the best bitter leaf soups I have ever eaten," remarked Odera.

"Thank you for the compliment, but you know that when you are very hungry, every food you eat tastes good," remarked Father Jude jovially.

"True, but this soup is very good. Thank you for a great meal and the kind reception."

"My pleasure," said Pastor Jude, acknowledging Odera's gratitude.

"Tomorrow, my mother will be here to prepare a special delicacy for us," continued Father Jude.

"It's becoming like I came here for a feast," remarked overwhelmed Odera.

Odera was indeed excited about the promised special delicacy because his mind went straight to ukwa (breadfruit), which he loved to eat. Ukwa is a natural delicacy for most people in Achara even though it is a very long process to prepare. If you have done something great, people are likely to comment that you have done a job that deserves cooking ukwa for you. Ukwa always made Odera's mouth water.

The two Priests then retired to the parlor over tea.

"How receptive are Achara natives toward the Church?" asked Odera.

"The Church has indeed grown greatly in the five years since I arrived here. They are beginning to see that my inaugural message that we are partners in progress is indeed true," replied Father Jude.

"Besides, they used to be unperturbed when their sons whom they considered lazy and lackluster became converted. But over time they have discovered that the church usually transformed those children into responsible prosperous sons and daughters. So now they even want their supposed good children to be converted also," remarked Father Jude.

"When I first arrived here, there were frequent conflicts between the Church and Achara people, especially during their traditional feasts," continued Father Jude.

"Masquerades often chased our members into the Church compound, which shouldn't happen."

"When I discovered that certain fanatic traditionalists purposely used that to foment trouble between the Church and the community, I directed our members to ignore any such intrusions for peace to reign. And it worked out very well," Father Jude continued.

"I also have organized a monthly meeting between the Church and some Achara elders who are our point people. During these meetings, I inform the town through them that the mission of the Church is not to condemn their tradition but to compliment it. I have told them, with the permission of the Bishop, that we will no longer forbid Ozo titled men from coming to the Church. We have instituted "Ozo-Uka" which means the Church's brand of Ozo title." Odera listened with rapt attention.

"I can see that God has an extra purpose for my visit because I have learnt so much from you that I can use in Akpu Parish," remarked Odera.

Although Father Odera praised Father Jude for the strides he made in Achara for peace between the Church and the Achara heathen, he noted that the Ozo title contradicted Christian doctrine of the Church in that Ozo was a purely heathen title. He felt very uncomfortable with it, but he kept that thought to himself.

"I am flattered, but thank you. The bible says, 'Iron sharpeneth iron,'" replied Father Jude.

"Now my brother, let us hear the main purpose of your visit," requested Father Jude.

Odera then narrated the purpose of his visit to a surprised Father Jude.

"Holy Mary!" remarked Father Jude.

"God will help us solve this riddle," continued Father Jude.

"I don't know about Akpu tradition, but remember that in all Igboland, suicide is an abomination, and even if you locate his burial place, it is forbidden to touch the corpse," warned Father Jude. This made Father Odera very uncomfortable, and he began to wonder if there was any wisdom in embarking on this trip and in his attempt to find Ekigwe's burial place.

He was beginning to be ashamed that he left his work in the Parish for a purposeless adventure. But he consoled himself with the thought that he needed to keep close to Adaobi in order to eventually meet Nweke toward discovering his identity.

"However, tomorrow we will go to the Primary School to see the Headmaster," concluded Father Jude. The two Priests retired to bed. But in Odera's room, though he was tired, he was up most of the night as he kept pondering the outcome of his trip as well as the riddle of his own origin which had consumed him for a season. It was a very long night for Odera.

The following morning, at the breakfast table, "I hope you had a restful sleep?" Father Jude inquired.

"Oh yes, I did," lied Odera. "Thank you again for the

wonderful reception given me and the delicious bitter leaf soup," Odera continued.

"That's what I ought to do," remarked Father Jude.

"And don't forget that my mother has a special delicacy for us at dinner time," Father Jude continued.

"I have not forgotten, even though I was hoping we would finish on time for me to head back to Akpu today," assured Odera.

"You are so committed to your Parish, but one extra day away won't set them back please," remarked Father Jude, somewhat jovially.

"I'm looking forward to hosting you in Akpu in the near future," suggested Odera.

"Sounds like a great idea," agreed Father Jude. The two Parish Priests then proceeded to Achara Primary School to meet the Headmaster.

The Primary School was a short ten-minute walk from Father Jude's house which was part of the Roman Catholic compound in Achara. The Reverend Fathers knocked gently at the Headmaster's office door.

"Come in," responded the Headmaster.

"Wow! Good morning, Father" greeted a surprised Headmaster.

"Good morning," answered the two priests together.

"I hope all is well. It is not common to receive two august visitors like you at the same time in my office. But you are most welcome," remarked the Headmaster.

"There is no problem at all," replied Father Jude.

"Meet Father Odera, the Parish Priest of Akpu. Father, meet the Headmaster of Achara Primary School, Mr. Ngene."

"You are very welcome to our Parish, Father," the

Headmaster greeted Father Odera.

"Father Odera arrived our Parish yesterday for an enquiry about a member of his Parish.

So we came here believing you'll be able to help us," continued Father Jude.

"If you have some time, Father Odera will narrate his story to you," requested Father Jude.

"Of course. I have as much time as you need, my respected Fathers," promised the Headmaster, who was happy and considered it a great honor to host two Reverend Fathers. The Headmaster offered the Priests seats and listened to Father Odera's account of his mission to Achara Parish.

There was a teacher, Mr. Agu, who had spent many years at the Achara Primary School. The Headmaster summoned this teacher for a meeting with him and the Priests. Mr. Agu was visibly worried by the presence of the two Priests at the Headmaster's Office especially how the Priests focused their steady gaze on him. He couldn't remember in any way he could have erred. The Primary School was under the authority of the Parish Priest, so Mr. Agu thought that he was summoned for a disciplinary reason.

"Please be seated," the Headmaster gestured with his hand to Mr. Agu.

The meeting started with the Headmaster asking their Parish Priest, Father Jude to tell Mr. Agu why he was summoned.

"There's no reason to be worried, Mr. Agu. We have only come to make an enquiry." Everybody laughed, including Mr. Agu, who was now more relaxed.

Father Jude proceeded to tell Mr. Agu the objective of

their enquiry.

"There was a boy called Ekigwe who passed through this school several years ago. He was not from Achara but he lived with a teacher while attending this Primary School." Father Jude gave Mr. Agu a brief account of Ekigwe, including that he committed suicide. It was quiet for a moment as Mr. Agu raised his head in thought. Odera was a bit tense, wondering what would be Mr. Agu's response. All eyes focused on Mr. Agu. Finally, to Odera's great relief, Mr. Agu broke his silence after what seemed like an eternity, at least to Odera.

"I recall a boy called Ekigwe who was very intelligent but later left the school. He did not complete his primary school in Achara. This Ekigwe I knew did not commit suicide, God forbid," Mr. Agu concluded. This version brought another angle to the story of Ekigwe. Odera seemed to have hit a roadblock because there was now no telling if they were talking about the same boy.

"This Ekigwe and the suicide Ekigwe, are they the same?" Odera was confused. The teacher calmed his nerves when he remembered that there was a rich farmer, Nwankwo, whose son was very close friends with the Ekigwe he knew. The meeting ended with the Headmaster asking Mr. Agu to kindly direct the Priests to Nwankwo's compound during their planned visit the following day. It was only a twenty-minute walk from the Primary School. Odera had planned to return to Akpu the next day, but with the development of things, Father Jude advised him to save himself another long bicycle ride back to Achara and follow the lead of the story before returning to Akpu. Odera couldn't agree more given the promise of what they already achieved.

Father Jude and Odera got back to the Achara Parish house of Father Jude. Both priests had a shower, and Father Jude invited Odera to a well-prepared dinner.

"Mama, meet Father Odera from Achara Parish," said Father Jude, introducing his mother.

"Welcome my son," responded Jude's mother.

"How are your people?" she continued.

"They are very well, Mama, and thank you for all the love you and your son have shown me."

"I have not even done anything yet my son. The dinner has been set and you should eat because I know you must be hungry."

Soon, both priests were seated at the dinner table. It proved to be the most memorable dinner of Odera's life.

There were three sets of majestic-looking covered dishes. One dish contained pounded yam. The second dish contained bitter leaf soup. Both dishes were favorites of Father Odera. But the third and largest dish contained steaming hot pepper soup, the special delicacy that any Achara man would crave. In fact, the Achara people so loved this pepper soup that they called it "mmili tea" (liquid tea). It was said that they called it 'liquid tea' because when tea first reached Achara, only the white Reverend Father had it. The first Achara people to taste the tea at the Reverend Father's house told the story of a drink that was sweeter than honey. Only this pepper soup compared with tea in sweetness!

Reverend Father Jude gave a short prayer, which mostly revolved around the Virgin Mary. He then opened the covers of the first two dishes to Odera's delight.

"So this is what you enjoy from time to time?" commented Odera, not really expecting an answer.

"From my childhood," replied Father Jude.

"Your mother's bitter leaf soup is the best I have ever tasted," continued Odera.

Odera remembered briefly that he probably had never known his biological mother.

Momentarily subdued, Odera wondered what his life would have been like if he had a mother.

Overtaken by curiosity, Odera requested that Father Jude give him a glimpse of what comprised the last dish.

"The special delicacy is a surprise for you," answered Reverend Jude with a smirk on his face. Reverend Father Jude was pinpoint prophetic. Only it was more than a surprise.

At last, the two priests settled down to dinner. Though Odera enjoyed the bitter leaf soup and pounded yam very much, he was careful to reserve space for the special delicacy in the yet to be opened dish. Odera was convinced that the content of that dish was breadfruit. Soon, they finished eating the bitter leaf soup and washed their hands. Odera was now waiting for the meal of the day.

Finally, Reverend Father Jude opened the third dish with fanfare, smiling and gazing at Odera, expecting a smile of approval and some excitement. Father Jude definitely got the excitement from Odera, but not the type of excitement he imagined.

Odera, on seeing the celebrated content of the dish, gave a sudden involuntary gasp, screamed and sprang to his feet like someone ready to flee from danger. Then he momentarily stared at the dish with disbelief as he saw a portion of the contents of the dish. Father Jude was equally alarmed at Odera's behaviour.

"What's the problem, my brother?" queried Father

Jude, seriously troubled and also on his feet. In the dish, its unique skin pattern standing out was the cooked part of a python snake, a delicious delicacy in Achara. But it was an abomination to kill a python in Akpu village, let alone eat it. Python was the god of Akpu village. Odera trembled and a cold sweat enveloped him. Odera was speechless. Father Jude was perplexed and kept asking Odera what the problem was.

"Liquid Tea is certainly too sweet and delicious to be the problem!" reasoned Father Jude.

After Odera regained his composure, and after what seemed to Father Jude like an eternity, Odera spoke up.

"Python is the god of my village," declared Odera, very ashamed of himself that he reacted that way as a Priest.

"I am very sorry for my behavior," Odera apologized to Father Jude.

"I certainly have no intention to reward your magnanimity and kindness with unbecoming behavior," continued Odera, who was visibly embarrassed by his own reaction to the snake which turned a great reception into a near nightmare.

"My reaction was not because it's the god of Akpu, but because I found it scary and repulsive, which shows that people's culture has an effect on them, whether they admit it or not," continued Odera. Besides, from my childhood, I have had a mortal fear of snakes, not only python. Most people in Akpu are equally afraid of snakes.

"But snake is not and can never be my god," Odera reiterated.

Father Jude was also sorry and understood Odera's predicament. In his own Achara village, tortoise was their god and no one dared kill a tortoise let alone eat it. Father

Jude's mother, upon hearing Odera's scream, came in to inquire what the problem was.

"We were merely cracking jokes," Father Jude lied to his mother. Meanwhile, Odera's hunger had evaporated and was replaced by fear, anxiety and shame.

As Odera retired to his room, he reflected on the events of the evening.

"How could he, a Christian Priest be running from a dead snake?"

"No wonder my village worshipped the snake," he reasoned.

"But what a shame for the Akpu people, that the god of their village was served to me as dinner?"

"If the Akpu god can't protect itself from predators, how can it protect Akpu village?" Odera wondered.

CHAPTER NINETEEN

The next morning, Nwankwo was surprised to see two Christian Priests in his compound. Mr. Agu was with them. Mr. Agu had been in Achara for so long that he needed no introduction to Nwankwo. As soon as Nwankwo saw Mr. Agu with the Priests, he remarked aloud, "Teacher, as you are coming to my house with two Priests, I hope everything is ok?" Nwankwo was not a Christian, but he was not against the Christians in Achara. In fact, Nwankwo was very proud of his son who passed through the Christian primary school and was now working in the city. Every time his son came home and gave Nwankwo a good sum of "Ego Oyibo" (White man's money), Nwankwo would beam with smiles. Nwankwo had come to expect it at the end of every month when his son Udeh came visiting. He would often remark, "Eli m ana obu m'atalu aja." This meant that enjoyment was not when you ate sand.

Enjoyment was often called "Eli m ana," translated literally as "Eating the Earth or Land."

"Welcome to my house," Nwankwo greeted the Priests.

"I hope there is no problem," Nwankwo remarked.

"We have come in peace and we bring you greetings," replied Father Jude.

"Good to hear because if not that I saw Mr. Agu with you, I would have gone into hiding," said Nwankwo jokingly.

"A Priest has never come into my house and now two Priests together!" continued Nwankwo, still in a jovial mood. Both Nwankwo and the priests laughed.

Nwankwo then gave them seats in his Obi and brought kola nuts and alligator pepper to his august visitors.

"Bia nu butelum ite nmanya," called out Nwankwo to the women's compound.

Within a few minutes, a young boy brought a keg of foaming palm wine and placed it next to Nwankwo's feet. He used his right palm and removed the foam and some bees and flies which had died, probably from an overdose of good palm wine. The Igbo say that if palm wine doesn't attract flies and bees, it's not a good palm wine. Nwankwo offered his guests palm wine.

He also brought kola nut on a carved wooden tray and offered his guests.

That his guests were Christian Priests did not prevent Nwankwo from praying in his traditional way. He greeted the gods for the visitors in his court. He said, "Let the eagle perch and let the kite perch. Whichever says the other will not perch, let his own wings break,"

"Iseee (Amen)" he answered to his own prayer. He continued, turning the kola nut in his palm as he spoke as if he were inspecting it.

"Onye wetalu orji wetalu ndu." He said that, "He who brings kola nut brings life."

"Oye taa oji, Afor taa oji, Nkwor taa oji, Eke taa oji"

which meant, "Oye eat kola nut, Afor eat kola nut, Nkwor eat kola nut, Eke eat kola nut."

The Ibo week is a four day week, namely: Oye, Afor, Nkwor, Eke. These weekdays are not mere days. They each represent a spirit, and that is why he invited each one of them to come and eat the kola nut. The spirits of dead Ibo ancestors play a day-to-day role in their lives. These four weekdays are also the four market days in Iboland.

After he finished praying, he broke the kola nut, took a piece and ate. Then he proceeded to share the rest of the kola nut pieces. He poured a little portion of the palm wine on the red dusty ground, as a libation, a drink offering to his ancestors to drink with them.

"To our forefathers," he declared and spilled again.

"Oye, drink wine." Again, "Afor, drink wine." And again, "Nkwor, drink wine." And lastly, "Eke drink wine," he concluded.

Then he poured out the palm wine to his guests.

Finally, he brought out his snuff-box, scooped a portion into his left palm and offered the box to his guests. The two Priests and the Teacher declined and thanked him for the gesture. Snuff was fast going out of fashion for the younger generation.

"My sons, you can now tell me the purpose of your visit," requested Nwankwo finally.

Father Jude gestured at the Teacher to proceed.

The Teacher gave Nwankwo a brief account of the purpose of their visit and that they needed information about a certain classmate and friend of his son Udeh called Ekigwe. As soon as Nwankwo heard "Ekigwe," he was startled and quipped, "My own Ekigwe? What information? And for who?"

Immediately, Odera felt that they were chasing the wrong person.

"His family heard that he committed suicide," answered the Teacher.

"Tufiakwa," rejected Nwankwo of suicide.

"Who told you that vicious lie?" continued Nwankwo.

"The gods forbid that Ekigwe will do such an abomination," declared Nwankwo. The

Teacher defended himself, "Our father, I have already told them that the Ekigwe I knew did not commit suicide."

"That is why we came to find out the truth," said the Achara Parish Priest.

The Akpu Parish Priest was quietly very excited to hear Nwankwo's comments. But he was cautiously optimistic.

"So you know Ekigwe well?" asked Achara Priest.

"Oh yes, Ekigwe is my son Udeh's closest friend even to this day. But I have not set eyes on him for some years. But he usually sends greetings through Udeh," answered Nwankwo.

The Akpu Parish Priest became a little doubtful and confused now.

"If Ekigwe didn't commit suicide, why hadn't Nwankwo seen him for years?" he reasoned.

"Or are they hiding something?" continued Odera.

"So where is your son, Udeh?" inquired the Achara Parish Priest.

"He works in the city and may even visit this weekend," replied Nwankwo.

"If you come on Saturday you will likely meet him," continued Nwankwo. So the guests thanked Nwankwo and took their leave with a promise to come back Saturday.

Odera, the Parish Priest of Akpu, was full of

anticipation and decided to stay till Saturday. He just hoped they were all talking about the same Ekigwe. But he thought it had to be because he fit all the descriptions.

"But how did the suicide story slip in?" Odera wondered.

"There is no smoke without fire," Odera feared in his mind.

"There are just too many mysteries for me to grapple with in my life," he lamented.

CHAPTER TWENTY

On Saturday the two Priests came to Nwankwo's compound.

"Good afternoon, sir," they greeted Nwankwo almost in unison.

"Welcome, my sons. You kept your word," Nwankwo remarked and gestured for them to sit down.

"Who is there?" shouted Nwankwo at the wives' hut.

"Our father, I am here," answered his wife.

"Tell Udeh to see me in the Obi now."

"Udeh has gone out to his uncle Ozodi's house," replied Udeh's mother.

"Send somebody to fetch him. He has visitors," instructed Nwankwo.

Within minutes, Udeh came in and exchanged greetings with the guests. Nwankwo introduced Udeh to the guests, and all sat down to kola nuts and palm wine as usual.

"I understand you are inquiring after my friend, Ekigwe," Udeh remarked.

"Oh yes," replied the Priest from Achara.

Odera listened nervously but expectantly.

225

"My brother here wants to know about Ekigwe and would want to meet him in person," Reverend Jude remarked.

"That's right," confirmed Odera.

"Why do you want to meet him, please? Is there any problem?" queried Udeh cautiously.

"It is a long story, my good friend. His family is very disturbed and came to my Parish in Akpu village to make inquiries about him. I promised to do my utmost to help them. Hence, I embarked on this long journey. I thank my brother the Parish Priest of Achara who helped me locate your house."

"Ok, I will get in touch with Ekigwe and send word back to you through our Parish Priest here in Achara."

Udeh did not want to confirm or refute Odera's account of Ekigwe, now a top military officer, without first contacting Ekigwe for his approval. So he kept his feelings to himself.

Ekigwe had returned from England and was a senior military officer, a Major, and the Army Adjutant.

The two Priests left Nwankwo's compound satisfied and accomplished. Odera thanked Reverend Father Jude profusely for his help. The next morning Odera went back to Akpu village optimistic and happy. He thought about visiting Adaobi but wondered what he would tell her seeing that nothing was yet conclusive. He thought that a visit then would only serve the purpose of heightening her anxiety. So Odera waited.

One day a message came from Achara Parish Priest through the church courier. Odera's hands were shaking as he opened the envelope to read the message. But the message only said that Odera should be at Achara Parish

226

Priest's house in two weeks.

Two weeks seemed like two years for Odera. Eventually, it was time to return to Achara Parish. This time the bicycle trip to Achara was easier because Odera had past experience.

The Achara Parish Priest was very happy to receive his Akpu counterpart. Father Jude had become involved in Odera's complicated life story and now, just like Odera, was also anxious about what to expect.

Thoughts of the bizarre experience of both Priests at the python pepper soup dinner occasionally cropped up in the minds of both Priests, but neither mentioned it.

Both priests returned to Nwankwo's compound the next morning. The Achara Parish Priest had already arranged the meeting to be when Udeh was in Achara town. So they met Udeh at home.

"Welcome, Fathers," greeted Udeh.

"Thank you, my brother," replied the Achara Priest and Odera simultaneously.

"I hope you have good news for us," continued the Achara Priest.

They all laughed.

"Of course my news is always good news," commented Udeh, smiling.

Odera was quietly happy to hear Udeh's comment but very nervous in anticipation of the news about Ekigwe.

"How's Ekigwe?" asked the Achara Priest.

"He's very well and wished he could come with me," answered Udeh.

"Oh, we were hoping to meet him today," remarked the Achara Priest.

"You know Ekigwe is a soldier and they don't just go

off like that," Udeh replied to Father Odera.

"Did you say he is a soldier?" asked the Achara Priest in wonder.

"Oh yes," replied Udeh.

"He has asked me to arrange for you to visit him at the Army Headquarters at a convenient time," continued Udeh.

The two Priests looked at each other with an air of disbelief.

Although the two Priests were happy to hear that, Odera was particularly thrilled because at last, here was the opportunity he had dreamt of for a long time. Here was a chance not only to visit Adaobi and meet her parents with the great and unexpected good news that Ekigwe was still alive but also to advance his own quest for self-discovery. Before they dispersed, a date was agreed upon for Odera to visit Ekigwe. It was agreed that Udeh would communicate to Ekigwe, who was then a Major, the date Odera would visit him. Odera then went back to Akpu, happy that he had scored a major breakthrough in the search for Adaobi's brother Ekigwe, and a stepping stone toward unraveling his own identity. He hoped that Adaobi wouldn't visit before he met Ekigwe in person so that he would have concrete news for her upon her visit.

Soon it was time to travel to the Army Headquarters to visit Ekigwe, and as Odera wished, Adaobi hadn't visited.

CHAPTER TWENTY-ONE

Odera didn't know how to prepare for this trip. He had never had anything to do with soldiers all his life. It was a very emotional trip for Odera because his expectations were very high and potentially life-changing.

Odera arrived at the Army Headquarters as planned and asked for Ekigwe Nweke. He was asked by a stern-looking soldier why he looked for the Army Adjutant, Major Nweke.

"His sister Adaobi sent me to give him a message," he replied, wondering what to expect from this man he had never met in his life. The soldier gave Odera a seat and left the scene. The soldier stood before Ekigwe and saluted,

"Sir, a man is here to see you. He said he was sent by your sister called Adaobi."

As soon as Ekigwe heard that Adaobi sent him a message, he left what he was doing, excused himself and ordered they bring Odera in. Ekigwe was trembling with expectation. He couldn't believe his ears. Even though Ekigwe tried to mask his emotions, the soldiers were surprised at his reaction when they told him Adaobi sent a message. Then the soldiers ushered in Odera, smartly saluted Ekigwe and marched off. Ekigwe nervously ushered Odera to a seat. Odera himself was also very nervous, not knowing what to expect. They met and Odera told him he was the Parish Priest of Akpu and that his sister Adaobi had come to the Parish to inquire about him. Ekigwe was exploding with emotions but held himself from crying. Odera was amazed at the pomp of meeting Adaobi's brother, Ekigwe. He had never before been with a senior military officer. Odera was served some refreshments at Ekigwe's office.

"Where is Adaobi? Why didn't she visit with you?" inquired Ekigwe finally after he regained his composure.

"She promised to visit the Parish but hadn't visited before I left Akpu. I would have gone to her house but I don't know the location of her house," explained Odera.

"Besides, I didn't know I could locate you so soon," continued Odera

"Please next time she visits, follow her and find out her house," pleaded Major Ekigwe. "I will do exactly that," promised Odera. Ekigwe then ordered a soldier to wait and escort Odera outside. The two men shook hands and Odera excused himself from Ekigwe and traveled back to Akpu overtaken with excitement at what he accomplished and the promise of finally unraveling his own identity.

During the meeting with Odera, Ekigwe had promised to visit the Akpu Parish on an agreed date and requested Odera to bring Adaobi to the Parish on that day.

Thus started the journey back down memory lane. Odera calculated that this was the golden opportunity for him to visit Adaobi's family and confirm if Nweke and Mgbogafor, in Adaobi's family were the same as in church records, the parents of the Odera twin. He reasoned with trembling and anxiety that if indeed he was the twin the church rescued, and Adaobi's father was the father of the twin and Mgbogafor the mother, then Major Ekigwe could indeed be his younger brother also. But he held this to his chest.

The days went by and Adaobi hadn't visited the Parish. Only Adaobi could confirm that

Major Ekigwe was her brother and hadn't committed suicide. Odera was beginning to boil with anxiety and expectation.

"Could the notes he found in the church be referring to him or was he just building castles in the air?" he mused.

It had been exactly two weeks since his visit to Army Headquarters. Major Ekigwe had become too restless and just decided that to regain his peace, he must take a chance at visiting the Akpu Parish priest, Odera, even without notice. So Ekigwe visited Odera before the agreed date at the Parish to take him to his sister Adaobi and his family.

Odera was praying and preparing the mass for the coming Sunday when he heard an unusual noise around the usually quiet Parish. He looked out of the window and saw an unusual gathering of people. Major Ekigwe was with his Army retinue which caused quite a stir at the Parish as people gathered in wonder to see why there were so many soldiers there. Akpu Town had never witnessed so many soldiers visiting her before.

Odera came outside and saw a number of military vehicles and soldiers at the Parish compound. They were asking for the Parish Priest when Odera emerged and moved briskly toward Ekigwe. Major Ekigwe exchanged pleasantries with the Priest, who ushered him to the

Priest's residence. Odera offered some drink but Ekigwe declined, very anxious to get going. Ekigwe wasn't there for drinks but for Adaobi, his sister. Odera disappointed him with the news that Adaobi had not visited him since his return to Akpu. Odera did not know Adaobi's house in Offia. Ekigwe left Akpu village disappointed. Odera promised Ekigwe that as soon as Adaobi visited he would send him an S.O.S.

A few days later Adaobi visited Odera. Odera told Adaobi how he visited Ekigwe at the Army Headquarters in the City and Ekigwe's visit to the Parish. Adaobi said she could not believe until she saw with her own eyes.

"Why didn't you bring him to Offia and ask for the Nweke family?" Adaobi lamented aloud.

Adaobi consoled herself saying,

"It's only a matter of time." Then it was finally time for Odera to know Adaobi's house. Adaobi showed the Parish Priest, Odera, her house so that when Ekigwe returned, Odera would know where to bring him. Adaobi dared not allow Odera to enter her compound because her father would know that she was flirting with the Christians like her brother Ekigwe did.

Locating Ekigwe and confirming he was still alive was Adaobi's passionate and private pet project.

Reverend Father Odera and Adaobi fixed a date that Adaobi would visit Father Odera to meet Major Ekigwe. Both Odera and Adaobi had passionate interest in this project, but Adaobi did not know the reason for Odera's unusual kindness in helping her locate Ekigwe. She didn't have the slightest idea that Father Odera had a vested interest in locating Ekigwe's whereabouts.

CHAPTER TWENTY-TWO

Then came the d-day! Adaobi was in Akpu Parish early. Father Odera understood and wasn't surprised at Adaobi's early visit. She was filled with mixed tension.

"Would it be the same Ekigwe, really, or would it be a wild goose chase, a miserable disappointment?" wondered Adaobi.

Major Ekigwe was late in coming. Adaobi's anxiety was reaching a breaking point and she was sweating and palpitating when Odera announced that he sighted some Army jeeps through the window. Then a knock at the door!

Father Odera opened the door and let Ekigwe in the house. There was an uneasy silence for a few seconds as Ekigwe and Adaobi studiously looked at each other as if to confirm that they knew each other. Then an uproar. Adaobi rushed to hug Ekigwe and almost threw him to the ground. Both Ekigwe and Adaobi held themselves in a tight embrace, tears of joy running down their faces. Adaobi was actually crying, unable to hold herself. It was probably a release of years of suppressed, pent up emotion. Ekigwe had quite a job consoling Adaobi from her run-away emotions. Consoling Adaobi helped Ekigwe control his own years of bottled-up emotions. Father Odera watched in quiet satisfaction. But Odera had a satisfaction filled with tension and uncertainty. At last, he had united Ekigwe and his family. One mission accomplished.

"Will the second mission be accomplished also?" Odera battled within. Both Ekigwe and Adaobi were too emotionally spent to eat the food prepared by Odera.

The uproar caused such a stir in the Parish that people gathered to find out what was the matter.

Ekigwe suggested that they should fix a date to meet their father, Nweke and the entire family. Adaobi could not contain her excitement and wanted Ekigwe to accompany her to the family right away.

"Do you kill an elephant and leave its meat to sour before eating it?" declared Adaobi. Ekigwe, also overcome with excitement, succumbed. Time had healed the rift and the wound between Ekigwe and his father. It was like a dream to Ekigwe. He was too anxious to meet his father, and even more, his mother.

Father Odera excused himself, but Ekigwe insisted,

"You made all this possible. You must accompany us to meet our father Nweke because he will surely want to meet the man who made this miracle possible." Ekigwe wondered if his father had forgiven him. Finally, Adaobi, Odera and Ekigwe, with his military escorts, arrived at Nweke's compound.

Nweke and his wives were asking Adaobi if there was a problem that caused their house to be invaded by soldiers. Neither Nweke nor his wives recognized Ekigwe. Moreover, Ekigwe was wearing sunglasses.

Ekigwe saluted his father and knelt down before him to Nweke's bewilderment. It was now clear the soldiers came peacefully.

"Who are you, my son?" asked Nweke.

"Please rise up," he continued.

"I am Ekigwe," he replied.

"What town are you from?" inquired Nweke, thinking he came to ask the hand of his daughter in marriage.

"I am Ekigwe, your son."

"Akpu ukwu gbata oso oo (Let the village god 'Akpu ukwu' immediately come running)," Nweke exclaimed.

As if lost in thought, briefly Nweke stared at Ekigwe. Then suddenly, Nweke recovered himself and let out a loud cry like he did when his personal god disappointed him and allowed Ekigwe to go "stretching his neck" toward the Efulefus – the Christians. Nweke called the gods and his wives to come and witness and hear the wonder that he was hearing and seeing. He embraced Ekigwe and remarked, "No wonder. An eagle does not give birth to a chicken." That is to say, Ekigwe was his replica, which was why he had become so successful and a top military officer. This comment attracted a scornful laugh from Ekigwe's mother, Uduaku.

"He is now his son - ha- ha- ha."

"Wonders shall never cease!"

"Certainly, success has many relations," concluded Uduaku.

Nweke commanded that they bring him the biggest he-goat from the stable. The he-goat was put inside the army jeep as a gift to Ekigwe. Nweke told Ekigwe to return home in eight market days so that a feast will be made and his mother's brethren will meet his lost son who has been found.

"Does udala fall far away from its tree?" continued

Nweke in his exuberant self-praise.

"No father," responded Ekigwe happily. Odera nodded in agreement.

Ekigwe told Nweke how Adaobi and the Reverend Father made it all possible. Nweke thanked Adaobi and the Reverend Father. He gave a live hen to the Reverend Father. Adaobi's mother also gave some unhatched eggs to Father Odera. Reverend Fathers, especially European Reverend Fathers, have been known to be lovers of eggs. Nweke, who was already getting old and sickly, recovered instantly.

Ekigwe went into the women's compound and to his mother's hut. All the wives of Nweke gathered at Uduaku's hut to rejoice with her. They praised Adaobi's tenacity and perseverance and said that Adaobi was more than a man. They referred to Adaobi as, "Udor kpulu enyi," the rope that pulled an elephant. Emergency food was prepared and served Ekigwe and Odera.

Ekigwe remembered his half brother, Umeh, "Father, I have not seen Umeh. I hope all is well with him? Or has he built his house elsewhere?"

"Is been so many years I have not seen him, you know," continued Ekigwe asking his father many questions at the same time.

"Umeh is well," responded Nweke casually.

"He has either gone to the farm or he may be in his mother's hut," continued Nweke.

"Father, permit me to go to his mother's hut and find out please," Ekigwe sought his father's permission.

"Didn't he hear all the noise if he is in his mother's hut?" Nweke blurted out.

"Or maybe he is in a deep sleep this hot afternoon,"

continued Nweke smiling cynically.

"Stay put here let me send somebody to go and see if he is home," Nweke said emphatically. Then Nweke called one of his younger children to go and check if Umeh was in his mother's hut and fetch him.

To Ekigwe's surprise and delight, the kid came running back and said to Nweke, "Father, Umeh said he is coming."

"I told you," Nweke turned to speak to Ekigwe.

"I can't wait for him to marry that girl he has been eyeing but couldn't raise the bride price," continued Nweke.

"That will be great so that you will have more grandchildren," responded Ekigwe happily.

"Let me finish raising Umeh first before I start to raise his children," commented Nweke sadly.

At this point, Umeh came into the obi and greeted lamely,

"Greetings, Father."

Before Nweke finished asking Umeh if he knew the man seated there with him, Ekigwe jumped on his feet and embraced a cold and reluctant Umeh.

"Very happy to see you, my brother. Quite an age!"

"Happy to see you too," responded Umeh sounding in every way lackluster. Nweke watched them and smiled ominously.

Umeh had always had a complex about Ekigwe when Ekigwe was a mere school kid. Now Ekigwe was undoubtedly the most important personality in the surrounding towns. Indeed, Umeh could not come near him if they were not family. Umeh remembered his comment about Ekigwe years back that meant Ekigwe was good riddance to bad rubbish when he said that Ekigwe's absence was better for the family than his presence because Ekigwe had caused the family enough problems to last them a lifetime. Umeh wished he could take back those words and lamented in his heart,

"If those words were not so wicked and poisonous, I would have loved to swallow them back and have some peace of mind!"

"While I was here eating new yams and enjoying festivities, Ekigwe was in a strange land suffering but making a name for himself," continued Umeh in his silent lamentation.

Then Ekigwe excitedly told Umeh,

"I understand you are getting ready to get married?"

"Yes," responded Umeh sounding a little brighter. Umeh almost wished he could ask Ekigwe for the bride price, but pride and guilty conscience were stumbling blocks.

"I am very excited for you, my brother. Please send me a message when you fix the date for the first traditional ceremony," pleaded Ekigwe.

"I will surely tell you, my senior brother," replied a refreshingly changing Umeh, even adding 'senior' to address Ekigwe. Umeh had never treated Ekigwe as his senior brother.

Ekigwe's attitude proved how powerful love could be and that love is indeed more powerful than hatred.

Nweke watched his two sons and the instant transformation of Umeh with utter disbelief.

"I thank the gods for a son like Ekigwe," declared Nweke in his heart.

A wholly more brightened Umeh respectfully took leave of his brother to the delight of their father, Nweke, and returned to his mother's hut.

"Father, please let me know where and how I can help as regards Umeh's marriage, especially the bride price," requested Ekigwe.

"His god is still awake," remarked Nweke about Umeh.

"I hope another more capable man has not paid his fiancee's bride price. Good things don't wait for anyone," concluded Nweke.

"He is indeed fortunate to have you as a brother. And you have shown great leadership as the eldest son, and you have changed him for good," continued Nweke.

"May the gods continue to promote you," Nweke prayed.

"Iseee," agreed Ekigwe.

"But it is up to Umeh to humble himself and ask you for the bride price. All I can do is to remind him to ask you. It is him, not me, that wants to get married," stressed Nweke.

"Please be a little easier on Umeh," pleaded Ekigwe.

"He will turn around. He has actually started to turn around," continued Ekigwe.

"My dear son, if I am not easy on Umeh, do you think I will be feeding him into manhood?" asked Nweke.

"It is not our tradition that a man of Umeh's age will still live in his mother's hut. And all his age-grade are married," continued Nweke

"A few days ago, I looked at Umeh and I said that the gods have punished me for my bad deeds and made sure I don't have a son. And as if to prove me wrong, you surfaced like I was dreaming.

Now looking at you, I know that most times, we don't understand the mind of the gods," said Nweke philosophically.

"I thank the gods that Umeh seems to be turning around and opening up to you. So please advise him if he will listen, to call his age-grade to go and march on the mud and build a hut where he will enter with his bride. I will give him a piece of land where he will build. He is not going to take a wife into his mother's hut. It is not done in this clime," concluded Nweke.

But Ekigwe agreed with Nweke that Umeh should come and ask for the bride price and left some money with his father toward Umeh's transportation to the Army Headquarters should Umeh decide to go and see Ekigwe.

"Thank you, my son, for your kind gestures. Our people say that 'lack of expression is the fault of the mouth,'" said Nweke, insinuating that it would be up to Umeh now to ask so that progress will be made.

For days the dramatic change of Umeh was trending in the family. Nweke's wives, especially the mates of Umeh's mother, were so happy and discussed it daily. They said that it was a new dawn in Nweke's family. Even Umeh himself noticed that he had and was still undergoing a great metamorphosis. He believed that the presence of Ekigwe would lift up his family's and his own standing before his bride's family.

"No girl can now afford to bluff or refuse me when she hears that Ekigwe is my brother," reasoned Umeh unprecedentedly.

All this while, Father Odera was watching the drama and excitement all over Nweke's family and thought that it was not the appropriate day to discuss the abandoned twins. But Odera was agonizing to sort out his own identity. He thought it would be great if he actually belonged to this family. Neither Adaobi nor Ekigwe knew what Odera was going through.

After the impromptu celebrations, Major Ekigwe and his entourage went back to the Army

Headquarters in the city. Odera went back to the Parish, pondering his life and his next moves.

"I need to see Nweke when he will be composed enough to listen to me," Odera reasoned.

"For now, the euphoria of Ekigwe's return is still very hot and has carried the day in everybody's psyche," continued Odera.

"Who will believe my story?" Odera lamented in a barely audible soliloquy.

"Thank God for the note I found in the Church records," Odera thought.

Thoughts ran wild in Odera's mind. Besides, Odera thought about the consequences of telling Nweke that one of the twins he threw into the Evil Forest as an abomination and taken for dead did not die after all.

"Wouldn't it be akin to accusing Nweke of murder?" Odera thought it was preferable telling Adaobi or telling Ekigwe his story and even show them the Parish records. Nweke was more likely to listen to a man than a woman.

Odera chose Ekigwe over Adaobi to hear his story. Neither Ekigwe nor Adaobi was privy to throwing away any twins. They were not yet born then. Besides, such deeds were kept away from children.

Nweke already had the guilt of Ekigwe's exile hanging around his neck.

"Will he stand another guilt, this time the murder of his twins, even if it was tradition?" Odera feared Nweke's reaction, but he had no peace as long as he kept this information to himself. But with this Igbo proverb in his thoughts,

"A person does not climb an Iroko tree twice in his lifetime. Therefore anyone that succeeds in climbing an Iroko tree better bring down all the fruits therefrom," Odera was resolute about narrating his story to Ekigwe.

After Ekigwe and Odera left the Obi and went back to their stations, Nweke was alone and reflected on the events of the day. Of particular interest to Nweke was Ekigwe's loving attitude and generosity toward his brother, Umeh, especially his promise to provide the bride price if Umeh needed it. Hitherto, the issue surrounding Umeh's inability to marry had been a thorn in Nweke's flesh. Umeh was Nweke's only son before the return of Ekigwe.

Nweke thought, "It is expedient to look for a black goat while it is still daytime."

"I will eat this food while it is still hot," Nweke continued in reference to Ekigwe's offer. So Nweke immediately sent for Umeh.

"Greetings father. You called me," said Umeh.

"Yes, Umeh. I called you. Please sit down."

"I continued to talk with Ekigwe after you left. He left some money for your transportation should you want to visit him," Nweke reported.

"Very kind of him, Father. I'll let you know when I am ready," Umeh agreed.

Umeh went ahead to plan the date of the first ceremony which was the payment of the bride price. But Umeh did not ask Nweke for the money left for him by Ekigwe, neither did Umeh visit Ekigwe during that period.

Umeh had selected a date for the visit of Umeh and his

family to the house of his fiancée to negotiate, agree and pay the bride price. Nweke went around and told his family and clan that they should get ready for the visit to their prospective in-laws according to tradition. Nweke also sent a message to Ekigwe giving him the date set aside for the occasion. Nweke made arrangements for palm wine from the best palm wine tappers in Offiah for the memorable occasion.

On the set date, food was lavishly prepared for the entertainment of the people who would accompany Nweke and his family on the trip. The marriage party was scheduled to leave Nweke's compound at noon. By mid-morning, people were arriving. The first to arrive were family members. They were seated on the chairs arranged for them and were served food and palm wine. A little later, elders of Nweke's mother's family, his adopted family, arrived with some Red Cap Chiefs. Nweke's compound was abuzz with preparations for the marriage trip.

Just before noon, the noise of a military convoy was heard outside Nweke's compound.

"That must be your great son," announced one of the Red Cap Chiefs for the benefit of Nweke.

"He is one son that is worth more than ten sons," added another elder, and everyone chorused agreement. Soon Ekigwe, accompanied by his soldier escorts, marched into the compound amidst low noises of acknowledgment.

"Greetings, my father," greeted Ekigwe.

"Welcome, my son," responded Nweke with obvious pride.

"Greetings my elders and chiefs," continued Ekigwe, greeting all the guests.

"I am sorry for arriving a little late," Ekigwe apologized to the admiration of all the seated guests.

"See how humble and respectful he is!" remarked an elder.

"I can't thank the gods enough," added Nweke and all the elders agreed that the gods had been very good to Nweke. Just then, Umeh walked in and greeted Nweke, Ekigwe and the elders.

"Ononenyi," an elder acknowledged his greeting by calling him "the man who sits on top of an elephant." All the elders agreed that Umeh was sitting on top of an elephant. Of course, everyone understood the underlying meaning. Of course Ekigwe was the elephant! Ekigwe and Nweke had a quiet discussion. Nweke conveyed the subject of his discussion with Ekigwe to a young man who acted as the Master of Ceremony on the occasion. The man immediately announced that the benevolent man, Ekigwe, had lived up to his name.

"He has provided a ride for everyone to the house of our prospective in-laws," he announced. There was a great applause in the compound. An observer would have thought that the occasion was all about Ekigwe if not for the colorful marriage attire put on by Umeh.

"My fathers and elders, this way," the Master of Ceremonies directed them toward a military jeep.

"Others, please, this way," he directed the rest toward a military minibus. Nweke and Umeh rode with Ekigwe in his official car. Without Ekigwe, the normal thing would have been a trek to the next village, which was the venue of the marriage.

The party then drove off to Umeh's fiancée, Ije. As they drove away, Nweke's neighbors gathered and looked in amazement. They had never witnessed anything of that nature and never thought they would witness it in their lifetime.

After what seemed to Nweke and his entourage a few minutes, they arrived at their would-be in-laws'. Usually, this trip would have taken an hour of sweaty trekking and dust to get there. As the military entourage arrived at Umeh's fiancée's family, a similar crowd of curious villagers gathered in amazement to herald them.

The party alighted from the cars and entered into the fiancee's compound where they were being expected. Chairs were already arranged in expectation of them. The hosts exchanged greetings with Nweke and his party. It was a very warm reception, and soon all were seated, ready for the business of the day. The fiancée of Umeh did not come out because it was the tradition of the people that bride price negotiation and payment was a man's business and women had no input there. The two parties sat facing each other, and the business of the day was set to start.

The family of the fiancée of Umeh brought kola nut and presented it to their guests. The chief spokesman of the bride's family then spoke,

"We welcome you into our family. Your journey will be a good journey which is climaxed with success."

"Iseeeee," was the overwhelming response.

"The feet with which you entered our compound, the same feet will take you back to your homes in peace," he continued to pray over the kola nut.

"Your feet will not stumble against a stone during this trip."

"Iseeeee," was everyone's response.

After all the ceremonies, and the bride price was

agreed upon, it was time to pay the bride price. Umeh had not asked Ekigwe for the bride price cash. So it was assumed that Umeh had the bride price. On the contrary, Umeh's pride or inferiority complex did not allow him to humble himself and ask for help.

So Umeh's in-laws-to-be waited in vain for the bride price. The hosts were in palpable shock and embarrassment as it seemed that this great family couldn't raise the bride price for their daughter. Nweke was embarrassed but exuded confidence because he was sure that his son Ekigwe was more than capable of raising the pride price several times.

"What do we call this?" asked a very vocal member of the bride-to-be's family.

"Is this a joke or a play?" he continued to the embarrassment of the visitors, most of whom were now visibly troubled. The man, who according to tradition was responsible to pay the bride price, Umeh, was just sitting down with a melancholy disposition, a victim of empty pride.

Suddenly, Ekigwe got up, excused himself, and went outside to his car. Everyone, except probably Nweke, was wondering what he was up to and whether he was leaving the venue in anger. He walked back into the meeting almost immediately, bag in hand, and placed the bag on the small table containing the kola nut. There was immediate applause from both camps as everyone imagined it was the bride price. The chief spokesman of the host family opened the bag, and with the help of two other men counted the money. Then the chief spokesman of the bride's family stood up and with much excitement and fanfare greeted,

"Ibeanyi kwenu!"

"Yeeaaaa," answered all.

"Kwenu!" he continued.

"Yeeaaa," he called again and concluded,

"Kwezuenuoooo!!!"

And then came an explosive answer, "Yeeeeeaaaaaaaa."

"There is no scarcity of goods in a great warehouse," declared the spokesman with much fanfare. Then the bride's father commanded that a big he-goat be brought to him. The he-goat was promptly brought to him. He carried the goat and kept it under the legs of Ekigwe. A group of band boys who had been quietly sitting at a corner excitedly started their music, entertaining everybody. The atmosphere became electric.

Before they got up to go back to Offiah, Nweke, who was exuberant, spoke to their in-laws and thanked them for the great reception shown them. The party got up and went back as they had come. They thanked Ekigwe profusely for rising to the occasion when they were about to be disgraced. The elders told Umeh that he was indeed 'Ononenyi,' meaning 'he who is riding on an elephant.' Umeh thanked Ekigwe at their father's Obi and apologized for the show of shame that almost ruined the day. Then Umeh escorted Ekigwe to his car and he went back to the city with his military entourage. Before Ekigwe left, the next marriage ceremony was fixed by Umeh, Nweke and Ekigwe.

After Ekigwe went back to the city, Nweke sent for Umeh to come and see him in the obi. It was time for Nweke to comment on the happenings before the marriage trip as well as at the marriage ceremony.

"Umeh," Nweke called his second son.

"Ogbuefi, my father," answered Umeh.

"I thank the gods that today you have started your marriage to your beautiful bride, Ije."

"Before the return of your brother, Ekigwe, nobody would have considered this day possible. I was not willing to sell my seedling yams to advance you the bride price. Even if I did what was considered foolhardy, would I be the breadwinner of your own house?" continued Nweke.

"Will I be the one to provide for your wife and your children?" asked Nweke. Umeh said nothing but simply shook his head in the negative.

"Now, will you tell me why you did not ask Ekigwe for help toward the bride price as we agreed well before the date of the marriage ceremony?" Nweke asked Umeh.

"Father, you already answered the question when you said that if you brought the bride price, would you feed my family for me?" and Umeh continued,

"If Ekigwe brought the bride price, what is the difference?"

"Will Ekigwe feed my family for me after the bride price?" continued Umeh.

"You sound so ungrateful my son," remarked Nweke.

"So should Ekigwe go back and collect the bride price which he was so selfless to part with for the sake of his brother?" Nweke asked Umeh.

"No father," answered Umeh.

"Then why not?" asked Nweke.

"Because it came out of his own free will. I did not ask him for the bride price," was Umeh's shocking reasoning. Nweke was bewildered because he thought that Umeh had been healed of his rotten attitude toward Ekigwe.

"A tiger never changes its stripes!" Nweke hopelessly thought. Then without any further discussions, Nweke dismissed Umeh.

"I have to consult the oracle before somebody goes out to the Oye market square stark naked," muttered Nweke to himself in reference to Umeh. Nweke thought about the rest of the marriage ceremonies and how Ekigwe was obviously going to shoulder all the responsibility and shuddered with this resolve,

"I'll make sure that Ekigwe does not waste his hard-earned money on behalf of this ungrateful Umeh."

"But if I prevail on Ekigwe not to help him, Umeh will stop at nothing until he has disgraced my family," thought Nweke, getting very frustrated.

"The best option is to help him get married, after which he would relocate to a land outside our compound so that we will know peace in this family," concluded Nweke. Nweke then resolved to fast-track the plan for the rest of the marriage ceremonies and discuss his ideas with Ekigwe. But Nweke's plan had to wait till Ekigwe visited again.

Meanwhile, the news of Ekigwe's return had spread like bush fire even to Akpu. One morning, an old man was walking gingerly into Nweke's compound. Adaobi sighted the man and said to her mother,

"Is that not Akilika coming into our compound?"

"That is very true my daughter. I didn't know that he still moved about. I wonder what brings him," concurred Uduaku.

"Welcome, our father," shouted Uduaku in greeting.

"Thank you, my daughter. Is Ogbuefi at home?" asked Akilika.

CHUKWUDUM OKEKE

"Yes Opulozo, he is in his obi," responded Uduaku.

Akilika continued his slow walk into the obi. He was the most familiar visitor from Akpu since Nweke's exile. Nweke was shocked to see Akilika walking into his obi. It was over a year since the last visit of Akilika.

"Am I seeing Opulozor or am I seeing his spirit?" joked Nweke in excitement, obviously happy that his long-time friend came to visit.

"You are seeing your ancestral spirit. Your father sent me a message from the great beyond to deliver to you," joked back Opulozor. Both laughed and embraced.

"But Opulozo, even though I am obviously happy to see you, what made you drag yourself on this long, taxing journey? Does a frog run in vain in broad daylight?" queried Ogbuefi proverbially.

"Ogbuefi, I thought you would first of all give me a chair to sit down before your many questions," commented Akilika.

"I am so sorry Opulozor for my inept attitude," Nweke apologized awkwardly.

"Our people say that a foolish man does not realize that his brother visiting in his house, is a guest." pleaded Nweke further. Then he promptly offered Opulozor a carved stool fit for an Ichie to sit down.

"Who is near?" shouted Nweke at the wives' compound.

"Nnanyi, I am here," answered one of the wives.

"Hurry and catch a big fowl and bring it to me. A great thing has happened," declared Ogbuefi.

"I have heard you, Ogbuefi," answered the wife and hurried off.

Soon the frightened cries of chickens were heard as

they chased after the hens to catch a suitable one. If there was a chicken interpreter, you could surely have heard their lamentation,

"When men are merry, chickens become victims!"

It is normal in Igboland for a rare and important guest to be received with something more than just kola nut. Sometimes even with a ram or goat depending on the caliber of the visitor. Nweke brought kola nuts and a keg of fresh palm wine from his favorite palm wine tapper, Mgbechi. After a routine prayer to the gods, they broke the kola nuts and settled in on the palm wine. Opulozor could not resist the urge to comment on Nweke's mastery of good palm wine,

"Ogbuefi!"

"Opulozo," Nweke answered Akilika.

"You would have been greater as a wine tapper than a farmer," Akilika complimented

Nweke for his recognition of great palm wine both in Akpu and now in Offiah.

"Rather palm wine taster," corrected Nweke jokingly, and both laughed heartily.

"Now can I hear what made Opulozor endure through this arduous trek?" requested Nweke.

"Nothing flies faster than good news," commented Opulozor.

"And bad news too may be even faster," added Nweke matter-of-factly.

"Even though most young people in Akpu don't know you, and not all the old men remember you, they know that the son of one Nweke from Akpu who was thought to be dead many years ago has reappeared. While that news was still spreading like wildfire, a bombshell followed that the resurrected son has become the new Governor," stated Opulozor.

"Should I hear such news about my lifelong friend and sit down in my house quietly?" asked Opulozo, expecting a confirmation from his friend Nweke.

"Or is there another Nweke from Akpu as big as Ogbuefi?" continued Opulozor

Nweke listened attentively and kept quiet for a while. Nweke and his family had not known about Ekigwe's appointment as the new Governor. But Nweke was cautiously and happily surprised to hear such news and didn't want to show he was not informed about it if the news was indeed true. Nweke pretended he knew about the news brought by his friend.

"Thank you, my good friend, for all the trouble you took to come and find me here," declared Nweke, thanking Opulozor.

"They gossipped that it is one Nweke from Akpu. Are they swallowing their words that they banished me?" asked Nweke rhetorically.

"Opulozor," Nweke called his friend.

"I am here," responded Opulozor.

"You are now in my house in Akpu to visit me or are you in my house in Offiah?" asked Nweke.

"Ogbuefi, I know that I am in your house in Offiah right now," agreed Opulozor.

"So leave Akpu people to worry themselves to death about Nweke. When the time comes, they will know what to do. This is just the beginning of their worries," concluded Nweke.

"Congratulations, Ogbuefi, for the return of your son, Ekigwe. The gods are to be praised for bringing him back like a king."

"Thank you Opulozor," responded Ogbuefi, acknowledging the congratulations and pretending he knew about his son's new appointment.

"Ekigwe has shown that he is a true son of Ogbuefi," continued Opulozor.

"It is also rumored that the elders are afraid of what the new Governor will do to Akpu Town," continued Opulozor, talking a lot like the parrot.

"Well, only the Governor knows what his plans are. He only comes here to visit his father and his family. I am not even sure that he knows that this town is not Akpu, but Offiah," continued Nweke, smiling.

"When he settles down and asks me about our town, I will explain to him," Nweke assured Opulozor. Opulozor was noticeably uncomfortable about the comments of Ogbuefi, his friend. Opulozor was hoping that time had healed the wounds inflicted on Nweke and his family, but it seemed that the return of Ekigwe had reopened the wound if it ever healed. Opulozor was wondering where he belonged in this equation,

"Did Nweke consider Akilika part of Akpu Town which threw him out of his hometown?" worried Akilika.

"After all, I was an Akpu Elder when Nweke and his family were disgraced and thrown into exile," reasoned Akilika.

"Now that his son has become the Governor, will Nweke seek vengeance?" continued Akilika, thinking about the new developments.

Meanwhile, Nweke was waiting for Opulozor to leave so that he could scream for joy and let out the steam of excitement, which had been building up inside of him since Opulozor spilled the beans. He couldn't wait for Ekigwe to visit again and confirm Opulozor's story. Once in a while, thoughts would creep into Ogbuefi's mind that it could be a mere rumor. But Nweke would quickly dismiss the thought with, "There's no smoke without fire!"

Finally, Opulozor was ready to start the long trek back to Akpu. He was happy that he was still a friend to the father of the new Governor. But Opulozor didn't know that his friend didn't know his son was made Governor. He did not realize that he let the cat out of the bag! In their generation, rumors were more effective in news transmission than media.

Ogbuefi saw his friend off, walking with him a reasonable distance before turning back to return home. Ogbuefi felt like dancing as he walked back home, but he kept the information from Opulozor to himself. Nweke considered it unmanly to flippantly peddle an unsubstantiated tale like that without first getting confirmation from his son, Ekigwe. But since then, his countenance changed. He was always so happy that his wives wondered whether it was just the return of his son or something else.

"Whatever it is, it is better and safer to be around a happy Ogbuefi than an angry one," declared one of the wives.

CHAPTER TWENTY-THREE

One day, Odera, fed up with waiting, set out to meet Ekigwe. Odera was no longer a stranger to Ekigwe, having brought Ekigwe back to his long-lost family. So he went to Ekigwe with new confidence. He was armed with the Parish notebook containing the records of the rescued twins. Odera arrived at the Army Headquarters, still vibrant from an otherwise long and tiresome trip. He requested to see Major Ekigwe.

"Do you mean His Excellency Col. Ekigwe Nweke?" the soldier corrected.

Odera was confused but said, "Yes."

"Is His Excellency expecting you?" the soldier demanded with a probing countenance, looking very stern.

"Yes," answered Odera confidently.

Odera was given a seat where he sat for over an hour pondering the meaning of "His Excellency" and "Col."

"Has Ekigwe been promoted since I visited?" he wondered.

"But what is the meaning of 'His Excellency?'" he

continued to ponder.

When Ekigwe was told that Odera visited, he was troubled because he thought a serious problem had occurred in his family, as there was no talk that they would meet so soon.

Nevertheless, he sent for Odera.

Odera was ushered into Ekigwe's office in military style. The soldier who escorted Odera to Ekigwe's office saluted and marched off to Odera's fascination. Ekigwe welcomed Odera and beckoned on him to sit down.

"What will you drink?" asked Ekigwe.

"Thank you very much for the offer. Maybe later," answered Odera.

"Is all well with my family?" inquired Ekigwe almost nervously, studying Odera's countenance for any signs of trouble.

"Yes, all is very well," replied Odera, even though his personal problem with identity was reporting trouble in his countenance. So from Odera's countenance, Ekigwe felt that Odera was concealing a serious problem from him.

"Any message from my father or Adaobi?" Odera inquired

"I have not visited them since you left," replied Odera.

Ekigwe was very surprised. "So what brought the Reverend to my lowly office today?"

"On the contrary, Major, it is an honor for me to be welcomed into your highly esteemed office."

Ekigwe noted that Odera still called him Major because he hadn't known of his recent promotion and appointment. But he was so anxious to know the reason for his visit that he reserved informing Odera of the recent developments for later.

After they exchanged pleasantries and Ekigwe thanked him again for connecting him back to his long lost family, Odera asked him for some time to discuss the reason for his visit and a very critical subject. Ekigwe then took Odera to an inner and more relaxed office. As Odera described the subject of his visit as critical, Ekigwe concluded that somebody, maybe his father had died and Odera was trying to conceal it but could no longer hold it. Ekigwe was nervously all ears when Odera proceeded and narrated practically the story of his life. Odera interrupted himself intermittently with tears. Ekigwe's shock was complete when Odera handed him the old notebook of the Christians at the Akpu Parish of that time. Ekigwe noted in amazement that the notebook was older than him. Every atom of doubt harbored by Ekigwe concerning Odera's account of his relationship to Nweke was erased by the old notebook. Ekigwe got up and hugged Odera, calling him "my brother." The two men were in tears as they hugged each other.

"It has become very clear that the village gods could not change destiny," Ekigwe remarked after he recovered from the shock.

"Now I understand why the Church named you Odera (Destined)," continued Ekigwe.

Odera pleaded with Ekigwe not to tell Nweke or Adaobi the story, but to first of all ask

Mgbogafor if she ever had twins at the approximate period which was then thirty-two years before.

The plan was that both Ekigwe and Odera would go to Nweke's compound. While at Nweke's obi, both would excuse themselves from Nweke and go over to the wives' huts to greet the wives. They would then go alone to Mgbogafor's hut and ask her in private if she ever had twins, and if necessary, tell her Odera's story. The day to visit Nweke was fixed to be a day before the day selected for Nweke to introduce his son Ekigwe to Nweke's mother's brethren and his adopted village. But before Odera left, Ekigwe told him that there was some good news in the Army.

"You are aware that there was a bloodless military coup de tat a week ago?" Ekigwe asked Odera.

"Yes, and I actually wanted to ask you about it," remarked Odera.

"I was not among the coup plotters, but I gave them my support and access to my area of control. Fortunately, the coup was successful," continued Ekigwe.

Odera listened with rapt attention. The correction given him about Ekigwe's rank by soldiers was beginning to make sense to him.

"The new military ruling council promoted me to the rank of Colonel and appointed me the Military Governor of our state, the Amagu Central State," continued Ekigwe.

At this point, Odera jumped to his feet and saluted and embraced Ekigwe.

"Your Excellency," Odera addressed Ekigwe.

"God has done wonders in our family," declared Odera, indicating he now considered himself a member of Ekigwe's family.

"Truly when it rains it pours!" declared Odera about their family.

Ekigwe then assigned a military car to take Odera home. Odera was trembling with excitement at yet another explosive and unexpected development.

CHAPTER TWENTY-FOUR

On the appointed day, Nweke and his wives were already preparing for the celebration the next day of Ekigwe's historic return home and introduction to Nweke's mother's brethren and his adopted village. A big cow was tied to an orange tree waiting to be slaughtered for the occasion. The look on the cow's face suggested it understood that it was not part of the celebration, but only a victim. The women were busy preparing the soup ingredients and sifting the breadfruit to be cooked overnight. Nweke's compound was as busy as a beehive. It was as though they were preparing for the great Opoto feast. Ekigwe and Odera arrived at Nweke's compound in an unusually long military convoy of vehicles. Nweke was too excited to ask questions. Nweke received the august visitors, oblivious of another bombshell, this time concerning Odera, that was to follow. On noticing the unusual convoy, Nweke reminded Ekigwe that the appointed day was tomorrow but that they were nevertheless welcome every day if possible. The wives and the children, as well as the helpers helping to prepare the cooking, and neighbors gathered to look at the big military convoy outside. Little did the community know that it was the Governor in their midst which accounted for the long entourage which included journalists. Even Nweke, as well as his household, had not known that their son was the new Governor. Nweke ordered kola nuts, alligator peppers as well as fresh palm wine to be brought.

These three were never scarce in Nweke's Obi. The best palm wine tapper in Offia village was Nweke's customer and friend. So the best fresh palm wine was a constant in Nweke's Obi.

After Nweke lavishly entertained Ekigwe and Odera, they excused themselves to greet the wives. Ekigwe had not yet told Nweke about his promotion and appointment. Nweke attributed the unusual convoy to his son being a top military officer.

Ekigwe and Odera went straight to Uduaku, Ekigwe's mother, to greet her. Uduaku was surprised but happy to see them.

"My son, I think you forgot that your reception is tomorrow and not today," stressed Uduaku.

"Nevertheless, you are most welcome. You should stay till tomorrow," pleaded Ekigwe's mother excitedly. Ekigwe explained he had to be in his office early the next day but assured his mother they would be back. They then visited the huts of other wives and ended up at Mgbogafor's hut.

Ekigwe explained to Mgbogafor that they came to greet her last because they wanted an audience with her. Mgbogafor was the most senior wife although she didn't have any children. You must accord the senior wife the honor due to her. Mgbogafor was surprised at Ekigwe's request for an audience with her.

"What's important to discuss with a childless woman?" thought Mgbogafor.

Nevertheless, she gave them each a seat and listened. Ekigwe and Odera greeted Mgbogafor. Ekigwe then asked Mgbogafor if she ever had twins. Mgbogafor lied. She shook her head in the negative. Mgbogafor admitting she had a set of twins would be akin to leaking a cultural secret, almost like killing a masquerade, an abomination. Worse still, it would be the same as accusing her husband Nweke of murder! On hearing Mgbogafor's answer, Odera almost passed out. What saved the moment for Odera was the sudden change in Mgbogafor's countenance. Ekigwe didn't believe Mgbogafor. Before Ekigwe could repeat the question, Mgbogafor had drooped her head and tears started to drop from her eyes. Ekigwe knew that his question had touched a sore point but asked Mgbogafor what the problem was. Mgbogafor in her sob said she hoped they didn't come to mock her childlessness. Odera and Ekigwe consoled Mgbogafor and told her that she was not childless after all. Instantly, Mgbogafor lit up, cleaned her eyes and listened attentively to Ekigwe and Odera as if to say,

"I believe, say it."

Ekigwe then told Odera to narrate his story. By the time Odera told Mgbogafor the year that the twins were thrown into the Evil Forest and the rescue of one of the twins by the vigilant Christians, Mgbogafor sat up trembling.

"Where is the twin child?" Mgbogafor asked, screaming and visibly shaking.

At this point, Ekigwe dropped the bombshell:

"You are looking at the child," Ekigwe said, pointing to

Odera and unable to control his own tears. Odera was like somebody in a trance, speechless and just staring at nothing. Mgbogafor was screaming and rolling on the floor. She was asking repeatedly and turning the question into a song,

"Where is the child? Where is the child?...............?" and dancing to her song.

And soon the other wives rushed to Mgbogafor's hut in fear of what could have happened.

At first, the other wives were afraid and confused. But soon they understood the happy development and joined Mgbogafor to sing her song and dance,

"Where's the child? Where's the child?...............?"

Nweke's compound erupted in jubilation and commotion. The uproar in the wives' compound was deafening.

"My fellow women and people of Offia, please come and follow me to see and hear what I am hearing oh!"

"Come and witness the moon in broad daylight oh!"

"Offia oh, come and see another wonder oh!"

"My twin didn't die oh oh oh oh oh!" Mgbogafor sat on the bare dirt floor of the compound and threw her hand up to beckon on the ancestors to come and witness with her.

As Nweke heard the commotion at his wives' compound, he wondered what the uproar could mean.

"The other day, it was Ekigwe's reappearance. What has happened again?" Nweke wondered. Soon there was mass hysteria in the compound as villagers trooped in from all directions and gathered inside Nweke's compound at the alarm of his first wife, Mgbogo. Even the soldiers were perplexed at the cause of the commotion but made sure the Governor was alright.

"Strange happenings never seem to cease in Nweke's house," remarked a neighbor.

"Just a few weeks ago, his soldier son that was missing and taken for dead suddenly came home. And tomorrow is the day fixed for his welcome home party, and now this! What are we going to call this one? His son too? Wonders never cease! His soldier son must be in the house. See soldiers everywhere," the neighbor continued.

Nweke inquired about the cause of the commotion and was told it was about Odera, one of Mgbogafor's twins rescued by the Christians. He quietly walked back to his obi and took out his snuff-box. While all this wild celebration continued, Nweke drooped his head in thought, speechless to the extent that people became confused and were even afraid to congratulate him.

Nweke had mixed feelings. He was inclined to be happy but each time, a spirit of guilt and vengeance had the better of him. Among the things that worried Nweke was the man, Anayo from Okwe, who he killed as an ancestral spirit. He wondered whether the curses rained on him by the parents of Anayo had started to work. Then Nweke reminded himself,

"But it was not me, Nweke that killed the stranger from Okwe. He was killed by an ancestral spirit."

"Whatever curse they released is on their own head," continued Nweke.

"Ugbu (I reject)!" Nweke concluded.

CHAPTER TWENTY-FIVE

"It has become obvious that often foolishness is dressed up in a flowing garb and christened as wisdom. And the reverse is also the case," declared Nweke to himself concerning Akpu tradition and his own actions over the years.

Nweke thought that his gods in Akpu village had betrayed him again! They had lied to him and were a complete failure and disaster. Nweke listed a catalog of evils done to him by his gods. First, they called his twins an abomination. Next, they led him to throw away his twins and he left them to die in the despicable Evil Forest, making his first wife childless. He even had to drive away his wife back to her parents. Then the gods caused his son Ekigwe from his second wife to go on exile. Finally, the gods drove him from his fatherland to this place where he was today. And now the Christian God had rescued both Ekigwe and one of the twins, thereby exposing his wicked and ignorant deeds against his own family. How could he stand the shame?

Even though the happenings in Nweke's house were good and happy things, Nweke could only see his ignorance, his weakness and the exposure of his evil deeds.

"The gods have done their worst," he sighed.

"The gods have misled me to a three-way road, and I don't know which one I should follow," continued Nweke in his lamentation.

"Somebody has to pay for these wrongs meted out to Ekigwe and Odera. It is either the gods or myself," concluded Nweke with a suicidal tone and with vengeance.

It was certainly not between the gods of Offia and Nweke. It was between the gods of Akpu and Nweke. Nweke has no reach anymore to the gods of Akpu. So Nweke concluded that he had to pay. He planned to hang himself when everyone had gone to bed.

"An abomination is now a Priest of the Christian God."

"Somebody is lying!" continued Nweke viciously. Meanwhile, Nweke just had a melancholy smile hovering about his lips, chewing away on kola nuts and inhaling his snuff. Most of Nweke's family thought that he was overwhelmed by the successive good news and was simply yet to digest all the good news.

Ekigwe's and Adaobi's mother, Uduaku went into the obi to congratulate and rejoice with Nweke about yet more great news. Uduaku didn't like what she saw. She met Nweke in a strange mood. Among Nweke's wives, Uduaku understood Nweke the most. She smelled danger. She became terrified because she knew what such emotions could lead to, especially with Nweke, who should be happy rather than sad.

Uduaku called her son, Ekigwe, and Odera, warning them that unless they met their father and arrested whatever the problem was, anything was possible.

"Disaster looms," she told them.

"What do you mean by disaster?" queried Ekigwe, who looked completely perplexed.

"Disaster in the midst of rejoicing?" wondered Ekigwe aloud.

"Did you not see your father's mood?" Uduaku answered Ekigwe.

Ekigwe was now beginning to understand and snapped his fingers in disbelief.

Ekigwe and Odera then rushed to the obi to meet Nweke. Nweke's mood was sinister and melancholy. Odera pointedly asked Nweke if he was unhappy about his return. Nweke did not lie to them. He told them that he should be happy, but the gods had betrayed him.

Ekigwe was shocked, but Odera understood. Odera told Ekigwe that Nweke was suffering from a very serious guilt complex which if not carefully handled could lead to destructive tendencies. Ekigwe and Odera took Nweke to the ime obi (inner court) and talked with him. Odera started their meeting with prayer.

"In the name of the Father, of the Son and of the Holy Spirit," declared Odera in Igbo language. When Odera finished praying, Ekigwe answered, "Amen."

Nweke, who through the prayer session had been carefully observing his sons also answered "amen" after Ekigwe.

Then Nweke excitedly asked Odera, "My son, your god has a son and so he must have a wife and maybe a daughter also just like the Awuka masquerade," commented Nweke. "The only probable difference is that Awuka's son is a buffoon," continued Nweke.

Nweke was privately amazed and convinced that he had finally found a perfect connection with his sons' God in the famous Awuka masquerade. The Awuka masquerade was composed of husband, wife, son and daughter. It also had a police officer who could be the family orderly. Besides, Nweke wanted to create the impression that all was alright so that they would leave him alone to carry out his nefarious plan.

"Father, our God has no wife," corrected Odera. "He is a spirit and the creator of husbands and wives, and all flesh."

"But that's not why we came to meet you," continued Odera. "Let us discuss why we are here and not be distracted," Odera concluded.

"I'm all ears. You may go ahead," Nweke answered Odera.

"Nnayi (our father), why are you unhappy that your son came back alive, and how did the gods betray you?" Ekigwe asked their father.

"I am happy and unhappy at the same time," replied Nweke truthfully.

"Why are you unhappy," inquired Odera.

"Because I listened to the wicked gods of Akpu that you and your sister were an abomination. So I threw both of you into the Evil Forest to die."

"And why are you happy?" continued Odera.

"Because my eyes have seen you alive and the Akpu gods have been put to shame. They have been proven wrong. But where is your twin sister?" asked Nweke.

"I will tell you when the dust settles, father." And Odera immediately started shedding tears. It was now Nweke's turn to shelve his problems and console his son, helped by Ekigwe.

Odera in between tears said he had all his life longed

to call somebody father. But he was devastated because after searching for years, he had discovered his father, but it was like his father didn't want him.

"He has been moody since I came back home," Odera complained tearfully.

"I will leave so that he will be happy," concluded Odera.

"Tufiakwa," shouted Nweke. "The gods forbid."

At this point, Ekigwe brought out his handkerchief from his pocket and started to dab his own wet eyes. Maybe the soldier in Ekigwe prevented him from crying loudly. Even Nweke was broken, but it was unmanly in Ibo culture to cry. So he reached for his snuff-box while gnashing his teeth.

Odera's tears proved to be the psychological therapy that Nweke needed to save him from his suicide trap. It was the game-changer, turning the table of victim from Nweke to the real victim, Odera.

Odera's tears and threat to leave the family brought about a spirit of defiance in Nweke. It was no longer that somebody had to pay for these evils between Nweke and the gods.

"The gods have to pay," Nweke resolved.

Nweke had forgotten that his attempted assault on his personal god (Chi) failed, and now he had no more access to the Akpu gods. Besides, even if Nweke succeeded in smashing the head of his personal god against that iroko tree stem, he would have only succeeded in breaking a piece of wood. His personal god was not the wooden idol, but a spirit residing inside that wooden image.

"Why will Nweke commit suicide?" asked Nweke rhetorically.

"It's the gods that are guilty, and it's the gods, not

Nweke that must commit suicide," determined Nweke in his heart.

Then Nweke addressed his two sons.

"The gods of Akpu have misled me, not once and not twice," Nweke told his sons.

"I want my vengeance on the gods," Nweke concluded with clenched teeth.

"My God, the Christian God says that we should not seek revenge. He says that vengeance belongs to him," admonished Odera.

"In fact, He says that if somebody slaps you on one cheek, you should turn the other cheek and let him slap you also," continued Odera.

"The gods have given me a dirty slap," remarked Nweke.

"Are you saying I should turn the other cheek too for them to slap?"

"I want to hear you clearly," continued Nweke.

"My father, the village gods have wooden hands which cannot move. Suppose their hands could move, I won't advise you to turn the other cheek because they will break your jaws." Odera said, finally smiling. Ekigwe was suppressing the urge to laugh loudly.

Odera's comment about the wooden hands of Nweke's gods took Nweke by surprise. Nweke never really thought about that but was pensive for a while. Then he lamely replied to Odera.

"The gods have invisible hands."

Yet he was now confused concerning the wooden hands of his gods. It suddenly dawned on Nweke that his gods had actually never moved those hands.

"Our father," Odera called to Nweke.

"I am here, my son," answered Nweke.

"If you are indeed happy that your sons, Ekigwe and myself, have come back home alive, then listen to my advice," requested Odera.

"I am all ears," replied Nweke expectantly.

Then Odera proceeded to tell Nweke how the Christians rescued him alive, but his sister wasn't so fortunate because she had died before the Christians reached them. Nweke's countenance immediately changed on hearing about Odera's twin sister. It was obvious that Nweke was broken by that account and was seriously fighting tears like a man should. Odera proceeded to tell him how he was adopted and raised by the Christians. He told Nweke about his travel to Rome and how he became a priest of the Christian God.

Ekigwe also told Nweke how Adaobi smuggled him out of their house through the back village path to the Christians. Ekigwe told him his travails and even his attempt at suicide. Nweke was shocked but listened with rapt attention. The climax was when Ekigwe told his father that the Army had promoted him and made him Governor of the state. At this, Nweke rose up and did the cadenced dance of Ozo titled men in jubilation.

"So my son is now the governor of Akpu, Offiah and every town and village?"

"Yes father," confirmed Ekigwe.

Nweke continued his dance.

"Are your mothers aware of this?" asked Nweke.

"No father, you're the first ear to hear this besides Odera," answered Ekigwe to Nweke's delight.

Nweke then remembered that his friend Akilika heard it before him. "My son, you are now greater than all the

270

kings in this region put together. You are the one to approve their installation or disapprove even in a hereditary kingship," continued Nweke.

Nweke continued his dance before he settled down again for Odera to continue his story.

"So father, you can see that our God only does good things," Odera continued.

"He makes people happy, not sad," continued Odera.

At this point, Odera did not have to do the preaching as Nweke took over.

"I've heard with my ears and now I have also seen with my eyes, my sons."

"My sons, you are the living evidence of what your God can do and His power," remarked Nweke.

"Only Okwe Town understood my Akpu gods. They are nothing but delicious meat!" "Akpu gods, unlike your God, are full of lies and deceit," continued Nweke.

"They told us that nobody can survive in the Evil Forest. So they gave the Christians the Evil Forest to build the house of their God so that all the Christians would die and we won't have to fight them."

"But is it a secret today that all the Christians are still alive, including my own sons?

Instead are they not waxing stronger?" asked Nweke rhetorically.

"They even cleared the Evil Forest and made it a beautiful town so that the Evil Forest does not exist today," Nweke continued.

"Akpu gods commanded my twins to be thrown into another Evil Forest to die, but Odera was saved by the Christian God and is sitting right here with us today."

"Akpu gods wanted Ekigwe dead. Is it not Ekigwe that

is right here with us and is the Governor of the state?" Nweke continued.

"Remember Nwaforcha?" asked Nweke

"Akpu gods cast Nwaforcha away from the village and from his family."

"Nwaforcha was rescued and raised by the Christian God and returned to Akpu like a king."

"Nwaforcha became the richest man in this region.

"And finally," concluded Nweke.

"The gods uprooted me from my ancestors and exiled me to another soil where I am today!"

"Am I not today the father of a Reverend Father and the Governor?" Nweke kept going on and on.

"The Christian God will return me to the land of my ancestors again," prophesied Nweke.

Ekigwe and Odera said, "Amen"

"The list goes on....." Odera continued.

"Our people say that when two elephants fight, the grass suffers," said Odera.

"But father, the angels of my God have obviously overpowered the gods of Akpu which is why we are here today celebrating. It was a vicious battle, but he gave Ekigwe, myself, Nwaforcha and even you the victory," concluded Odera.

"But father, the gods of Offiah are not different from Akpu gods. They are all the same and evil. They have eyes but they don't see, ears but they don't hear, hands that don't move. Have you ever seen Akpu Ukwu move from its shrine or your Chi move out of your compound with its legs?" asked Odera.

"No, I have not seen them walk my son," answered Nweke, privately startled that it had never occurred to him.

"Do you know why father?" continued Odera

"No, my son," answered Nweke again.

"It is because these gods are made of wood, and carved by man's hands. Sometimes they are made of clay or mud. At best they could be made of iron but it doesn't make them different," concluded Odera.

"Does your Christian God move?" inquired Nweke expecting to get an affirmative response.

"Our God does not have to move because He's everywhere at the same time," answered Odera.

"He sits on His throne in heaven, yet is everywhere!" continued Odera.

"Is that not wonderful?" asked Odera.

Nweke was confused and surprised but kept quiet.

"My God that made heaven and earth and everything in them, wants to help you," Odera continued.

"That is why he saved your children and made you see them again. And that is also why he has today made you a father of the Governor!"

"He is the great and true God," remarked Odera.

"You said your God sits in heaven?" asked Nweke

"Yes, father"

"Our Chukwu-Okike also sits above in heaven. But the gods who are his agents are here with us like Okochi and Akpu Ukwu," proclaimed Nweke with an air of 'yeah, we're on the same level.'

"Father, there goes the main difference between your gods and our God. The agents of your Chukwu-Okike are man-made. The agent of our God is the Son of our God and He is equal with our God. He is not man-made but He created all men, including you."

"If you notice, Akpu gods which are made of wood are simply houses for the devil, who you cannot see with the ordinary eye," continued Odera.

"Odera my son, what are you still waiting for? Show me the Son of your God and your God."

"I want to follow the Son of your God. Let me sacrifice a cow to the Son of your God. What is He made of?" asked Nweke.

"He must be made of iron because He is such a powerful God," Nweke concluded. Nweke was asking so he could make his own god out of iron also. But Odera told Nweke his God is not made of wood or iron.

"If your god is made of gold, please don't ever say it aloud because these young men of today will steal your god in a blink of an eye," Nweke advised.

Odera and Ekigwe burst out laughing but then Odera remembered the shiny statue of Mary in front of the Offiah church and reasoned that Nweke might be referring to it. Then Odera remembered the Ten Commandments.

"Thou shall not make unto thee, any graven images......for I am a jealous God." Odera became subdued and wondered the difference between his father's wooden idols and those graven images molded by the church. Odera and Ekigwe looked at each other as if Ekigwe was also thinking the same thing. Ekigwe told his father that the most important development in all this was that out of the embers of Akpu tradition had risen a new hope for him in the persons of Odera and Ekigwe.

At this point, Ekigwe looked at his watch and begged to excuse himself. Ekigwe believed that the dark cloud that hovered over his father was dispersed. He went to the hut of his mother and the other women and said bye. His convoy made its way back to the Army Headquarters, leaving the community wondering at Nweke, his family and all the drama.

Odera got himself back and told Nweke,

"Your gods are made by hands and by men."

"Our God is invisible and is not made by any man. Rather, He created all men."

Unknown to Ekigwe and Odera, Nweke was desperate to mold the God who made Nweke's wealth look like poverty in comparison to Nwaforcha's wealth and who rescued and made Ekigwe and Odera prosper. Nweke wanted to replace his failed gods with this God.

Then Nweke asked Odera,

"What is the name of your God and where is he? Let me sacrifice to him."

"We don't sacrifice to our God," answered Odera.

"Our God is not a hungry God. We don't give Him chickens and cows. He doesn't eat them. He gives to us," Odera continued.

Nweke chuckled,

"Do you think our gods ate those chickens?" asked Nweke, amused at the apparent ignorance of his son.

"My son, we ate the chickens. The gods took the blood only," Nweke continued, answering his own question.

"But don't worry, just tell me the name of your God." insisted Nweke.

Odera, frustrated but amused, answered his father,

"Your insistence in knowing the name of my God suggests something to me. Do you determine the power of a god by its name?"

"My son, use your tongue to count your teeth," replied Nweke.

"Well my father, the name of my God is not Tortoise; it is neither Python nor Ikenga.

The name of the Son of our God and the name of our God is the same. His names are Chukwu-Okike, Jehova, Jesus Christ." Odera left that food for thought with Nweke and got up to leave. He went to the huts of the wives greeting them and promised to be back the following day for Ekigwe's reception and now his reception also. Odera went back to Akpu happy and accomplished.

But once again alone in his hut, Nweke had a lot of reflection to do. First, he muttered to himself that though it was wise for him to be careful in embracing his sons' God, nothing is left to doubt that his gods, both Akpu gods and Offiah gods were a great misadventure. He reasoned that he would be gradual in disengaging himself from the weaker gods to avoid any clashes with the village elders. He figured he would be able to do that safely after Ekigwe was entrenched as Governor.

"Secondly," reasoned Nweke, "wisdom is not by age anymore because my sons have almost made rubbish of all the wisdom of our forefathers within a short period because they were pragmatic and followed the wisdom of the moment rather than blindly follow the status quo.

"Who can challenge the Government today even in matters of culture. Is it not the Government that controls the soldiers, the police and even approves the appointment of the Paramount Chiefs, the very head of the tradition? When Ekigwe was disobeying me and refusing to follow our culture with me, there must have been something he saw that I didn't see. I think he saw the future. He saw the new yardstick for wealth and nobility. Who can argue with him on that? After all, Ekigwe is the highest power in the state today. He challenged the tradition and got away with it. It will be foolhardy for you to challenge his tradition today. His brother Umeh, who was the good boy because he followed me in our tradition cannot even pay the bride price for his wife. If Ekigwe did not come to the rescue, it would have been the family shame to be told from generation to generation. It would have been retained as folklore in Akpu Town.

"Tufiakwa! No wonder, Nwaforcha was the first into the future and disagreed with his father. He then insisted on transferring it to Ekigwe. But how did both Nwaforcha and Ekigwe get the wisdom to see into the future? Was it not through the Christian God and the Christian school? Wow! This whole mystery is finally unraveling," concluded Nweke.

Pragmatism seems to be the new definition of wisdom.

CHAPTER TWENTY-SIX

Ekigwe was no longer the oldest son of Nweke, but Odera. Realizing this, Odera paid more attention to Akpu Town, especially salvaging whatever was left of the heritage of his father Nweke in Akpu Town, Akpu culture and Nweke's larger Akpu family. Odera had quietly traced the original home of his father, Nweke, in Akpu when he was still researching about Ekigwe for Adaobi. He was in tears when he revisited it and saw the wreckage of what used to be his ancestral home now overgrown with weeds and remembered the story behind Nweke's exile to his mother's town, Offiah. But Odera never tried to enter the remains of the compound as he did not want neighbors to start wondering what the Parish Priest was looking for in that abandoned compound. Odera was particularly interested in rebuilding their father's Akpu home and restoring Nweke's glory in Akpu. He dreamed of the eventual return of his father and entire family back to Akpu. He reasoned,

"Now that Ekigwe will be inaugurated as Governor, the Chiefs and Elders of Akpu will be too happy to welcome my family back to their roots." But that was for Nweke to decide.

"Who wouldn't want to claim the Governor as their son? Certainly, Akpu will jump at that," continued Odera, very excited at the thought. Odera was now back from Offiah to his Parish house at the Akpu Church. Throughout that evening and the following days, Odera reflected on his life history starting from when he was thrown into the Evil Forest, his rescue by the Church and his travails in search of his real family. And now his full discovery of his identity and all of it left Odera completely overwhelmed. For days, Odera shed tears severally, sometimes tears of joy and sometimes tears for his twin sister who he never met. Odera thought he ought to write a story of his life's travails and triumph, not necessarily for himself, but at least in memory of his twin sister.

"What should I title this book?" Odera thought.

"I should have titled it after my sister, but she wasn't even named before she died!

Nobody rejoiced over her birth." Odera continued almost aloud, tears beginning to well up in his eyes. After Odera calmed down, he mused over several titles and settled with "The Embers of Tradition." Odera said within himself that he chose that title because,

"My sister was the victim of a vicious tradition, fueled by ignorance, leaving destruction and death in its trail." He continued,

"My greatest sadness is that she could neither complain nor seek redress for the damages inflicted on her."

Finally, it was time for Odera to get down to work towards forging a strong bond with Akpu Town and the eventual restoration of Nweke's Akpu family home.

"But for me to accomplish this mission, I need to forgive Akpu Town concerning my sister so that I can heal," reasoned Odera.

"But where do I start?" he pondered.

"The Parish!" he shouted, punching his clenched right fist into the air.

Odera was well-liked by the Parish, and Odera believed that the elders in the Church would be very willing to work with him in reaching the elders of Akpu. So he had that settled in his mind as a great strategy. Odera felt that once he captured the goodwill of the town towards the Church, he would have gone halfway in restoring his father's estate.

The following Sunday after Mass, Odera invited some Church elders to a meeting in his office. Odera was careful to avoid linking his family with Akpu or the story of his life. He felt that it could breed bad blood with the Traditional elders of Akpu who he was trying to woo, as it could seem like an accusation. Odera outlined the purpose of the meeting and told the elders that he wanted a united Akpu where the Church and the Traditionalists would coexist in peace. He pointedly requested their help in reaching out to the Traditional Elders to meet with him at the Church premises. The response of the Church elders was unanimous. They agreed that two weeks was enough for them to reach out to the Traditional Elders and bring them to the Church meeting. So Father Odera fixed the meeting for the next two Sundays. The elders were only too happy to help with reaching out to the Akpu Traditional elders on behalf of their Reverend Father. Above all, the Church elders were privately happy to discover that they had indirectly been connected to the new Governor through their Priest. But they had not summoned the courage to ask Reverend Father Odera about the rumor concerning him, which was making the rounds in Akpu, especially among the Christians. Because of that rumor, unknown to Odera, Akpu Church elders and the whole of Akpu Church were very eager to help plan to bring back their Priest's family from exile in Offiah. Akpu Church elders did not want Offiah to claim ownership of the new Governor even though they had no proof of their assumptions. Odera's standing as the Parish Priest of Akpu had a brand new dimension since the rumor that he was the direct senior brother of the new Governor. In Akpu, rumor was more powerful than the newspaper! An elder commented while gossiping with another elder concerning whether the hardcore traditionalists of Akpu would welcome Nweke back from exile:

"Don't you know our people again?"

"How do you mean?" queried the other elder.

"The majority of the so-called die-hard traditionalists are mere sycophants," he answered.

"Just wait and you'll see that they will all be at the Priest's beck and call," he continued.

"They all have a price on their heads," concluded the elder, both men looking at each other knowingly.

"Besides, the law of the land today is very clear. It is no longer at the whims and caprices of Akpu chiefs or Akpu tradition," commented the other elder in agreement.

"At our first meeting with the Priest, I remember him telling us that he is a survivor of the horrors of tradition," continued the second elder.

"What did he tell you all?" asked the first elder, looking very curious.

"He did not elaborate, but it is rumored in Akpu that his father escaped death in the hands of the Masquerade Cult or the Ancestral Spirits. Just before the arrival of the ancestral spirits, his daughter ran to his mother's brethren to tell them that her father was stubborn and had refused all entreaties to leave his house but instead loaded his Dane gun to confront the ancestral spirits. Men from Nweke's mother's family rushed to Akpu and took him away by force to Offiah where he is still today in exile. Thus, Nweke was saved from being burnt alive in his home."

"Why would they want to burn him alive?" queried the first elder.

"His offense was that his son, who is now the new Governor killed a masquerade! They actually wanted to burn down just his home, but he refused to leave. Instead, he loaded his gun and waited for the Ancestral Spirits to come rather than dance naked at the market square. That was when his daughter sent an S.O.S. message to his mother's people. They came and took him away by force and saved his life," continued the second elder.

"You know that Nweke is not the kind of man you can disgrace. He would rather die than do such a thing like dance naked in public. His love for tradition does not go that far," he emphasized.

"Our Parish Priest and his twin sister were thrown into the Evil Forest at birth to die according to our tradition but vigilant parishioners rescued him. His sister did not make it before the Christians arrived," continued the second elder.

"I already told you that his brother, the new Governor killed a masquerade. His father wanted him to face the wrath of the ancestral spirits, but he was smuggled out to the Christians, leaving his father to face the ancestral spirits. The story sounds like a fairy tale," he concluded.

"But please if you quote me, I will deny you. It is just the rumor going on in town. I don't know this Nweke, but I heard he was a tough man," he warned.

The first meeting between Odera, a select number of Church elders and some key traditional elders of Akpu Town took place inside the church hall. It was unprecedented to have heathen Akpu elders inside the Church premises in peace.

The Church elders ushered the Akpu heathen elders into the church hall and gave them seats. There was a brief exchange of greetings in Igbo language between the Christian elders and the heathen Akpu elders. While they waited for the Parish Priest, the heathen elders roamed the church hall with their eyes on the colored glass decorations and the graven images. Of particular attention was the statue of Mary carrying baby Jesus as well as the statue of Peter. They said nothing, but one could imagine them saying,

"That statue resembles the shrine of our god Igodo."

Just then the Parish Priest entered the hall. He was fixated on the heathen elders and seemed to be momentarily also wondering what was on their minds. Father Odera entered the hall accompanied by his assistant, a young Catechist who was to act as the secretary. The meeting was held in the native Igbo language. Odera's discovery of his identity clearly showed recently in his happiness and self-confidence.

The entry of Odera took both elders by storm. What happened next shocked both the Church and the heathen elders, though pleasantly,

"Ibe anyi Kwenu!" declared Father Odera, with a raised clenched right fist toward the perplexed elders who were witnessing this type of greeting by a Reverend Father for the first time.

"Yeaah," came the inevitable and enthusiastic response.

"Akpu kwenu!"

"Yeaah!"

"Kwenu!"

"Yeaah!"

"Kwezuenuoooo!"

"Yeaaaaaah!"

"Greetings, my beloved elders," greeted the Parish Priest in the native dialect.

"Greetings, Father," responded the Church elders.

The heathen elders mumbled something in Igbo, apparently unsure of how to greet a Reverend Father. The mutual glance among the heathen elders suggested that they were saying among themselves concerning the Reverend Father's greeting,

"Did you see what I just saw? This is surprisingly a familiar and friendly terrain my fellows!"

Father Odera took his seat facing all the elders. He thanked them for answering his call.

"I am not a white priest, but one of you. I did not greet you in the white man's language," he declared. Odera remembered his discussion with Father Jude during his visit to Achara Town Parish in search of Ekigwe. How the Parish allowed the heathens to convert to Christianity while retaining their traditional practices like polygamy and the Ozo title. Father Odera was not comfortable with the practice of allowing heathen converts to retain their ozo titles inside the Church. However, he had not settled on how to deal with it without sending the wrong signal to the heathens of Akpu, especially when most parishes practiced it. Besides, Father Odera remembered that he hadn't dealt with a rumor in Akpu that the Church collected levies. They asked what the Church did with church offerings, and it was rumored that they collected it to send to the Pope. The rumor claimed that the white man brought the Church to exploit the people financially, just as they imposed taxes on every adult.

Father Odera signaled the Catechist to go and fetch the kola nuts accompanied with garden eggs and the peppered groundnut source. The Catechist soon came in with the kola nut and the rest. A boy accompanied the Catechist, carrying a big keg of foaming fresh palm wine. He dropped the keg and rushed out to bring the gourds for drinking the palm wine. Then Father Odera continued,

"My fathers, I have brought you kola nuts to welcome you to Akpu Parish." Surprise and happiness were written on their faces, and they thanked Father Odera for the great reception accorded them. As they settled down to eat the kola nuts and drink palm wine, Father Odera addressed them,

"This meeting is the first of its kind in the history of Akpu Town. It is evidence of great unity in Akpu and united, we will make Akpu a very great town," declared Father Odera. There were mumblings of agreement on the Father's assertion. Then Odera continued,

"I request that everyone should feel at ease to contribute his ideas. Two good heads are better than one. Is that not true, my people?" There was another unanimous agreement, "You have said the truth."

Odera went on to tell Akpu Traditional elders the position of the Church concerning traditions like polygamy, masquerades, Chieftancy titles like the Ozo and the village feasts. On polygamy and chieftaincy titles, Odera told them that the Church had no problems with them. He told them that the Church would not forbid them from converting and cited some Church elders seated at the meeting as examples. He told them to feel free to approach him and find out things for themselves rather than depend on rumors. On the masquerades and the village feasts, Odera assured them that the Church did not come to Akpu to condemn or destroy the tradition of the people but to strengthen it.

"What we ask for is mutual respect. The masquerades should respect the Church premises whereas the Church respects the freedom of the masquerades outside the Church premises. The God of the Church, our God, has commanded us to love our neighbors and to help them in every way possible." Odera declared. He continued,

"One of the things we plan to do in helping to develop Akpu is to build schools so that Akpu children will be trained for important positions in our society." He cited the son of an Akpu heathen who rose to become a police Sergeant after going through Akpu Church school and later the police academy. He then asked the elders,

"Who is today benefitting from the police Sergeant's education, his high position and his wealth?"

"Is it Akpu Church or the Sergeant's father?" continued the Parish Priest.

"The Sergeant's father of course," agreed the elders in unison.

"So we can see that we can educate our children and still enjoy our tradition within the laws of the land." Odera was making a veiled reference to the killing of twins.

"Do you realize that the richest people in Akpu today all went through the Church school? And they still enjoy all the benefits of Akpu tradition. Do they not enjoy the jokes of Atunma masquerade or the dance of the Ogbangbada masquerade?" Odera continued.

Most of the heathen elders didn't know when they nodded their heads in agreement to the obvious delight of the Parish Priest. They discussed amongst themselves in low tones about the many possibilities in Akpu with this Parish Priest. When the euphoria died down, the Parish Priest told them that the floor was open for suggestions and ideas, and he was all ears to hear contributions on how to move Akpu forward.

A Traditional elder said that on behalf of other Traditional elders, that it was his pleasure to inform the Parish Priest that the Traditional Ruler, the Paramount Chief of Akpu was aware of their participation in the meeting and gave his blessings to the meeting as well as his greetings to the Parish Priest.

When the Colonial Masters came to the region, they found out that these Igbo people, unlike the other peoples, did not have kings but were republican in nature. They found that to be very inconvenient for what they came to do on these shores. They did not want to waste their time in administering these people. So they appointed what they termed Paramount Chiefs. So they passed instructions through the Paramount Chiefs who served the same purpose as the kings, which was obtainable amongst the other peoples of the region.

The Traditional elder further said that the Parish Priest should give them some time to go round to all the Akpu elders and hear them out first, after which they would come back. Odera agreed that it was a reasonable thing to do and said he hoped that they would be through with that in time for a follow-up meeting. The elders gave the Parish Priest assurances of their loyalty in that regard. Father Odera declared the meeting a great success and told the elders that the meeting was over. He told the elders that he had some gifts for them to thank them for answering his call.

Father Odera gestured for the Catechist to bring the gift of Schnapps and tobacco leaves wraps which the Parish Priest kept as a gift for the elders. The Catechist gave every elder the gift, which was arguably the best thing you could give an Igbo elder. The elders made the indispensable snuff from the tobacco leaves. Both Traditional and Church elders were speechless at the generosity and reception of the Parish Priest. A spokesman emerged immediately for the elders,

"We the elders of Akpu carry our load of thanks to you. We have seen that God has good things lined up for Akpu because since you came to Akpu, it is only good things and peace that Akpu has known. It is our prayer that our relationship with you and the Church keeps growing to the benefit of the whole town, both the Traditional and the Church citizens."

"I say a resounding amen to that," responded Father Odera. The elders started to leave for their respective villages. It was very obvious that they were happy from the meeting, as they walked along out of the Parish courtyard in a jolly mood. Tobacco and Schnapps were exactly among what the colonial masters used to entice the natives after which they took many precious things, including slaves, from them. The story of the Parish Priest's generosity and acknowledgment of Akpu tradition went around Akpu Town very fast.

Two weeks later, approximately four Akpu market weeks, the elders assembled again at the Parish hall for a follow-up meeting. This time they were all familiar with each other and with the Parish Priest.

The Parish Priest welcomed them, "Akpu Kwenu!" greeted Father Odera.

"Yeaaaaaa!" was the elder's response.

"Kwenu!"

"Yeaaaaa!"

"Kwezuonu!"

"Yeaaaaa!"

"I am sure that you know that you are always welcome to Akpu Parish. It is my pleasure to host you again," Odera assured the elders.

The Parish Catechist served the elders kola nuts and palm wine and the meeting started.

"The first part of the agenda for today's meeting is to detail how the Church and Akpu will work together to benefit the good people of Akpu," declared the Parish Priest.

"The second part is how Akpu will take part in the inauguration of the new Governor," continued Father Odera. "The inauguration of the Governor will take place in about three weeks. This part is indeed for Akpu to decide. But I simply want to state that the Church is ready to offer whatever help she is asked to give in this regard. I mentioned it here because representatives of the elders of

Akpu, as well as most Ichies, are here, and the Igwe listens to you," continued the Parish Priest.

The Traditional elders, the Igwe, as well as Akpu Town had not known that the new Governor was their own son who they caused to run for safety in exile. So far it was only known by a few people in Akpu as a rumor. But they had no idea whatsoever that the Parish Priest was a son of Akpu, albeit an abomination. Neither did they know of any connection between the Parish Priest and the new Governor. Even Ekigwe, the Governor, had not addressed the issue of which town to actually call home with his father Nweke. Nweke expected Akpu, which drove them out in the first place to request for them if they so desired, and they must conduct all the necessary rites to reverse what they originally did to Nweke and his family. But Nweke's friend Opulozor cautiously hinted on the matter of Nweke's return to Akpu when he visited Nweke with the gossip that Ekigwe was rumored to be the new Governor of their State.

"Concerning the first agenda, the Church has obtained the approval of the Bishop to establish another school in Akpu, specifically in Obinagu village so as to bring the school closer to all parts of Akpu Town." There was thunderous applause.

Then the Parish Priest who hitherto had been speaking in Igbo added,

"The ball is now in your court, and it is up to you to enroll your children in the school nearest you."

There were some unsettling grumbles and chit chat among the elders. An elder visibly disturbed by the Parish Priest's suggestion about the ball murmured to another elder,

"I thought that this Priest is a good man. But how can he say such a thing?"

"I wonder," agreed the second elder.

The Parish priest observed the murmuring among the elders and noticed the uncomfortable expressions on their faces and asked,

"Is everything okay?"

One of the Christian elders replied,

"Mazi Oji is asking if you said that our children can now play football when you build the new school? Because Ekene's son broke his leg in the process and is yet to recover."

"I did not say that, my elders," replied the Parish Priest laughing. I said that it will then be up to you to send your children to the nearest school," explained the Parish Priest, and everybody joined him to laugh. Father Odera asked the elders if anyone had another question or desired more clarification. Nobody had any more issues, so Father Odera thanked the elders and brought the meeting to a close.

Akpu Town started to prepare for the inauguration of the new Governor. As expected, every town was also preparing and trying to outdo the others in impressing the Governor. Akpu obtained permission from the State capital city to set up the biggest masquerade, Ijele, at the venue a day before the event. The Ijele masquerade was massive and needed a lot of time and effort to set up.

Finally, the day arrived for the new Governor to meet the people. The capital city of Amagu Central State, Obodo Ukwu was bustling with an unusual amount of people and vehicles as delegations of different towns arrived. Some came with dances as well as masquerades to entertain and impress the new Governor. By noon, all the delegations from various towns had settled down at the spaces allotted them and waited for the Governor to arrive. Only Akpu Town had the Ijele masquerade in tow.

The long motorcade of the Governor snaked through the city into the stadium. There was an announcement that the Governor had arrived. As he proceeded to take his seat at the VIP stand, he was greeted with a deafening ovation. The Master of Ceremony introduced Governor Ekigwe Nweke with fanfare,

"People of great Amagu Central State, let us rise up and give our young and able Governor, Colonel Ekigwe Nweke, a rousing welcome." Immediately thousands of people rose up for a tumultuous welcome for Governor Ekigwe Nweke. The Master of Ceremony continued with the reception,

"His Excellency, you can see that the people of Amagu Central State are very happy and have great expectations." He now handed over the microphone to the Governor.

"I greet you, great people of Amagu Central State. I thank you for this great gathering to welcome me. I promise that I will not disappoint you, but we are going to be partners in progress to build up our state. Am I speaking your mind?"

There was a thunderous applause and agreement. Then the Governor handed back the microphone to the Master of Ceremony. The Master of Ceremony started to call the towns in alphabetical order to come and march past and entertain the Governor. Akpu Town was one of the first called, "The great people of Akpu should please proceed to the VIP area, please." Akpu Town led by the Paramount Ruler, Igwe Odogwu, rose and went around, stopping at the VIP area and greeting the Governor, dancing to the Ijele rhythm. The crowd roared in admiration of the Ijele masquerade. The march past continued till the turn of Offiah Town. Only Akpu displayed the majestic Ijele masquerade. There was no mention of the home town of the Governor by the Master of Ceremony. At the end of the day's event, it was obvious that Akpu Town gave a good account of herself.

Later that week, Akpu received a letter from the Governor's office that Akpu Town was one of the first official visits of the Governor. Akpu prepared for the Governor's visit very seriously, proud that the Governor chose them for his first visit.

"Was it because of our Ijele masquerade display at his inauguration?" wondered the Paramount Ruler. Also, the Church elders kept wondering what would happen when the Governor visited,

"Will the Governor confirm the rumors that he is from Akpu Town, or will he still keep us in suspense? Will he claim Offiah as his hometown? Will he introduce our Parish Priest as his brother?" Even Odera knew that his dreams about returning to his ancestral home, Akpu Town, depended more on Nweke than on either himself or Ekigwe. But Father Odera prepared for the Governor's visit because he knew that the Governor must stop over at his Parish during his visit, not because he was the Parish Priest, but because they were brothers.

Akpu Town prepared to receive the Governor at the main market square, Oye Market, were Akilika once reported to Nweke that he saw Ekigwe stretching his neck admiringly at the Christian boys playing football. A few days into the Governor's visit, the Paramount Ruler and his council invited the Parish Priest to the occasion.

It was early morning in Akpu on the day of the Governor's visit. There was unusually heavy human traffic on the main road of Akpu. All roads led to Oye market, and both human and masquerade dancers were seated at allocated positions at the market square. Of course, the Ijele masquerade had a prominent presence at the market square. Later the Paramount Ruler and the Red Cap Chiefs were seated surrounding the High Table. Father Odera was now also seated at the High Table, and everybody waited patiently for the Governor's arrival. Akpu Town had a carnival atmosphere.

The noise of the Governor's entourage could now be heard from the distance. The Governor entered the venue greeted by loud applause. The Governor acknowledged the greetings by waving his hands towards all angles of the gathering. The Paramount Ruler, surrounded by Red Cap Chiefs and top elders of Akpu delivered the welcome address,

"His Excellency, the Governor of Amagu Central State, it is a great honor and privilege to Akpu Town that you chose us as your first official visit. I, on behalf of Akpu Town, welcome you to our great town. It is our hope that you find this august visit memorable." The Paramount Ruler then sat down. It was now time for the Governor to give his address. As the Governor stood up, the square for the first time became quiet and pregnant with great expectation.

The Governor looked round the square, cleared his throat and shouted greetings, "Akpu kwenu!"

"Yeaah!" responded the crowd.

"Kwenu!"

"Yeaaah!" responded the crowd again.

"Muanu!"

"Yeaaah!" answered the crowd.

"Zuanu!"

"Yeaaaaah!" came the final response of the crowd.

"Thank you, thank you, thank you for your kind reception," repeated the Governor, feeling emotional. "Eze Odogwu, the Paramount Ruler of the great people of Akpu probably did not realize that he was right on point when he said that he hoped I find this visit memorable," said the Governor. Again the arena became extremely quiet as if the people were in great expectation. They soon got more than they expected as the Governor continued, his voice almost breaking down with emotion, "Except for two brief visits to my senior brother who is your Parish Priest seated here, this is my first visit to Akpu since I left it as a young boy twenty years ago," continued the Governor, dabbing his eyes with a handkerchief. The shock in the arena was so thick you could touch it. Even the Governor's entourage was in shock at what was unfolding. Then the Governor continued,

"I was falsely accused of killing a masquerade. When uncountable ancestral spirits amassed at my compound, my sister helped me escape to the Church. Then my father was told to produce me or dance naked in my place at this very market square. He refused and eventually went in exile to his mother's town, Offiah, till today. My senior brother and I met for the first time less than a year ago, as he was thrown into the Evil Forest at birth because he was a twin, but vigilant members of Akpu Church rescued him alive. His twin sister wasn't as fortunate. She had died before help came. If my brother was not posted to Akpu and still wasn't inquisitive enough to investigate a very old record of his rescue from the Evil Forest, I would never have known he is my brother."

The Paramount Chief was shaken and troubled by the Governor's bombshell.

"Will he seek vengeance?" worried the Paramount Chief. Even the Parish Priest was not prepared for the Governor's revelation of the family's ordeal at the hands of Akpu Tradition. Father Odera was equally very uncomfortable. Besides the Governor, a lot of people were also teary-eyed.

The Governor controlled his emotions a bit and continued with his address, "Beloved Akpu fathers and brethren, my tears are not tears of agony but tears of joy that I am today standing on Akpu soil again. Just like Joseph in the bible told his brethren, the sons of Jacob who sold him to Egypt, I tell you today, "Be not grieved or angry with yourselves that you caused me to escape into exile, for it was not you that did it, but God did send me before you to preserve you in posterity." With that, the Governor concluded his speech and thanked the people of Akpu for their reception, "Thank you. Thank you. Thank you," and sat down.

The rest of the evening was more relaxed. The Paramount Chief and the elders felt better after the Governor revealed that he bore no grudges toward the Akpu people for his life's ordeal. The various dance groups performed to the delight of the Governor and all that gathered at the market square.

The Paramount Chief spoke again, thanking the Governor for his revelation and magnanimity. He said that the Governor demonstrated the true spirit of a noble Akpu man.

"His humility and spirit of forgiveness are unprecedented," declared the Paramount Chief.

"The true blood of Akpu runs in His Excellency, our great Governor. He has shown that he is indeed God-sent," concluded the Paramount Chief.

After the closing remarks of the Paramount Chief, the Governor and his entourage rose to leave the square. As the Governor rose from his seat, a deafening ovation erupted in the square. The Governor drove straight to the Parish to visit Father Odera. Father Odera entertained his brother the Governor and his entourage. Father Odera had a private meeting with the Governor where they fixed a meeting with their father Nweke at Offiah in a week. The Governor and his entourage left Father Odera to reflect on the historic event of the day.

The next day, a delegation of Akpu elders led by the Paramount Chief paid a surprise visit to the Parish. They came to seek Father Odera's consent to take a delegation of Akpu elders to Offiah, "We have come to let you know that the revelation of the Governor yesterday was deeply felt in our hearts. We are thankful to God for the kindness of the Governor. The Governor displayed a great spirit of humility in speaking out and forgiving us. We hope that you share his feelings of kindness and you have also forgiven us."

Odera gave them his assurances, "I don't even have a choice because our God said that if you don't forgive people who sin against you, God will not forgive you your own sins against Him."

The Paramount Chief thanked him and pleaded, "We therefore request that you take us to go to Offiah and see your father and also ask for his forgiveness. We are ready to do what your father requires from Akpu and what your father's family in Offiah requires of us in order to bring back your family to Akpu even though the evil of years past cannot be reversed and we cannot remove the agony, the shame and all the losses already suffered by your family. Now we know that we did all that we did to your family in ignorance. What our fathers thought was wisdom, we now know to be utter foolishness. But even that foolishness was passed on to them by their forebears. They could not see it because they were not blessed with visionary youth like the Governor and the Parish Priest who could see the woes of it and be bold to stand up against such practices."

The Paramount Chief was referring to the throwing away of twins into the Evil Forest.

"We have come to ameliorate the past actions of our forefathers and undo all that is undoable," concluded the Paramount Chief.

Father Odera then thanked the Paramount Chief and all the elders with him and assured them that the family had forgiven them and were looking forward to a happy future relationship with Akpu Town.

"We look forward not backward and what is on our mind now is how we can move Akpu to greater heights," Father Odera assured Akpu elders.

Father Odera discussed with the Paramount Chief and the elders and both agreed on a date which the Parish Priest would escort them to his father in Offiah. Father Odera and the Governor had already agreed to return to their ancestral home in Akpu. Even though that decision lied on the lap of their father, Nweke, they knew that based on recent interactions with him, convincing their father would not be a tedious task.

As Father Odera bade farewell to the Paramount Chief and the elders, he remembered his last discussions with his Father Nweke, which clearly showed that somebody had mistaken foolishness for wisdom. Nweke had told Odera that Akpu gods deceived him into believing that his twin son was an abomination, and now the abomination had become a Priest of the Christian God. And also that his son Ekigwe had committed an abomination because he 'killed' a masquerade. Again, the Christian God had made the same one that committed the abomination become the Governor of the state. The same town where the abomination occurred was under the jurisdiction of this state! Then Nweke asked Father Odera a second time, "What is the name of your God?"

Odera remembered his answer to his father Nweke, "Jesus Christ."

A GLOSSARY OF IGBO WORDS AND PHRASES

Chukwu: Almighty God

Chukwu Okike (Chineke): Almighty God the Creator

Chi (Ikenga): Personal god

Efulefu: Lost and worthless person

Ogilisi: A tree usually used as a place and land marker

Oyibo (Onyeocha): A white man

Oyibo DC: White District Commissioner

Ego Oyibo: White man's money

Ego Ayolo: Cowries used as the local money

Kotma: Court Messenger

Oba ji: A barn of yams

Ogbuefi: Killer of cows (An honored title)

Mmuo Osisi: Flogging Masquerade

Ekwulo: A flogging masquerade dressed in sack cloth

Mkpuke: Wives' courtyard

Odonigwugwu: Whatever (Your headache)

Oliaku: Popular name for girls meaning consumer of wealth

Ogwe Nso: Neighborhood Playground

Mmuo Akuko: Storytelling masquerade

Ogba Mgbada: Dancing Masquerade (Also called Ojionu)

Akataka: A flogging masquerade dressed in outfits made of ropes

Ogolo: A flogging masquerade dressed in cloth

Izaga: A masquerade that stands on stilts

Ijele: The biggest masquerade

Okwonma: A masquerade that wields a matchet.

Agu Mmuo: Spirit Tiger

Ogbadu: A spirit forerunner that precedes Ayaka

Ayaka: A group of nights only masqueraders chanting as ancestral spirits

Egwu Onwa: Moonlight night play

Udu: A musical instrument made like a clay pot

Ogene: A metal Gong, musical instrument

Igbu Uga: A play for girls involving clapping and stomping of feet

Ukpaka: Oil bean seed or oil bean tree

Adaobi: First daughter of the family

Ududo: Spider

Opulozo: Worthy of ozo title

Akwu: Palm fruit

Akwu chalu n'odu igu: The unusual, the impossible has happened

Okochi: Nweke's Ikenga (Personal god)

Uli: Igbo Ink for body art

Akpu Ngu: Igbo delicacy made from sliced cassava

Eke: One of the four Igbo market weekdays

Eke: Python snake

Nna Anyi: Our father

Udala: A type of Igbo apple

Nne: Mother

Nna: Father

Nnwa: Child

Uwa (Enuwa): World

Olili: Merriment

Daa: Fall down

Obi: Man's courtyard

Ututu: Morning

Ugani: Famine

Alu: Abomination

Osu: Outcast

Nenya lie: Come and eat it

Akala: Fried bean cake

Odera: Once it is written

Uzo: Way, road, pathway

Akpa: Bag

Ubiam: Poverty

Ego: Money

Ajuju: Question

Ewu: Goat

Isee: Amen

Orji: Kola nut

Egbe: Kite (Also a gun)

Taa: Chew

Lie: Eat

Oye: An Igbo weekday (also a market day)

Afor: An Igbo weekday (market day)

Afo: Stomach

Nkwo: An Igbo weekday (market day)

Tufiakwa: God forbid

Bia: Come

Nmanya: Palm wine

Ukwa: Breadfruit

Njakili: Acidic jokes

Ngwa: Okay

Nwantakili: A kid, child

Ihe: Something

Nwam: My child

Ogini: What is it?

Okpoko: Very noisy specie of bird

Oga: Boss

Osipaka: Rice

Odu-okike: Elephant Tusk

Oja: Flute

Ogbuagu: Killer of tigers

Egbenu Mbu (First Cockcrow): After 1:00 am

Egbenu Abuo (Second Cockcrow): 2:30 am

Egbenu Ikpeazu (Last Cockcrow): 4:00 am

Mpio: Deep hole in the earth

Okuko: Chicken

Onu: Mouth

Mbelede: Emergency

Otolo: Running Stomach

Nsi: Excretion (Also Poison)

Obodo: Town

Igwe (Eze): King (Paramount Chief)

Ichie: Minister (Chief) in the King's Cabinet

Alusi: Idol

Nmuo: Masquerade

Mazi: Mr.

Onwa: Moon
Nkita: Dog
Mmiri: Water
Agu: Tiger (also Wilderness)
Aguu: Hunger
Akwa: Egg (also bed, cloth, cry or mourning)
Oloma: Orange
Ibeanyi: My brethren/fellows

ACKNOWLEDGMENTS

I thank my wife Bridget, who constantly nudged me out of my laziness to get to work. She takes care of me like I am one of her children. She is such a blessing. Many thanks to my niece Kem, author of *Locked Gray/Linked Blue* for teaching me that there is more to Novel writing than the village moonlight night folk tale. My beloved daughter Oge helped with typing the initial manuscript and together with my beloved younger daughter Dika, gave me no rest till I put pen on paper. My son Ifeanyichukwu gave me useful suggestions. Thanks immensely.

Many thanks to Professor Bertram Okpokwasili and his wife, Eunice my sister for their encouragement. I thank my niece and New York Actress Okwui who out of her busy schedule read part of the novel and encouraged me. Much thanks to Rutgers Professor of Writing Alex Dawson and his wife, Kristy for being such kind neighbors. Alex humbled himself and tutored me at no cost on readying my book for publishing.

Thanks to Nick and Kyle at Atmosphere Press. Kyle worked patiently and steadfastly editing the novel.

I have a good remembrance of my close friend, Emma Okocha, author of *Blood on the Niger.* He wrote a comment for the back cover of my novel but died few days before he was to send it.

I started seeing myself as a writer when my Freshman English Professor, Dr. Edith Schor, put my first essay in the College magazine and told me pointedly that I could write. God bless her.

Finally, to all who helped me in seeing this story published, especially my students at Perth Amboy,

Piscataway and Highland Park Middle Schools, I say a big thank you for your love and encouragement.

To Jesus Christ, my God, thank you for without you I can accomplish nothing.

ABOUT ATMOSPHERE PRESS

Atmosphere Press is an independent, full-service publisher for excellent books in all genres and for all audiences. Learn more about what we do at atmospherepress.com.

We encourage you to check out some of Atmosphere's latest releases, which are available at Amazon.com and via order from your local bookstore:

Relatively Painless, short stories by Dylan Brody
Nate's New Age, a novel by Michael Hanson
The Size of the Moon, a novel by E.J. Michaels
The Red Castle, a novel by Noah Verhoeff
American Genes, a novel by Kirby Nielsen
Newer Testaments, a novel by Philip Brunetti
All Things in Time, a novel by Sue Buyer
Hobson's Mischief, a novel by Caitlin Decatur
The Black-Marketer's Daughter, a novel by Suman Mallick
The Farthing Quest, a novel by Casey Bruce
This Side of Babylon, a novel by James Stoia
Within the Gray, a novel by Jenna Ashlyn
Where No Man Pursueth, a novel by Micheal E. Jimerson
Here's Waldo, a novel by Nick Olson
Tales of Little Egypt, a historical novel by James Gilbert
For a Better Life, a novel by Julia Reid Galosy
The Hidden Life, a novel by Robert Castle
Big Beasts, a novel by Patrick Scott
Alvarado, a novel by John W. Horton III
Nothing to Get Nostalgic About, a novel by Eddie Brophy

ABOUT THE AUTHOR

Chukwudum Okeke was born in the Township of Onitsha and grew up in Ukpo Town both in the South Eastern Nigeria. After secondary school and the Biafran war, he proceeded to New York City for higher education. His first interest in writing was as a columnist with his College newspaper. He taught briefly at the City University of New York before going back to Nigeria with the Nigerian National Petroleum Corporation.

Upon retirement from NNPC, he returned to the USA and gave more attention to writing. In his life, he has encountered some extreme experiences with tradition which contributed to his focus on culture in his writings.

The Embers of Tradition is his first novel. He has some yet to be published short stories and is writing his second novel.

He lives in New Jersey with his wife, Bridget and has three children, Ogechukwu, Ifeanyichukwu and Onyedikachukwu.

CPSIA information can be obtained
at www.ICGtesting.com
Printed in the USA
LVHW030043150521
687443LV00005B/233

9 781637 528952